CHAMELEON

CHAMELEON

WARRIOR WOMAN OF THE SAMURAI BOOK THREE

INDIA MILLAR

RED EMPRESS
PUBLISHING

Red Empress Publishing
www.RedEmpressPublishing.com

Copyright © India Millar 2019
www.IndiaMillar.co.uk

Cover Design by Cherith Vaughan
www.ShreddedPotato.com

ALSO BY INDIA MILLAR

Secrets from the Hidden House

The Geisha with the Green Eyes

The Geisha Who Could Feel No Pain

The Dragon Geisha

The Geisha Who Ran Away

The Song of the Wild Geese

The Red Thread of Fate

This World is Ours

Warrior Woman of the Samurai

Firefly

Mantis

Chameleon

Haiku Collections

Dreams from the Hidden House

This book is humbly dedicated to Baizenten, the Japanese Goddess of writers and geisha. May both you and she enjoy the words written herein!

PREFACE

Though the sex to which I belong is considered weak you will nevertheless find me a rock that bends to no wind.
Queen Elizabeth I of England, 1558—1603

PROLOGUE

*E*very living heart that is born has only so many beats within it. When the moment comes—as it must for all of us—when our body has used the very last beat, our time in this incarnation, in this world, is through.

I have heard it said that when that moment comes, another heartbeat is the only thing that cannot be bought or sold in the Floating World. Anything else—anything at all—is available. At a price.

Those who are not acquainted with Edo's capital of pleasure, the Floating World, laugh at this. Surely, they say, the human soul cannot be purchased! Neither can happiness. Or any other thing that cannot be perceived by the five known senses. Such people are foolish. Those who know the Floating World's secrets understand that everything has its price. That if one is prepared to pay enough for it, then it can be purchased. Everything except one more heartbeat beyond the last.

Everything in life and everything in death.

But also, it is well to remember that little in the Floating World is as it seems. Take this tiny merchant's shop wedged between two larger buildings. It has nothing to commend it particularly. No sign hangs outside to say what the merchant has to offer. The shoji screen door hangs at an untidy angle and is partially shut, allowing little of the bright morning sun to penetrate the interior. Rather than enticing passersby to stop and look inside, the whole shop has a secretive air about it. Almost as if the merchant who owns it is reluctant to sell any of his wares.

Anywhere outside the Floating World, passersby would dismiss the shop as being of no importance. One might think it's probably an apothecary, with dusty shelves covered in herbal remedies that have been there so long their once vibrant colors have merged into a uniform grey. Or possibly one of those shops that sells nothing in particular, just a collection of curios that the owner has picked up for a song and hopes to sell on to a gullible visitor for a profit. There is that element, of course. After all, this *is* the Floating World, and everybody here is happy to make a profit.

In spite of its unwelcoming appearance, should you be sufficiently intrigued to tug and pull the shoji back and enter the shop, please be sure to mind your step. There are items everywhere, spilling from the counter and the shelves onto the floor almost covering the tatami. Scrolls and woodblock prints; some of them very fine examples of their kind. A few pieces of Satsuma ware. Old kimonos, once exquisite but now sadly faded. Mismatched zori; one wonders what happened to the matching shoe. You think you see a stuffed cat, sadly moth-eaten, then a pair of green eyes turns to you and you realize the cat is not dead at all, just old and content in her patch of sun.

Most people turn around and tread carefully out of the curio shop at this point. They have seen enough. There is nothing to tempt them here. Those that venture further in do so because they know what they have come here for, and that their desires are not available anywhere else. And they know that if they wait patiently long enough, the merchant will part the beaded curtain that leads into the back of the shop and he will attend to them.

If he likes the look of his customer, he will listen patiently to them when they ask him if he has what they want. Often, he will shake his head sadly and tell them he does not possess what they are looking for. Occasionally, if his instinct tells him he can trust this customer, he will nod quietly and a bargain will be struck.

It will undoubtedly cost the customer dearly.

Because this is the Shop of Dreams, and dreams are more valuable than anything else in the Floating World.

Only the truly desperate shop here. If you must seek a bargain with the merchant, be careful. The price of realizing your dream may be far higher than what you are prepared to pay.

ONE

> Were you watching? If
> You were, how is it that you
> Did not see me pass?

I was so worried about my missing younger sister, Niko, that I had forgotten I was still dressed as Jun the kagema and not Kamakiri the top-flight oiran. If anybody bothered to give me a passing glance, they would see only a young man. One of the many youths in the Floating World who were available to fulfill the desires of their own sex. At a price, of course.

Not that I expected to attract any attention. The streets of the Floating World were already packed with people going about their business. Geisha tottered past me in high geta, their maids following behind. Yujo lounged about, their eyes flickering constantly in search of customers. As she passed me, one paused as if she recognized me and then shook her head and frowned as she moved on, as if she had been mistaken. I remembered her well enough. Effet, the yujo who had helped entrap me for Hana. Almost did I turn back and call out to her, hoping that she might have some information about Niko. I bit my tongue, knowing it was pointless as soon as the thought flickered across my mind.

I doubted Effet would know any more than I already did. Thanks to the help of Aisha, the kannushi at Jokan-Ji Temple, I was sure I knew that Niko's disappearance had nothing to do with Hana, and curiously, very little to do with the Floating World itself. I was almost certain I knew who had taken her and why. But where she was, I had no idea. The helpless sense of frustration that arose from knowing half the puzzle, yet at the same time not knowing enough to act, burned like acid in my belly.

It was all my fault. If I hadn't been so blind to everything other than getting my revenge on the men who had wanted to buy me, the men who had humiliated me, I would never have left Niko alone. But what else could I have done? My thoughts were anguished. I was onna-bugeisha. I lived by the samurai code of bushido. It had been a question of honor, of adhering to the code. At the same time, my conscience pointed out that I also had an equally great obligation to Niko, my adopted younger sister. If I had not left her, she would have been safe. I was riven in two, feeling my thoughts tangle themselves into knots.

I found as I walked that the rhythm of my steps helped clarify my thoughts. I had done what I had thought was right. No man—or woman—could do more. Or so I told myself. And I truly had no idea that Niko would be in any danger. Slowly, I became a little calmer. I could not undo the past. The important thing now was to get Niko back, and quickly. I concentrated and began to make sense of what had happened to my younger sister. Before the picture could clarify completely, a voice disturbed me, shattering my carefully built up concentration.

"Hello, young man. Why are you in such a hurry on this fine morning? Won't you stop and take some sake with me?"

I ignored the man who had spoken and kept on walking, causing squawks of annoyance as I shouldered aside those who didn't want to move to let me through. But the man who had accosted me wasn't so easily ignored. If anything, my disdain seemed to increase his interest.

"Oh, come now." He had lengthened his stride to keep up with me. He put his hand on my arm and tugged. "Don't be so difficult. We could have such fun together. Look, I have plenty of cash." He patted a heavy purse hanging from his obi, which was suspended by rather a fine netsuke. "What say I spend some of it on you?"

That did stop me. I could barely believe that anybody in the Floating World could be so innocent—and stupid—as to wear their wealth where it could be seen. I glanced at his face and saw he was sweating. The day was cool, so I doubted it was from the exercise of catching up with me. He grinned nervously and I guessed he was a stranger to the Floating World.

"Go away," I snapped. "Leave me alone. I have nothing you want."

I walked away from him. He was at my side in a moment, his expression pathetically eager. Did he think I was playing games with him?

"Oh, don't be so horrid to me," he whispered. "I'm a stranger here. I need somebody to show me the sights, if you get my meaning."

His hand was on my sleeve again. We were passing the entrance to a narrow, shadowed alleyway. Suddenly, the hand that was on my arm was sliding around my waist.

"Come on, you dear young man. I've heard all about you delicious kagema here in the Floating World. I'll pay you well, I promise. Just a few moments of your time, that's all I want. And the pleasure of your beautiful lips around my tree. What do you say?"

He was literally drooling. He licked a thread of spittle from his lips and tugged hard on my waist. We were attracting attention. The Floating World loves any form of entertainment, and if it happens to be free, so much the better. Two brightly dressed yujo were watching us avidly, nudging each other and giggling. A merchant lounging in his doorway thrust his hips forward and made an obscene gesture with his clenched fist. The man who had accosted me didn't even notice. His whole attention was on what he thought was his prize.

I glanced down at the front of his robe and saw his tree almost parting the material. A man in lust is a fool. A man as deeply in lust as this one appeared to be is not just a fool, but is as single-minded as a dog that has smelled a bitch in heat. Nothing would shake him off until he had slaked his desires.

Normally, I would have found his antics entertaining. I might even have been tempted to lead him on to amuse myself. It would surely have been worth spending a few minutes of my time to see his horror when he discovered that his bargain was entirely different from what he had hoped for. Today, I had no time at all to waste. But the more I tried to shake him off, the tighter his grip grew.

"Let go of me," I growled. "I've got important business to take care of."

"Oh, so have I!" The man rubbed his sweaty cheek against my face and I cursed my choice of words. "Do come down here. I'm sure we'll be safe and undisturbed."

A small crowd had gathered around us. The yujo had been joined by a noodle seller and a man with a performing dog. A beggar was peering over the noodle seller's shoulder, standing on tiptoe to get a better view. The merchant was pretending to gossip with a prospective customer. They were all watching our performance avidly.

I was rigid with fury. I could dispose of my admirer easily enough. An elbow jabbed hard just below his rib cage would leave him breathless and doubled over in pain. I could walk away from him and leave him gasping in the roadway. I itched to do it, but I knew I could not. An unwilling kagema was unheard of and would attract a great deal of attention. People would remember, and I rather thought I might want to become Jun again at some time in the future. If I had need of him, it would be important that he went unrecognized. Apart from that, my wretched conscience wouldn't allow me to leave this innocent and idiotic stranger to the mercy of the Floating World. I could never forget that I was a samurai warrior woman. Just as the code of bushido bound me to help my dear Niko, so did it insist that I show compassion to those who were less fortunate than I. All life must be given equal respect. Even this irritating creature who was grinning hopefully at me and almost dancing with impatience. I grimaced as I acknowledged that even though this idiot probably deserved all he got, fate had decided that it was up to me to try and save him from himself.

I am so sorry, Niko! I apologized silently to my younger sister. I had already let her down. I could not leave this fool of a man to be devoured by the Floating World as well. A man who was obviously a stranger to the Floating Worldly would be easy prey. If he lost only his purse, he would be very fortunate. I wondered sourly if perhaps the gods had decided that keeping him safe was my responsibility as punishment for abandoning Niko. *I will hurry, little sister*, I promised silently.

I glanced around the crowd and smiled cunningly, as if letting them know that I had led my admirer on long enough and was finally satisfied that I would get my price. Without a word, I allowed him to tug me down the alley. A ripple of laughter followed us and I heard the murmur of the crowd resuming its business in the street.

The man was jittering with eagerness. He had hold of my hand and pulled me forward into the shadows where the houses on each side almost met they were so close.

"I do hope you don't think I make a habit of this sort of thing." His voice was high-pitched with anticipation. "It's just that I've heard so much about the kagema in the Floating World, I thought I might give it a try. I daresay you've noticed I'm a visitor."

I closed my eyes in despair. I had been right. The gods had clearly directed this innocent to me. A genuine kagema would have had a dagger at his throat and his purse emptied by now. We had reached the end of the alley. Cursing to myself, I pulled him toward me. He trembled and moaned with pleasure and anticipation. I almost felt sorry for him as I slipped my hand into the front of his robe.

"Listen to me," I said. My fingers slid inside his loincloth and cupped his kintama. He yelped as I pinched them, hard. "I told you, I do not have time for this nonsense."

He groaned and I sighed in irritation as he snuffled at my neck.

"Oh, yes, please. Do carry on doing that." His tree nudged my thigh. The stupid man thought I was being playful. I gritted my teeth and stopped pinching. Instead, I squeezed hard. His groan of pleasure turned instantly into a howl of intense pain.

"Listen to me," I repeated. I loosed my grip just enough to allow him to register what I was saying. "The gods are smiling on you today. You are fortunate that you chose me. Any other kagema in the Floating World you would have had a knife in your ribs by now and your fat purse would have gone."

"Please, take my money. Anything, just let me live," he panted. I felt like banging my head on the wall in exasperation.

"I don't want your money. I'm going to walk away from you now. You will stay here until you have counted to thirty." I thought that would be long enough to let me get well away, but not too long to entice anybody down the alley. "In the future, if you must have the company of a kagema, don't approach one on the street. Visit one of the houses where they can be found. And do not take a full purse with you."

"Thank you. Thank you," he spluttered. I shook my head in disgust and walked briskly away. As I emerged from the alley, the merchant who had watched us called out, his voice ripe with amusement.

"By the gods, but that was quick! Come and spend some of your fee with me, young man."

I shrugged, smiling at him over my shoulder. "Perhaps some other time," I called. He rolled his eyes in pretended disappointment and disappeared back into his shop. Nobody else gave me a glance.

Although I was walking quickly, it wasn't fast enough to explain the way my heart was beating as I came to the cul-de-sac that sheltered Akira's house.

TWO

You say you share my
Grief. How can you? Can you read
My innermost thoughts?

*A*kira was delighted to see me. His face gave nothing away, but his light grey eyes were warm and his body open and relaxed. I wondered if it was no more than that his curiosity was piqued at my unexpected visit. I was so on edge, worrying nervously about Niko, that I wasn't sure about anything.

Had I made a mistake in coming here? I had been so very sure that I could trust Akira, but now I began to wonder if my instincts had been wrong. It took considerable effort to smile courteously at him.

I relaxed slightly with relief that he was here. I had given no thought at all to what I would have done if he had been absent. Would his servant have admitted me? Unlikely. People in Japan never visit each other uninvited. To do so would be seen as being extremely odd, to the extent that an uninvited guest was unlikely to get past the shoji. And Akira was the leader of the most powerful yakuza gang in the whole of Edo. He would surely be surrounded by enemies. In his case, an unexpected visitor could mean trouble, and I was sure the door would have been kept firmly closed to me.

But he was there. And I had been admitted. The first hurdles had been surmounted.

"Kamakiri-chan." He glanced at my robes and top-knot and smiled. "Or perhaps I should say Jun. I had no idea you were back in the Floating World. What brings you here so unexpectedly?"

I spoke quickly and bluntly. I might as well tell him the truth. I would know in a moment if I made a mistake in giving him my trust.

"Niko's gone. She wasn't at home when I got back," I blurted. Akira blinked, but other than that his expression did not change.

"I see." He stared at me curiously. "Why are you so worried? People disappear in the Floating World all the time. Niko's very young. You're sure she's not just playing a game of her own? Perhaps she just got bored waiting for you? If she wasn't expecting you back, she might just have gone out for a walk perhaps?"

"No, she's been gone for some time. I could tell that by the state of the house. And Matsuo was locked in the garden. She would never have gone out without him. Besides, look." I held out the doran and kiseruzutsu I had found in Niko's futon. Akira looked at them calmly. I wanted to shout at him, to make him understand that something very bad had happened to Niko. I took a deep, slow breath and spoke only when I was sure I had control of myself. "These were tucked in the folds of her kakebuton. You can see where the cord that tied them to an obi has been ripped.

She must have managed to tug it off in the struggle to get away from him."

Akira handled the pipe holder and the tobacco pouch. I saw a brief expression of distaste flicker over his face and guessed that, like me, he thought the doran felt too much like human skin for comfort. I waited, forcing my impatience to die down. He was intrigued, I could see that; if he were not, he would simply have shrugged and told me not to worry. Any other man would have rattled off pointless questions, demanding to know how I knew there had been a struggle and who I was talking about. But Akira was no ordinary man. He considered my words and the items I had given him quietly, ordering everything in his own mind. I began to understand why he was the most dreaded yakuza in Edo. He was completely in control of himself, concentrating totally on the question I had posed to him. His discipline was icy. I was suddenly very glad that I had nothing to fear from this man.

I would make him help me find Niko. Between us, we would get her back safely. I prayed to all the gods that it wouldn't be too late. I closed my eyes for a second, feeling relief flood through my body.

"You're certain that she's has been taken," he said. It was a statement, not a question. I nodded. "You said 'he,' so you think you know who did this. So, who has her? One of your enemies out for revenge?"

"I don't *think* I know. I'm sure. He is most certainly one of my enemies. I believe she's been taken by one of the men who tried to buy me from Hana. But that's just a coincidence. I don't believe him stealing Niko has anything to do with me at all."

"I don't understand." Akira looked at me intently. "There were three men in the final bidding for you. I imagine each would know who the others were. They would have asked Hana about that to get an idea of the strength of the competition. Out of those three, I have already dealt with our mutual acquaintance, Hara. I promise you, he is no longer in a position to take any interest in Niko."

He raised his eyebrows, inviting me to ask. I did not. When I had discovered the man who now called himself Hara had betrayed Akira's father many years ago, I had handed Akira the information to do as he wished with it. Just as I adhered to the code of bushido, I knew that yakuza had their own code of honor. The need for vengeance against anybody who had betrayed their family would have strengthened over time, not weakened. Akira had been the final instrument of my vengeance. I had felt that it had been a fitting revenge for Hara at the time, but now I shuddered as I discovered I was still woman enough not to want to know what had actually happened to him.

"Thank you," I said stiffly.

Akira shrugged. "No need to offer me thanks, it was my pleasure. But that still leaves the other two men who were bidding for you. I wonder, is it possible that one of them has heard of the sad fate of Hara-san? If he has, he may be asking himself if it's purely coincidence that one of the other men who were interested in you has met with such an unfortunate accident. Is it possible that he thinks you caused Hara's misfortune and he's taken Niko as insurance? Might he be holding her for ransom to keep you away from him?"

"No," I said wearily. "I wish it were that simple. But I told you, I don't believe it has anything at all to do with me. It's pure coincidence." Akira looked at me cynically. I spoke slowly, setting out the facts carefully. "I think the man who has Niko—Hana called him Ikeda-san—knows me only as the girl who was offered for sale by Hana. I suppose Hana must have told him I managed to escape, and I doubt he will have given me a second thought since then. I think he's seen Niko with Kamakiri the oiran, but not made the connection with me in either case. There's no reason why he should; I've covered my tracks very carefully. It doesn't matter anyway. I'm sure it's Niko he's interested in. Not me at all."

"Why him and not the remaining man who was in the bidding for you?" Akira said briskly.

"The second man who wanted to own me will not trouble me any longer. He has been dealt with," I said evenly. I saw admiration flare in Akira's eyes. At any other time, I would have been delighted by his respect, but at this moment I had no time for anything but Niko. "But the remaining man—Ikeda—I'm sure it's he who has taken Niko."

"I hear what you say. But I don't understand why you think it must be him if taking Niko has nothing to do with you. That doesn't make sense," Akira said thoughtfully. He was leaning forward slightly. Every line of his body said he was interested in what I was saying. I took a moment to order my thoughts and spoke only when I was sure I had everything right.

"Bear with me. I'll explain. The main reason Ikeda wanted me was because Hana had convinced him that I was a virgin. And not only that, but a virgin who came from an excellent family." I paused, glaring at Akira as I challenged him to ask. His lips twitched, but he said nothing. "He could have bought a girl from the streets, of course. But he would always have had his doubts whether she was really whole and not tainted with some disease or other. I imagine he would think that Hana's involvement offered him a guarantee that I was...whole. I suppose the fact that I'm samurai would have delighted him as well." I grimaced as I remembered Ikeda, hiding himself in the shadows like the monster he truly was. "His face was horrible. His nose had been eaten away and his voice was so odd. I think he had something wrong with his mouth as well. Hana told me he was badly infected with baidoku, the plum poison disease, and that he had tried everything to be cured but nothing had worked. He was stupid enough to believe in the old idea that the only true cure for his disease was to have intercourse with a virgin girl. That was the real reason he wanted me so badly. Hana had convinced him I was still whole—and who in the Floating World would ever doubt her word?

"When I escaped, he had to look elsewhere. And I'm sure that's why he's taken my poor Niko. He must have seen her in the streets with me when I was walking out as Kamakiri the oiran followed by her sweet, young maid. I'm sure he would have thought that I had kept Niko pure for my own profit so I could sell her to a tea house as a maiko or possibly auction her virginity off myself. The fact that he saw me at Hana's really is just a horrible coincidence." I shuddered as a thought came to me. "He probably probed her thoroughly before he took her to make sure she really is a virgin."

The idea of those red-blotched hands touching my poor Niko made me feel ill. I swallowed and closed my eyes. I think Akira must have seen my distress. He spoke quickly, and I was grateful that he had changed the subject.

"There are no coincidences," he said crisply. "Everything that happens in this life has a purpose. It's karma. It was karma that led you to Hana and, hence, to me. It was

karma that led Hara-san to you, and karma that allowed me
to punish him for his treachery after so many years. One
cannot argue with what is right. What is preordained."

The air between us was suddenly alive. I stared at a
point just above Akira's head as I thought about his words.
He was right, of course. Every person in Japan understands
that one has a red thread—invisible to mortal eyes—that
runs from the heart to the littlest finger on the left hand.
This thread is your karma. It connects each of us to every
person who has an impact on our lives. Sometimes the
thread becomes tangled and knotted, and when that
happens, there is trouble. But always, eventually, the thread
runs smoothly again. We do not choose who we love and
hate. It is simply that our red thread has led us to them.
One's thread is broken only upon death, and many people
believe that even then the same thread is simply taken up in
the next life.

As if he had read my thoughts, Akira held up his left
hand, the little finger crooked. He was right, but this was
not the moment for philosophy. I needed action, and now.
Niko was all that mattered. I had made myself accountable
for my little sister when I rescued her from the men her
father had sold her to. And now, just as her father had done,
I had betrayed her. Not intentionally, but by my neglect in
leaving her. Still, she was my responsibility. She trusted me,
and I had betrayed that trust. I had to find her, and when I
did, I would keep her safe at my side.

I realized that Akira was waiting patiently for my
answer. I nodded and spoke quickly.

"You may be right. But coincidence or fate, it doesn't
matter. The reason I came to see you today was for Niko's
sake," I said firmly. "We have to find her before it's too late."

I would not say what I was thinking, that it could

already be too late. I tried to think logically. Ikeda was clearly desperate. He could have taken Niko on her own futon. He had not, I reassured myself quickly. If he had, he would have murdered her then and there to cover his tracks. He had taken her with him instead, and I supposed I should be grateful for that. Akira's calm voice broke in on my thoughts.

"Yes. Of course we must find her. But one step at a time. I hear what you say, but I still don't understand why you're so certain it's Ikeda who has her."

I pointed to the doran and kiseruzutsu that Akira still held in his hands. "Those," I said simply. "I believe Niko tore them off in the struggle to take her. She's a clever girl. Somehow, she managed to hide them in her kakebuton so that when I found them, I would know she hadn't just gotten bored and gone off on her own. I've seen them both before. Ikeda wore them on his obi when he came to view me. I remember Hana held a candle for him to light the pipe with, so I saw them both clearly then. The kiseruzutsu in particular is very ornate and very old. I can't believe there could be two like it in the Floating World."

Akira put both objects down and rubbed his fingers together as if he found their touch distasteful. "In that case, you're right. It must be Ikeda who has taken her. What do you want me to do?"

I stared at him, so shocked I had no words for a moment. Surely it was obvious? I had been unable to find any trace of Ikeda in the Floating World, but Hana knew him. I wanted him to talk to Hana. Find out where we could find the monster. And once we knew that, I hoped he would help me to get Niko back.

"I want you to make Hana tell you where Ikeda lives," I

snapped. "Then get some of your men together and we go get her."

It was so simple. Why, I wondered, was Akira shaking his head?

"Hana doesn't know who he is," he said quietly. I laughed incredulously, wondering why he was lying to me. My brother, Isamu, had introduced me to Hana's tea house. He had boasted that it was the best in the whole of Edo. He had told me that Hana refused to allow any man over the threshold unless he had been introduced by an existing patron. And even then, she had to be certain that the newcomer was not only rich, but high-caste and very well connected. And above all, she had to approve of him. If Hana didn't like a prospective client, then no matter who or what he was, he would not be allowed to enter her premises.

"Of course she does," I said angrily. "Hana knows everything there is to know about all her patrons. She would never let an unknown enter her house. You must make her tell me who he is. Where we can find him."

"Kamakiri-chan, listen to me." Akira reached toward me and clasped my hands between his palms. I realized I had been rubbing my hands together as if I was washing them, and I was angry with myself for showing my distress. I forced myself to breathe slowly and evenly. "Generally, you're quite right. Hana has not made her tea houses the most exclusive in Edo by allowing just anybody to enter. But Ikeda is one of the very few exceptions to her rule."

I shook my head, dazed. How was it possible that the one patron Hana didn't know was the man I had to find? I stared at Akira, willing him to explain and wondering why he seemed to be so reluctant to speak. I was deeply suspicious, wondering if Hana had simply lied to him for her own reasons. Or was he lying to me? My head ached with uncertainty.

"I don't understand. She must know Ikeda," I said.

"Give me a moment and I'll explain. You know that Hana was my father's lover?" I nodded impatiently, wondering why Akira had chosen this moment to tell me ancient gossip. "My own mother died when I was very young. Hana and I have always been very close."

"Hana told me that herself," I interrupted. "But what does it have to do with Ikeda?"

"It's important that you know I'm telling you the truth," he said urgently. "The Hana you know, and the Hana the world sees, is not my Hana. To me, she has almost been the mother I never really knew. Others see her as a cold, ruthless woman. I know she has a softer side. And very occasionally, it gets her into trouble."

For all my seething impatience, I was becoming fascinated. I waited silently for him to continue. When he hesitated, I prompted him.

"Tell me," I demanded urgently.

Akira hesitated and then spoke reluctantly. "A while ago, Hana fell deeply in lust with a man who was slightly younger than her." Akira stared at his hands as he spoke. I understood instinctively that he was reluctant to tell me this. "He was handsome and charming and also penniless. She was a fool, and when I found out about the affair, I told her so. The man was an adventurer, out to make his fortune in any way he could. When I realized she hadn't taken my advice, I warned him off. And trust me, Kamakiri, when I tell somebody to stay away, I am obeyed. He disappeared, and I thought no more about it. But Hana didn't forget him. She went behind my back and kept on seeing her lover in secret. She was very discreet, you understand. If I had heard about it, the man would have been dead." He said the words so calmly I shivered, wondering if I had been right in putting my trust in him. Had my instincts failed me badly this time?

"What's this got to do with Ikeda?" I asked suspiciously.

"Listen for a moment. I'm getting there," Akira said curtly. "Hana hadn't listened to a word I said about her lover. And she certainly didn't believe me when I told her he was just using her for her wealth. She was infatuated with him and showered him with gifts. Very expensive gifts. And even worse, she was so taken up with him that her business began to suffer. Before too long, she found she was short of money. And at that point, her lover began to cool on her. She was desperate to keep him. She couldn't ask me for money. I would have wanted to know why she wanted it, and she wouldn't dare tell me. So instead, she borrowed it from one of her patrons. This particular man had been a patron of both the Green Tea House and the Hidden House for years. Hana thought she could trust him. She was a fool yet again."

Akira's voice was bitter. I wanted to comfort him, but his face was so tight with anger that I kept my voice neutral.

"What happened?" I asked.

"He lent her money. He's a rich man; it would have meant little to him. But of course, it did no good. Once she had money, her lover was suddenly interested in her again. He took everything she could offer, and eventually even Hana came to her senses and realized she was at risk of losing everything she had built up. At that point, she had the sense to tell her lover to get out of her life. She said he went without a word of regret. Hana managed to pay back the money she owed to her rich patron. But of course, that wasn't the end of it.

"She owed him more than money. She owed him a debt of gratitude that she could never repay. From that day on, he never paid for any of the services of the geisha in either of her houses. She never even asked him for payment, of course. And even worse, he began hinting that Hana should give the services of her geisha free to those of his favored cronies who happened to want to taste their joys. It was a matter of honor. Hana couldn't refuse him, and for the first time, she was forced to allow men to visit her girls who were unknown to her. Fortunately, most of them were respectable, high-caste men. But they were still largely unknown to her, and that was a bitter pill for her to swallow."

"And Ikeda was one of the unknown men?" I asked slowly. Akira nodded. "How do you know?"

"I am a cautious man." Akira smiled at my incredulous expression. "I had the idea that it might be necessary to keep an eye on the three men who had been so very interested in you they were prepared to spend a huge amount of money to possess you in case they caused trouble for both you and Hana in the future. When I asked Hana about the three men, because she knew nothing about Ikeda other than his name, she finally had to tell me the whole, pitiful story of how her lover had betrayed her and she had been forced to open her doors to complete strangers. I was extremely angry with her, but there was nothing I could do, especially with regard to her lover. It seemed he had the sense to flee far from Edo. I haven't found him yet, but I will. And when I do, he will be very sorry he ever hurt my poor Hana."

I supposed I should have felt at least a little sorry for Hana's lover, who had no idea the direction his karma was leading him in, but I did not. Instead, I felt a flash of sadness for Hana herself. Any woman could make a mistake. And we all suffered for it. But how much worse would it be for a woman like Hana, who was thought invulnerable by everybody around her? I guessed what Akira was thinking, and I spoke to his thoughts.

"None of this will ever pass my lips," I promised. "When you do find her lover, whatever you decide to do to him, please, don't tell Hana about any of it. She's been punished enough by his behavior. To tell her what happened to him would demean her."

"Thank you. I would never give Hana greater distress than she has already suffered. When I find her lover—and I will find him—I will deal with him. She will never know of his fate." He smiled, and for a second, we enjoyed a silence of mutual understanding. I was unhappy that I had to break it.

"You knew who the other men who were bidding for me were?"

"I had heard about Sato. Everybody in the Floating World knows about that nasty young man. But I could understand Hana admitting him. He's well connected, and very well off. And Hana said he could be very amusing when he wanted to be. For some reason, she took a liking to him. I have no doubt he curbed his excesses when he was with her."

"And Hara-san? You didn't connect him with your father's old enemy?"

"Why should I?" Akira shrugged, but I could see my words had stung. "He was new to Edo, but he was generally accepted as a very rich merchant who had retired here peacefully. Apparently, he was very free with his money, and Hana said he was introduced to her by an existing patron, so she had no reason to distrust him. He didn't draw my attention to him in any way, so I didn't give him a second thought. You must remember I was little more than a child when he betrayed my father. I don't believe I ever met him then. Hana didn't remember him either. She would have told me at once if she had. I haven't told her the truth about him. It would only add to her burden of guilt. You have my undying gratitude for giving him to me and allowing me to avenge my father after all these years."

"Find Niko for me, and there will be no obligations between us," I said crisply. Akira stared at me. When he spoke, his words were not what I expected, and I was surprised.

"I've already asked Hana if she knows anything at all about Ikeda." He smiled briefly. "Because he was totally unknown in the Floating World, he was something of a mystery. I don't like loose threads, and I wanted to know about him. But she insists she knows nothing about him but his name. She assumes he must be wealthy to be friends with Endo-san—the man who lent her money—but she says he's unknown in the Floating World."

"I see." I started to rise. "If you don't know anything about Ikeda, then you can't help me find him. In that case, Kamakiri the oiran will pay a visit to Endo-san and find out things for herself."

"No." The single word stopped me instantly. Akira's face was expressionless, but those cold, grey eyes were bright. Was it with anger or some other strong emotion? "What will you do? Simply arrive at his house and start asking questions about his friends? You haven't thought this through. Sit down, Kamakiri-chan, and listen to me."

THREE

I wonder if fish
Sleep. Should I dive into the
Ocean to find out?

I knew Akira was right. But it didn't stop me from being angry. With myself for my foolishness, and with him for daring to tell me about it. I wanted to walk out, but when he spoke again, I knew I had to be sensible for Niko's sake and sat down reluctantly.

"I understand how frustrating this is for you," Akira said reasonably. "And I also know that you blame yourself for allowing Niko to be put in danger. But listen to me. Kamakiri the oiran has very quickly become widely known and admired throughout the Floating World. Gossip has it that many men have already admitted they have tried to secure you and failed. The word in the Floating World is that you are playing a deep game. That you will only be satisfied with the richest, most powerful of patrons. Some have even whispered that you are waiting for the shogun himself to show an interest in you." I laughed incredulously at the nonsense. Akira smiled with me. "You have succeeded far better than you know yourself. You must remember that most people see only what you want them to see. Know only what you want them to know."

Echoes of Yo told me the same thing. I blinked and pushed the thought of my lover away quickly. Absurdly, I felt as if I was betraying him just by thinking of him in Akira's presence.

"I'm pleased to hear it." I bowed my head in acknowledgment. "But what's that got to do with Endo-san? If he's heard of my reputation, surely he'll be pleased to have a visit from me?"

"He would no doubt be delighted. He would also be deeply suspicious. You've rejected much richer and more powerful men than him. And if you suddenly approached him...I assume he hasn't contacted you?" I shook my head. "I thought not. In that case, he's unknown to you. And to add to the oddity of it, if you begin asking questions about Ikeda, a man who's a stranger to the Floating World, Endo would immediately be deeply wary. He's not just rich, he also has friends in very high places who trust him to keep their secrets. If you turn up unasked, asking searching questions, he would probably be so worried he would contact the authorities and have you arrested as a spy. The shogun is already worried about disturbances amongst the peasants. I've heard he's convinced it's caused by ronin rebels trying to cause civil unrest. If your true identity were discovered, he would be sure he was right. In any event, anything and anybody unusual is suspected. You would be taken into custody at once, and word would be passed to the shogun immediately."

The idea that I might be a spy was so laughable I shook my head in amazement. "I suppose I hadn't really thought about it properly," I admitted. "But what else can I do? If Endo has some illness, I suppose Kamakiri the anma might pay him a visit, but he might be just as suspicious about that."

I hadn't bitten my nails since I was a child. In fact, I had stopped when my brother Isamu had threatened to cut off all my fingers if I continued. At this moment, my thumbnail had found my teeth of its own accord. I turned the action into rubbing my lips. Oh, how the lessons learned in childhood do live with one!

"You can do nothing on your own," Akira said calmly. "But I know of a way where there is a good chance of getting the information you need without arousing any suspicions or putting you in danger."

"You mean you know of a way of acting without me? No," I said firmly. "This is my problem. I must resolve it. I will only accept your help if it is really necessary."

Akira was very still for a moment. He was staring at me in such a fixed way that I thought I had insulted him with my bluntness. I had spoken only the truth. I would not back down. I met his gaze calmly, and I saw a gleam of humor warm the coldness of his grey eyes.

"You may be a samurai, woman. And a warrior woman at that. But you forget. I hold the Floating World in the palm of my hand. I can find Niko for you, but you have to trust me and do exactly as I say."

I thought instantly that he was—not lying, precisely—but exaggerating to put me in my place. I stared at him angrily.

"Niko is my younger sister. I caused this trouble for her. If I had been here, it would never have happened. It's up to me to get her back safely. If you will help me, then I will be grateful. But I will not allow you to act without me."

Akira frowned at me. We glared at each other like a pair of dogs squaring up for a fight. Eventually, he took a deep breath and shrugged.

"You are a stubborn woman," he growled. "I am not accustomed to women telling me what they will or will not do. In fact, there is not even a man in the Floating World who would dare speak to me with such a lack of respect."

"But I am not from the Floating World," I said sweetly. "And as you say, I am not just a woman. Not even just a samurai. I am proud to call myself onna-bugeisha. Perhaps you've never come across a woman like me before, Akira-san."

I used his title sarcastically. I knew I had hit home when Akira flushed. He controlled his temper, and I admired him for it.

"I hear you. Such a shame that an honorable samurai woman must seek the help of this riverbed beggar of a yakuza," he replied tersely. Suddenly, I could see that his patience was exhausted. "Come. Enough of this nonsense. Do you want to find Niko or not?"

"I want you to help me find her," I said stubbornly. I could feel the heat of his body against my face as if I was leaning toward a fire. I was deeply ashamed as I realized I was excited by the situation, and that I was actually anticipating the struggle to get Niko back. I spoke coldly, determined Akira would not read my thoughts in my body's response. "Tell me what you're thinking of. If Kamakiri the oiran can't demand an audience with Endo, then how do you think you're going to get any information from him?"

I had spoken without thinking, and my words sounded sarcastic. I could see the emotions warring within him. His body was rigid. A muscle worked beneath his left eye. I held my breath; if he were going to refuse me, then now would be the moment.

But he did not. He spoke slowly, as if he was choosing each word with care.

"I will help you. But not because you need to uphold your honor as a samurai. Not even because I am in your debt over Hana's insult to you. I will help you because you are a brave, stupid, beautiful woman who will do anything to rescue her younger sister. And because I don't want to see your head taken off your shoulders by the executioner's sword."

I was surprised to find I was touched by his response. But I told myself that this was no time for sentiment.

"So, tell me what we are going to do," I demanded. Akira raised his eyes to the heavens in exasperation, but I could see he was clearly amused by my defiance. Had he really called me beautiful? I tried to be annoyed with myself for liking that far better than him calling me brave, but I could not.

"You are going to do nothing for the moment." He held his hands up as if he had anticipated my protests and was warding them off. "The way Endo-san has treated Hana has troubled me for a while. I intended to pay him a visit myself anyway. But now I think that can wait a while longer. Instead, I am going to tell Hana that she is to arrange a party at her tea house. The guest of honor will be Endo, together with any of his friends he may wish to invite." My lips parted in a sigh of satisfaction. I nodded to him to go on. "I hope he will bring Ikeda with him. Even if he does not, I don't doubt that Hana will find a way to bring the conversation around to that person. If Endo has had enough of Hana's excellent sake, she will be able to get the information we need out of him without him even knowing about it."

"Excellent," I said, clapping my hands in approval. Akira raised his eyebrows sardonically and gave me a small bow. "Kamakiri the oiran will be there, of course."

"She—you—will not attend." I glared, my good humor forgotten instantly. Who did Akira think he was to try and order me about like this? Before I could protest, he spoke over me. "You are still unused to the ways of the Floating World. Hana's most sought after geisha will be at the party. It will be proper for a couple of her maiko to be there as well, to pour the sake and make sure the patrons have enough food. But an oiran would never attend such an event. It would be unheard of. In fact, it would be almost as suspiciously strange as you barging into Endo's company uninvited."

There was the ring of truth about his words, and I spoke quietly, suddenly interested. All knowledge is power; this tidbit of information might come in handy at some time.

"Why? Explain it to me. A high-class oiran is just as talented as any geisha. And just like a geisha, she chooses who she...entertains."

We both knew the essential difference, of course. Geisha took a lover because they wanted a certain man. An oiran also chose those clients she wanted to make love to her, but unlike geisha, she expected to be paid very well for it. An oiran combined business with pleasure, but there was no real affection involved in the transaction.

"True," Akira agreed. "But you're missing the essential difference. You must understand, an oiran is for later. When the patrons have had their fill of the geisha's polite company, then they move on to a courtesan or an oiran if they can afford her. An oiran is the most beautiful, the most talented of even the high-class courtesans. And by far the most expensive. She chooses her clients; they go when they are summoned to her. You would be out of place in Hana's gathering, Kamakiri. It would be like throwing a stone into a quiet pond. The ripples would disturb things, set everybody on edge. Endo would be wary. He would drink very little, and say even less. I'm sorry. If you attend, we will never get any information."

"I see." And truly, I understood. Society in the Floating World was as rigid in its own way as it was amongst the ranks of the samurai. But Akira had to understand also that I had to be there. I had to hear and see for myself. I spoke very carefully; Akira held Niko's safety in his hands. "I understand now that Kamakiri the oiran would be out of place. But a geisha who is new to Hana's tea house, a geisha from outside Edo, perhaps from Kyoto? That would be different. Naturally, Hana would want to show off her new arrival."

"You?" Akira was smiling so widely I could see his very white teeth. I startled myself as I wondered how pleasurable it would be to have those sharp canines nipping my neck. "You really think you could manage to play the part of a geisha?"

"Naturally," I said calmly. "Like all samurai women, I was taught all the arts from a very young age. I can sing and dance. Play the samisen and perform the tea ceremony. With the correct dress and makeup, I could pass for a geisha easily."

"You think so?" Akira was obviously choking back laughter. "I don't doubt your talents, Kamakiri-chan. Not for a moment. But could you lower your head to a patron? Flirt with him from behind your fan? Pretend to be ecstatic at every stupid witticism he makes? And above all, not glare at him in the way you're looking at me now?"

I closed my eyes and made the gesture of smoothing my hands in front of my face that recalled instantly my sensei's teachings. Riku-san, the old warrior priest who had taught me to fight like a samurai, had also taught me that the greatest weapon I possessed was my mind. *Think of nothing at all. Clear your mind of everything. When you do that, you can do anything. Be anything.* Also had he taught me the gesture I used now. Just like a dog that learns to obey when his master clicks his fingers did the ritual cleansing of my face also cleanse my mind. I took a deep breath and tilted my head on one side flirtatiously.

"Akira-san, I don't know what you mean. Why would I have to pretend to be delighted by the wit of a patron such as you?" My voice was high-pitched and breathy, as though I was truly overjoyed to be in Akira's presence. I put my fingers to my lips and tittered as his jaw dropped in surprise. "I do not have my samisen with me, so unfortunately I cannot play for you. And to sing without it would be unthinkable. But perhaps you might like to have a game of mahjong with me? I am generally accounted a good player, so perhaps I might be able to entertain you. Although I'm sure my best efforts would never be good enough to beat you."

I lowered my eyelashes and pouted. I saw him blink and knew I had won.

"By all the gods, Kamakiri-chan!" Akira exclaimed. "You are far more talented than I ever suspected. Even though you're sitting in front of me looking more like a kagema than a woman, you managed to sound so much like a geisha that if I had closed my eyes, I would have believed you really *were* geisha." He was looking at me intently. I met his gaze and held it. "Your name should never be Kamakiri. You are more like a chrysanthemum bloom than a mantis. So many lovely petals, and each of them folded inward to hide the secret heart within. And what is in that heart, I wonder?"

"I am neither more nor less than what you see." He smiled, and I saw that he delighted in the subtle lie. "I assure you, just like the mantis, I use my disguise to lure my prey into a false sense of security. Then when it is close, I snatch." I made the snapping scissors motion with my fingers, which is the sound that gives the mantis its Japanese name. "And once I have my enemy in my grasp, there is no escape. The chrysanthemum may be beautiful to look at, but it cannot move, it has no skills."

"You think not? You're wrong. The chrysanthemum uses its beauty to lure the bee to it. And once inside that most lovely of flowers, the bee cannot escape until it has done its work and pollinated the bloom. The mantis may be an excellent hunter, but it lacks the allure of a chrysanthemum blossom."

"Then perhaps I should think of myself as the mantis that sits on the chrysanthemum bloom waiting for its prey." I laughed with pleasure, and Akira smiled with me.

"Even better, I think you're really a chameleon," he said.

I shook my head doubtfully. "I've heard of them, but I've never seen one. Do they really exist? I thought they were just creatures of legend," I said doubtfully.

"They are as real as you and I," Akira said. "In fact, when I was a boy, I had one of the amazing creatures as a pet. My uncle traded with the long-standing Japanese colony in India, and one day he came with a present for me in a small box. When I opened it, there was the most beautiful lizard inside, unlike anything I had ever seen before.

My uncle told me it had been found inside some cargo he had just received from India and he thought I might like it."

"And what was so special about this lizard?" I asked.

"He was a loyal pet. He loved to sit on my shoulder and walk with me." I shrugged, not at all sure I liked the inference. Occasionally in the Floating World, one saw men with large lizards perched on their shoulders or walking on a lead. It was fashionably iki to have such a creature. Whilst I admired their supple skins and jeweled colors, I was not at all sure I wanted Akira to compare me to a creature as cold and unthinking as a lizard.

"Yes?" I said mockingly. "And do you also expect me to sit patiently and obey at your command?"

"That would surely be a miracle," Akira said dryly. "As much a miracle as the very special talent my chameleon had. He was very like you in one way. He could camouflage himself at will. If I placed him on a green branch, his skin turned green. If he sat on brown earth, then he was brown. And he could see in all directions. Nothing could ever take him by surprise, nor did he ever allow any prey he had fixed on to escape from him."

I stared at Akira, convinced he was making fun of me. I had heard it said that these legendary chameleons were masters of camouflage, but surely this was too much to believe! He raised his hands, palms out, in a gesture that said clearly, *trust me.* For the moment at least, I chose to believe him.

"And what happened to this amazing creature of yours?" I asked.

"I gave him too much freedom. He slept in a cage at night, and one evening I forgot to close him in it. It was a warm night and I had left a shoji open, just a little. Come morning, he had gone. I missed my amazing pet, but if it was time for him to leave me, then so be it."

We looked at each other. I wondered about his words. Was there a message in them for me? I rather thought there was. I smiled and lowered my head. We could talk about futures and freedoms later. Today was Niko's time. I hoped Akira would be instinctive enough to understand that.

"Then Kamakiri the oiran shall be like your chameleon and change her color. You'll take Kamakiri the geisha to Hana's party?" I asked. I felt a spurt of anger when he shook his head. He must have sensed it, as he spoke quickly.

"I will not take Kamakiri, no. It's an excellent name for an oiran. Even for an anma, when you consider how a masseuse has to use her patience to find out where her patron hurts and then work quickly while she has her patient still. But to call a new, unknown geisha by the same name as a famous oiran could arouse suspicions."

"I hadn't thought of that." I relaxed, appeased. His words made sense. "Shall I go back to being Keiko, then? Lady Keiko was kept out of society. She wasn't very well known even amongst samurai. Shall I go back to being myself?"

"Keiko means 'lucky child,' doesn't it?" Akira asked. I nodded, wondering if one day I would explain to him that I had been given the name because my mother had died giving birth to me. Not only had I been lucky to survive, I had been twice blessed that my father hadn't exposed the useless girl child who had killed his wife to come into this world.

"Yes," I said simply.

"It's not a traditional geisha name, but as you're from Kyoto, nobody will think twice about it," he said thoughtfully.

I knew that I had won, then. I inhaled deeply with satisfaction and pushed thoughts of Keiko the geisha to one side. She was settled for the moment.

"Will you talk to Hana now? We must get to Niko as soon as possible. If that vile man takes her, she's as good as dead."

In my mind, I saw Niko struggling and screaming as she fought against Ikeda. My lips peeled back from my teeth in instinctive fury. It would not happen. I would not allow it to happen. Akira shrugged almost lazily. I was so pent up, I had to fight the urge to tug him to his feet and make him go to Hana at once.

"I'll speak to Hana today, I promise. But you must remember, it will take her a day or two to organize the event, and then she must ask Endo if the evening she has chosen is suitable for him."

I could barely sit still. I banged my knuckles together impatiently, wondering how he could sit so calmly. Didn't he understand a word I had said? Niko's life was in danger. We had to act. Now.

"We can't wait!" I protested. "We have to get to Niko."

"Yes. Of course. But things may not be quite as bad as you think. You say that Ikeda was very badly infected with baidoku? How do you know?"

"Hana said he was. Apart from that, it was clear to see. His skin was covered with red blotches. Even I know that's why the disease is called 'plum poison,' because the rosettes look a little like plum flowers. And his condition was so far advanced, his nose had fallen in. It was hideous." I grimaced at the memory of that ruined face. "I think there was something wrong with his mouth as well. When he spoke, his voice was muffled, as if he was speaking through a mouthful of food. Surely if he's so badly infected, if he takes Niko he'll pass it straight on to her."

"No, you're wrong." Akira spoke so calmly I felt a little of my own agitation die down. "It sounds as if his disease is in the last stage. His voice was probably odd because the roof of his mouth has collapsed, like his nose." His lips curled disdainfully at the thought. "I'm sure he must be in the third stage of baidoku. And if he is, that means his disease is dead within him, as is the case with lepers who have had their disease for many years. He cannot be cured, no matter what he thinks. But neither can he infect anybody else."

"Even so." I shivered as I recalled my own disgust when I had seen Ikeda. The thought of him even looking at my sweet Niko made me nauseous. "I am not prepared to allow that horrible man to deflower her. It makes me shudder to even think of him touching her."

I stared defiantly at Akira, praying all the while that he was right.

"I think she will be safe. For a while, at least." I stared at him, willing him to explain. Akira tapped his finger on his lips, obviously thinking carefully before he spoke again. "As far as I am aware, baidoku does not steal one's manhood. But I have heard sometimes that men who have the later stages of the disease find it impossible to make their trees rise for a woman. It may be that they know that they are so hideous in appearance that they can take no pleasure in being with a woman. I don't know. The mind is a strange thing. But that was probably why you found no evidence that he had taken Niko immediately—he simply couldn't. Because of that, I believe we have at least a little time."

There was a flaw in Akira's argument. I pounced on it at once.

"I hear what you say. But if his tree isn't willing to rise for a woman, why has he taken Niko in the first place? If he can't match the bird to the nest with her, then she's useless to him."

"Not necessarily. He has his virgin at last. I imagine he will have lived with his disease for some years, and if that is the case he will want to make sure he can do her—and himself—justice. He'll need some potion to make his tree rise, and I doubt that there's any apothecary in Edo who could promise him a result under the circumstances. In that case, he's likely to turn to a witch for help." He smiled briefly, anticipating my next question. "I doubt he will have a potion already. He would not have wanted to admit his lack until he was absolutely sure he had need of it. I think we have a little time. Trust me, Keiko. If I weren't sure, I would tell you."

I sighed deeply. Did I trust him? Did I have any other option?

"I will trust you," I said softly. "But if you're wrong and he takes Niko before we can reach her, then her death will be down to you and I will punish you for it."

Akira stared at me silently and I knew that he believed me. The knowledge gave me little comfort.

FOUR

When the moon conceals
The sun within his embrace
We should share their joy

*E*verything that was necessary had been said between us. Akira opened the door for me himself —such courtesy!—and Marika, his lovely shiba inu, bounded in and threw herself at my legs in an ecstasy of pleasure. I bent and patted her, pleased that she remembered me. The dog whined unhappily as I rose quickly. I would have loved to have stayed and fussed her longer, but I felt I had to get away. If I stayed, I would begin questioning Akira further. And I thought wryly that he was not a man who would take kindly to being nagged.

For Niko's sake, I would trust him. I shook my head angrily as I admitted to myself that I had no option.

My wandering thoughts were distracted by the sound of a voice raised in anger. The man was speaking Japanese, but with some difficulty. His voice was thick, the words slurred. I stopped and turned my head, seeking the source.

I knew that voice. Adam, the gaijin who had unwittingly allowed me to take my revenge on Lord Akafumu. I had stolen his morphine pills and used them when I was Kamakiri the anma to get Akafumu addicted to the drug. I was about to turn and walk away when I felt intensely guilty. Adam could never have known why I had stolen his pills and then simply disappeared. He had been very kind to me, and I knew that he had become very fond of the blind anma I had once been.

I had encountered him again when I had been Kamakiri the oiran. I shivered as an icy finger of superstition tickled my spine. Was karma pushing me toward him yet again?

It hardly mattered. An interested crowd had already gathered to listen to the dispute. If there were trouble, Adam would be dealt with very roughly. If I walked away, I would be adding to the debt I owed him.

And yet I wanted to walk on. Niko was my responsibility, my problem. Not this tall, muscular gaijin. Surely he could take care of himself. Then I saw heads were beginning to turn all around me. Two young men exchanged glances and stopped, staring intently in the direction of the source of the voice. A merchant retreated into his shop and pulled the shoji closed, as if distancing himself from any trouble. The atmosphere was beginning to tighten. I clenched my fists with indecision. Adam was not my problem. Besides, it would hardly be useful to him if he recognized me. He was so gauche it was entirely likely that he would welcome me as an old friend. If he did, the crowd would become enraged. Nobody liked the gaijin, particularly one who was so foolish as to think he had Japanese friends.

I glanced down at myself and sighed. Of course Adam would not recognize me. Jun the kagema was unknown to him; I was perfumed and painted and clearly not blind.

And above all, I was not a woman. There was not the slightest reason why Adam would connect a strange youth with his blind anma, and still less with Kamakiri the gloriously female oiran. Besides that, I was sure that the gaijin thought that all Japanese looked much the same, in exactly the same way as we found it difficult to distinguish one gaijin from another. That idea finally made my mind up. I could help him and walk away with no complications and a clear conscience. In that way, at least one debt would be removed from my conscience.

"I will not go!" Adam's voice was far too loud. "Somebody told me that you know everything about the Floating World and the people who live here. You must know where she is. If you tell me, I'll pay you well."

A couple of yujo in the gathering crowd turned to glance at each other. A beggar twitched his shoulders and tightened his grip on his begging bowl. I sighed; it did not do to show one's wealth in the Floating World. Discretion was everything. Let anybody know you had a fat purse, and even a samurai who had refused to give up his swords at the gate might wake up in a dark alley to find he was penniless. If he woke up at all.

I pushed my way through the crowd. One or two of the people glanced casually at me, but to my relief I aroused little interest.

Adam's voice was echoing from inside a shabby shop. I was vaguely puzzled. I was certain I had walked this way before, yet I didn't recollect this odd little shop. If I had seen it, I was sure I would have been interested enough to take a look inside. It was different enough to be intriguing; most shops in the Floating World displayed their wares enticingly. This shop seemed to have deliberately hidden whatever goods it had for sale from the casual passerby.

I paused in the half-open shoji to allow my eyes to adjust to the gloom. It was stacked with goods, but unlike most shops which dealt in only one thing—jade or porcelain or kimono—this place seemed to have a little of everything. I was instantly uncomfortable. There was something wrong here. Everything was dusty, as though none of the merchandise had been disturbed for years. And nothing was displayed enticingly. Rather, it was thrown down carelessly, as if the merchant didn't care whether it was purchased or not. I shrugged. None of this was any business of mine. I was here to rescue Adam from his own stupidity, not buy cheap trinkets or moth-eaten clothes.

I glanced at the counter and got my second surprise.

The merchant was very, very old. He was also small and his robes were wrinkled and looked as if they should be beaten to remove the dust that clung to them. Adam towered over him, looking even taller and more vigorous than I remembered him when compared to the small stature of the merchant. Oddly, the man behind the counter seemed not at all cowed by this shouting, obviously agitated gaijin giant.

The merchant looked past Adam as if he was invisible and bowed politely to me. His words made me stop as surely as if I had been turned to stone in the moment.

"Ah, Jun-san, how good to see you at last. I wondered when you would find your way to my humble establishment. Have you come to guide this gentleman out of danger?" He spoke so rapidly I guessed Adam hadn't understood him. Adam turned and glared at me, clearly not recognizing me at all.

"Do you know this man?" Adam spoke eagerly. "If you do, make him tell me what I need to know. Somebody told me that he knows everything about everybody here. He's pretending he doesn't understand me, but I know he does. I'm looking for an anma called Kamakiri. I have to find her, and I haven't got much time. Do you know of her? Please, help me."

I glanced at the merchant. His face was impassive. I tamed my own leaping curiosity and spoke quietly to Adam. I kept my tone low; he might not recognize me, but it was possible that he would remember my voice.

"If he doesn't want to tell you anything, then you won't get anything out of him," I said roughly. "Come away. You're wasting your time here." Adam's lips set in a tight line. He turned back to the merchant stubbornly. I spoke quickly, desperate to get him out. "I think I know the anma you want. Come with me. We can talk outside. It's so dusty and dirty in here, it's difficult to breathe."

And that was no more than the truth. A little sunlight penetrated the dirty shoji and lit dancing dust motes in the air. I took a deep breath and coughed. Adam was looking at me, his face alight with hope. I grabbed his arm and tugged him toward the door. Something was very strange in this place. I wanted him out of it. Come to that, I wanted to get out myself.

"Good day to you, Jun." The merchant's voice cackled with hidden laughter. "When you have resolved this gentleman's problems, I do hope you come back to see me very soon. I have something you might be interested in."

Adam paused in the doorway as if he might continue his argument, but I pushed him out with a firm hand in the small of his back. I was relieved to see that most of the crowd had become bored and drifted off. Only the beggar and the pair of yujo remained. The beggar immediately went into a practiced whine, scratching at his crotch and holding out his bowl. The yujo glanced from Adam to me and raised their painted eyebrows, radiating silent disapproval.

"You. Get away," I snarled at the beggar. I spoke quickly, hoping that Adam wouldn't understand my rapid Japanese. "This one is mine. He has nothing for the likes of you."

The beggar spat on the cobbles at my feet and turned away. The yujo gave us one last sneering glance and then tottered down the street in their high geta, walking arm in arm for balance as much as companionship.

"Please." Adam's voice was hopeful. "If you really know something about Kamakiri, will you tell me? I'll pay you well for any information you have."

I sighed with irritation. How had this innocent creature survived for so long in the Floating World?

"I don't want your money," I said firmly. "And keep quiet about it. If people hear you shouting about your wealth, they'll steal it. Do you live nearby? I don't want us to be overheard."

I knew perfectly well where Adam lived, and I had almost given myself away by simply telling him to take me to his house. He stared at me with his head on one side, and for a moment, I was sure he had recognized me. I breathed out on a long sigh when he shrugged and pointed.

"Down there. It's not far."

I would go with him. See him safely behind his own shoji. I owed him that much at least.

He was silent until we reached his door. I hesitated as he slid the shoji back. Adam tugged on my sleeve and I wondered whether now was the moment to slip away from him. I was uncertain. When I was a child, when my sister Emiko was in a good mood and had time for me, we had played with wooden koma—spinning tops. The aim of the game was to knock the opponent's top over. I was good at the game at first, but always lost in the end as my imagination filled me with the giddy motion of the spinning top and my fingers lost their sureness. I recalled that sensation now.

There had been so very much strangeness in this day. First, finding my poor Niko had been stolen from me. And then the conversation with Akira, raising the hope that I might find her again. And now encountering Adam again. Logically, I felt I should go home at once. Search the house to see if there was anything else that Niko had managed to leave for me to find. At the same time, I was deeply reluctant to walk into my own home, where the lack of Niko would be everywhere, calling to me in silent reproach that I had abandoned her here.

And there would be nothing else for me to find, I thought sadly. If there were any other traces of Niko's abductor, Matsuo would have found it for me already. No, all there was for me to go home to was a house that was no longer comfortable for me. Rooms that should have been full of Niko's chatter and her happiness would be empty.

Adam's voice broke in on my whirling thoughts. "Please, do come into my humble home. I am sorry everything is in such a mess. I've been recalled to my own country. I leave tomorrow. That's why I was so anxious to find out if my dear friend Kamakiri is safe and well. I didn't want to go without getting some word about her."

My guts clenched at his words. I had not thought it possible for my conscience to torment me any further. Now, I knew I had been wrong. Just as I worried about Niko, it seemed that Adam worried about me. Or rather, Kamakiri the anma. I could, I supposed, simply tell him cheerfully that of course Kamakiri the anma was alive and well. That she was sitting in front of him. Could his unobservant *gaijin* eyes not see that?

But I couldn't say that. If I told him the truth and revealed the lies I had told him, he would be bitterly hurt at my deception. He was very fond of his blind anma, I reminded myself. Besides, he was leaving Edo. I would never see him again, and I couldn't bear the thought that he would go thinking I had made a fool of him. Surely, the gods would not be pleased with me if I allowed this sweet-natured gaijin to leave us with his gentlest memories turned sour. And if the gods did not care, then I did!

"I'm sure that she's safe," I said finally. Adam gestured to me to sit down. He folded to the tatami unsteadily, and I guessed he had been drinking. Out of sorrow at his departure or because he was worried about his anma? Perhaps both.

"Do you know where she is?" he asked hopefully. "Please, I forget my manners. I don't know your name. I am Adam. Do you know Kamakiri? If you do know her, perhaps she's spoken about me."

I had always thought that Adam was half in love with his anma. Now, I understood that I was wrong. He was completely in love with his memory of her. I was filled with a great sadness for him.

"My name is Jun," I said. I set my face in an expression of polite regret. "I don't know Kamakiri the anma very well." I improvised wildly. I had to take his hope away. Better that I cut cruelly now than have him nourish hopes that even now she might still return to him. "But I saw her a few weeks ago, when she came to give me a massage, and she told me then that she was leaving the Floating World. She had become very close to a client whose health she had restored and he had asked her to marry him."

"I see." Adam's voice was toneless, but I felt his pain. "I am very pleased for her. He is a kind man, I hope?"

"I believe so. And quite well off. It will be a very good marriage for her."

Adam was close to tears. I was suddenly full of pity for him. And, oddly, for myself. I liked this big, clumsy *gaijin*. It would be sad that he was no longer amongst us.

"Ah. Well, that's good for her. But I forget my manners. Would you take a drink with me?"

I shook my head, but Adam didn't notice. He was already on his feet and moving to a chest against the wall. I remembered that chest very well; it was from there that I had stolen the morphine tablets. Then, the top had been bare. Now, it was adorned with a clear, glass bottle holding an attractively amber-colored liquid and several sake cups.

"Thank you, but no," I called. Adam was swaying slightly. I watched in growing alarm as he unscrewed the top of the bottle and slopped the contents into two sake cups. He brought them back unsteadily and sat down. He held one cup out to me and I took it reluctantly, guessing that if I refused it he would probably drink it himself. And I was sure that he had already taken too much when I saw him lick his fingers where the liquid had dribbled on them before he took a sip out of his own cup.

"Here's to you." He held his cup up toward me. I assumed that his words were an invitation for me to drink and I took a cautious sip. Instantly, I wished I had not. I rarely drank, and this strange stuff appeared to be infinitely more powerful than sake. It burned my throat and the fumes made me choke. Adam lurched over to me and patted me carefully on the back.

"What is it?" I gasped.

"Whiskey." Adam beamed at me and finished the contents of his cup. "It's a *gaijin* drink. Don't you like it?"

He sounded so concerned, politeness dictated that I finish my cupful and pretend to enjoy it. I closed my throat after I had swallowed to stop myself from coughing again. I placed my cup down carefully and put my hand on his sleeve to pat his arm as if he was a small dog. I surprised myself with my own familiarity; Adam's face was suddenly even more surprised. I glanced down and saw that my robe had parted when I leaned forward and that the swell of my breasts had been revealed.

I stayed very still. This foolish gaijin had felt tenderly for me when I had been a poor, blind anma. I was astonished to find that I felt very warmly for him now. Adam lurched to his feet and brought the bottle back to the tatami. He poured more in both cups and drank his off at a gulp. I was suddenly very thirsty and swallowed mine almost equally quickly. I peered at Adam and was astonished to find that he was sitting much closer to me than I had thought.

"Thank you for telling me about Kamakiri." Adam cleared his throat. His gaze did not leave my breasts. I sat back, well aware that the movement parted my robe still further.

"Not at all," I said politely. For some reason, I felt exceptionally cheerful. I would find Niko, and very soon, I was sure. Also, I was suddenly very concerned for Adam's welfare. "As you are to leave Japan tomorrow, I hope your memories of your stay here will be good," I said seriously.

"Oh, yes." Adam breathed. He was sweating, his face shiny. I giggled at him. He might think himself deeply in love with Kamakiri, but that obviously hadn't blinded him to my allure. Or was I doing him an injustice; was he so hurt that Kamakiri had found herself a husband that he wanted to punish her memory by taking another woman in her place? He was breathing heavily and I doubted he could be so subtle. Especially after so much of the potent whiskey.

I watched Adam's beaming face and felt a rush of affection. He was leaving us tomorrow. I knew what I was about to do was foolhardy and perverse and that I would probably regret it. But who knew what the next hour might bring? For a moment, I was astonished at myself, and then I stopped bothering about analyzing my thoughts and spoke instinctively.

"Perhaps I might be able to add another happy memory of your stay for you?" In response, Adam leaned forward and poured more whiskey into my cup. It overflowed and I looked at in dismay.

"Not to worry! Cheers!" Adam raised his glass. I assumed the word was some sort of *gaijin* salute and I raised my brimming cup carefully before I sipped at the fiery contents. Adam tossed his off at a gulp and then leaned forward, running his finger down the front of my robe, parting it completely.

"If there is one thing I have learned in the Floating World, it is never to take things at face value," he said seriously. I laughed at his witticism, and he smiled with me.

"What are you, Jun? When you came into the shop, I thought you were a kagema." He blushed ripely. "But I was obviously very wrong. Are you perhaps some sort of yujo I haven't come across before?" Would he never learn when he was overstepping the bounds of politeness? Still, what did it matter? He was going home tomorrow and I would never see him again. Besides, I was feeling extremely relaxed. More than relaxed, I was aroused. I decided I would forgive him for the gross impoliteness he had shown to me.

"The Floating World has many secrets, Adam-san," I said mysteriously.

He licked his lips and looked at me with hope in his expression. But he did not move. I had had enough of this play-acting. I took his hand and pressed it hard against my breast. I saw his tree tenting the front of his robe and my desires rose to match it, although how much of the desire had been provoked by Adam and how much was the spell of the whiskey, I didn't know.

He made a hoarse noise deep in his throat. A grunt rather than a word. His hand gripped my breast, and the sensation was very pleasurable. He squeezed harder and I bowed my head and bit his knuckles. My teeth left deep impressions in his flesh. So close, the fumes from the whiskey almost slapped me. If we had not both been the worse for drink, I would have worried that he might have seen through my disguise. As it was, I was reasonably confident he would not.

Still, it suddenly seemed a good idea to distract him. I grabbed his head and pressed my lips tightly against his mouth. I had noticed before that when he kissed he closed his eyes. Would Akira kiss? And if he did, would I want him to hide those cold, grey eyes from me? The thought was intriguing. But Akira was not here, and Adam was. I slipped my tongue between Adam's lips and caressed the tip of his tongue. He promptly bit it, quite hard. I luxuriated in the pain.

He released my breast and his hand slid down my belly. He made a curious circular motion with the palm of his hand on my stomach, and then his fingers were flirting with my black moss. In my turn, I reached for his tree. My memory had not played me false. His tree of flesh was as long and thick as I remembered; so thick that my fingers would barely meet around it. I had a fleeting thought; such a pity that I did not have longer to teach his tree how to truly please a woman! He moaned into my mouth, and I allowed my fingers to slip down to his kintama. I fondled their fleshy pouch, sliding the skin between my fingers.

Suddenly, I was taken with the strangest of desires to lick and caress his kintama, hairy as they were. My mouth salivated at the thought, almost as if I was starving and sitting at a table laden with the finest food. I put my hands on Adam's chest and pushed him away from me. I was barely surprised when he lost his balance and sprawled on the tatami in front of me. What did surprise me was the sudden surge of lust that his posture caused. This big, well-muscled man lay in front of me as helpless and submissive as a baby. He was breathing heavily, his mouth open and a thread of saliva shining on his chin. He did not speak, but his expression begged me to pleasure him.

I leaned forward and my balance deserted me. I put my hands quickly on the tatami at each side of him and flicked at his nipples with my tongue. They hardened immediately, and I wondered if that gave him as much pleasure as I would have experienced. His whole body jerked, and I guessed that it did. I allowed my tongue—just the very tip —to trail down his chest. I dabbed at his belly button and smiled as he groaned. His tree was pressing hard as wood into my breasts. The sensation was delicious, and I was reluctant to move until I thought of the pleasures to come and slid myself down. I licked the length of his tree briefly and then fastened my mouth around his kintama.

They hung like two ripe, fleshy plums, secure in their bag of flesh. I nibbled one experimentally; Adam sighed with pleasure and thrust his hips upward. Ah, but that was good! I opened my mouth far enough to allow one kintama to slide between my lips. I closed my mouth around it, sucking and squeezing it against the roof of my mouth. It tasted of clean skin, fresh from the bath. I turned my attention to the other plum, rolling it around my mouth and nibbling. Adam groaned as I allowed it to slip from my lips. I smiled to myself. I had enjoyed that. Perhaps if one gave me pleasure, two would give much more? I stretched my mouth wide and very slowly and deliberately sucked both kintama between my teeth. My cheeks bulged as I gulped them both inside me. They were huge. I had barely room to maneuver, but I tucked my tongue out of the way and moved my head back and forth, biting gently as I did so.

I heard Adam scream, as high pitched and breathy as a woman enjoying her yonaki, and then he was tearing himself out of my mouth. I gave his departing kintama a fond nip of farewell and suddenly found that Adam the submissive had vanished to be replaced by a roaring sea monster of a dragon, a dragon that breathed desire rather than danger.

He sprawled back on the tatami, at the same time clenching his hands around my waist and lifting me on top of him. His robe got in the way, and he elbowed it aside fiercely. I laughed silently with pleasure, allowing him to place me over his tree and lower me on to it. His urgency was too great and I slid over his tree, rather than on it. That was easily remedied. I reached behind me and grabbed his flesh, slithering forward to allow me to place it at the entrance to my black moss. The head of his tree bobbed against my sex and I almost screamed with frustration as we both fought to get it where we wanted it to be. A moment later and I relaxed with a sigh of pleasure as it slid deep and deeper still inside me.

I leaned forward and placed my palms on Adam's chest.

Already, his rhythm was galloping far too fast. I knew instinctively that the combination of strong drink and excitement was acting to bring him to his climax far too quickly. I tensed and gripped him hard, forcing him to slow down. I relaxed very slowly, rocking myself back and forth, allowing him to penetrate me deeply and then withdraw so that only the head of his tree was still imprisoned inside me.

In spite of my best efforts, I felt that Adam was approaching the moment when he would burst his fruit. I could do only so much to delay him. He was big and strong and very determined. I made up my mind in a heartbeat. If I could not delay him, then I would find my own yonaki with him.

I slid myself back up his tree and then wrapped my fingers around his exposed length. This time, I made no attempt to cup his flesh, but left my fingers extended. As he thrust himself back into me, he took my fingers with him. I felt the slight roughness of my own knuckles inside me and rubbed my sex in rhythm with his thrusts. It was delicious. I was so full, I felt that I could take no more. Then Adam thrust again, and again and I screamed my pleasure. I felt the moment of hesitation when he was still and I knew he was about to burst his fruit inside me. Then the moment was gone and I felt his seed hot and copious jetting against my tender flesh. I threw back my head and howled with pure pleasure as my yonaki matched his. We rocked together. I held him tightly clenched inside me until the last echo finally died to less than a whisper. When Adam finally slid away from me, I spread my fingers wide. His seed dripped down to my wrist and I put each finger in my mouth, licking his hot, thick juices from each one. It was delicious, and I jerked fiercely as the last tremble of my *yonaki* made my sex tighten with pleasure.

I thought Adam had fallen asleep. He was very still, his eyes closed and his chest rising and falling evenly. I was tempted to lie down at his side and nap for a few minutes. Surely there could be no harm in that.

Adam murmured something very softly. Almost giggling, I put my head close to his mouth to listen.

"Kamakiri." Just the single word, but it did nothing to hide a world of longing. Suddenly I was disgusted with myself, and not just because I had been pleasuring myself with Adam while poor Niko was in danger of being taken brutally by a monster I had unwittingly unleashed on her. I had allowed the whiskey to rob me of my judgment. Not just my judgment. I rather thought it had taken my wits with it. What sort of samurai warrior would allow themselves to be made the worse for drink? I had never seen Isamu drunk. And I could not imagine my father ever taking so much sake that he regretted it. I told myself I had not understood how strong Adam's whiskey was, but it did no good. It was not an excuse, and I was ashamed of myself. I would go now.

I gathered my robe around me quietly and slid my feet into my *zori*. Adam's voice froze me to the spot.

"Jun, are you leaving me as well? I seem to be fated to lose everything I find here in Japan that is precious to me," he said sadly.

"I must go." I hesitated. The cloud of intoxication was beginning to leave me. I felt dizzy, but now I was in command of myself. Still, his words cut into my heart. It was the right thing to do, I was sure. It seemed to me that Adam fell in love—or at least fell deeply in lust—far too easily. I would not want him to regret losing Jun as well as Kamakiri.

I had hurt him enough already. I would not inflict fresh hurt now. I knew I was right when he spoke again.

"Please," he whispered without opening his eyes. "If you should meet with Kamakiri again, tell her that I searched for her. Tell her I wish her great happiness."

I walked away without replying. I turned to glance at him as I slid the shoji back and saw that already he was deeply asleep. I wondered if he would be safe if I left him, then I saw he was breathing easily and I decided he would be fine. I should have expected his words, I supposed. But still, I felt...lessened. Not a word for Jun, who had rescued him and pleasured him so very well. All of Adam's thoughts were clearly with his blind anma.

I took a deep breath of the not so fresh Floating World air as I walked away. The spell of the whiskey lessened with every step. I was thirsty, but otherwise nothing seemed to have been permanently affected. This had been the first time I had allowed something outside my own body and mind to affect me. I vowed to myself that it was also going to be the last time.

Then I realized that my unconscious footsteps had taken me back to the grubby merchant's shop where I had rescued Adam earlier and my pace slowed.

FIVE

The past is gone. It
Cannot be brought back to life.
Why do you stay there?

*T*he shoji was still ajar, hanging at exactly the same angle. I wondered if it would ever be possible to close it properly, though I doubted if it mattered greatly. From the very little I had seen of the interior earlier, the old merchant had nothing that would tempt even a beggar to steal. Besides, there had been something about him that told me that no matter if he had truly precious things in his shop, nobody—not even in the Floating World —would dare to steal from him.

I hesitated in the doorway, allowing my eyes to adjust to the gloom inside. Adam had said that he had been told that this man knew everything and everybody in the Floating World. And the merchant had called me Jun even though I was certain I had never seen him before. How was that possible? I closed my eyes to shut out the street around me and tried to remember if I had ever heard anything about this strange little shop. I frowned and shook my head. There was nothing, I was sure. Why, then, did I still search my memory?

I stared at the shadows inside. The day was very still, without any breeze, yet it seemed to me that a pile of woodcuts inside the doorway lifted and fell as if they had been disturbed by a breath of wind. Fancifully, I wondered if the movement had been caused by an unseen spirit rather than the wind. I wondered with wry amusement if the effects of Adam's whiskey were still with me. I decided quickly that I was fine, but then I was immediately irritated with my own gullibility. If this was the effect the shop had on me, then it was time I moved on. I turned, but before I could take a single step, I heard the merchant's voice call out to me very softly.

"Jun, you have come back, and so very soon. I owe you my thanks for taking the gaijin away before he could cause trouble for me." I hesitated and his voice wheedled. "Please, do come in. I have something you may be interested in."

I was startled at the words and hesitated. I knew I was going to go in when I found I had convinced myself there could be no harm in it. It might even prove useful in my search for Niko. I remembered that Adam had been convinced that the old merchant knew everything and everybody in the Floating World. If that was truly the case, it might be possible to get some information about Ikeda from him. And besides, I did not like the thought that there was somebody in the Floating World who was a stranger to me yet called me by my assumed name. It made me deeply uneasy. I would go in. Just for a moment.

The old merchant was still standing behind his counter. He gave the impression that he had always been there, in that exact space. That no matter what time of the day or night one entered, he would be there. Waiting like a spider waits for prey to enter its web.

"How do you know my name?" I asked abruptly. There was a sound like a very old door creaking and I realized it was the merchant laughing.

"Didn't you hear what your friend the gaijin said? He said I knew everything and everybody in the Floating World. He was wrong, of course. Things change so very quickly here that it is impossible to know everything. But as knowledge is vital to my humble business, I do my best."

"You have the advantage of me. You know my name, but I have no idea who you are." I spoke politely. This merchant might be grubby and very old, but the code of bushido insisted that compassion and courtesy were due to all—in particular, those who had less than oneself. And a glance at his old, faded robe assured me that this particular man was very needy indeed.

"My name is Ota." The merchant paused, looking at me with his head on one side, as if he expected that his name would mean something to me. I smiled courteously, still on my guard. I did not know him. But if he thought he was important enough to be known to me, then I would tread carefully.

"Good day to you, Ota-san," I said politely. "You said you had something that might interest me?"

I kept my eyes firmly on him. I knew if I glanced around, I would be unable to hide a smile. Really, what could he have that could possibly be of any interest to me amongst the piles of junk that crowded his shop?

"You don't know me, Jun?" His face was impassive, but I thought I heard a note of surprise in his voice. I shook my head, beginning to be irritated. I was wasting my time here.

I should never have come in at all. "But perhaps you have heard of my humble shop?"

I did smile then. I glanced around and allowed my face to show my incredulity. Why should I have heard of a grubby little shop that sold nothing but what looked like other people's cast-offs? Ota said nothing, but rather than be rude to him, I pretended to be interested in yet another tottering pile of woodblock prints at the end of the counter. I pushed at them with my finger and the top prints slid to one side. Three prints fell together, leaving the print beneath them exactly in place, as if it had been waiting for me to see it all along. I dismissed the idea as fanciful and then caught my breath.

This was no print. It was an original piece of brushwork that would have been used to create a wooden block that in its turn would have reproduced numerous prints. And I knew it at once. I had one of the prints in my room when I had lived on our family's estate. A pang of nostalgia brought tears to my eyes for the second time this morning as I stared and stared at the original. My brother Isamu had purchased the print for me.

"Thought you might like this," he had said cheerfully. "It's by a young, up and coming artist called Hokusai. Lovely colors."

I had indeed liked the print, which depicted a bird about to land on a peony blossom. I had hung it where I could see it each day when I awoke. And truly, the colors—a blue background behind subtle shades of pink—were beautiful. But if I had thought the print lovely, then the original painting was stunning. I picked it up carefully, thinking that Ota had been right after all. Truly, he did have something of interest to me.

But how had he known? I shrugged the notion away. It

was a coincidence, of course. A faint echo of Akira insisting there was no such thing as coincidence raised the fine down on my forearms. I shrugged the memory away. In this case, Akira was wrong, and I was pleased; he was arrogant enough to think he was always right. I knew differently.

"You do indeed have something to interest me, Ota-san. This is lovely. How much is it?"

"It has no price." Ota smiled, showing stumps of brown teeth. I wondered for no reason at all how old he was. His face was as wrinkled as the beach when the tide has retreated, but the eyes that peered from beneath his bushy brows were as young and bright as a very young child's.

"Oh. I had hoped to buy it." I put the painting down reluctantly, putting it respectfully into place on the teetering pile.

"It has no price," Ota repeated. "For you, it is free. Please take it. I am pleased it is going to somebody who will appreciate it."

"Thank you." I bowed deeply. Courtesy insisted that I accept the gift. But at the same time, it made things awkward. Tradition insisted that I must also repay the gift by buying something of equal value and I doubted very much that there was anything else here that was worth more than a copper coin. Ota was smiling at me, and I suddenly recalled what he had said earlier. "I'm sorry, I don't know anything about your shop. Is there any reason why I should?"

"It has been here for a very long time. I have owned it for many years, but it was here long before that." His voice was very soothing and his words fell pleasantly on my ears. "Many people think it is nothing more than a legend, that it has either never existed or that it ceased to exist in our father's father's time. They are wrong. The Shop of Dreams has been here since the Floating World began. It will never close until the Floating World ceases to exist."

I drew a sharp breath. The Shop of Dreams. I had heard of it. Everybody in Edo knew of it, but most people—as Ota had said—dismissed it as no more than a legend. Those that did believe in it said that anything the heart desired could be purchased here, but the price was high. Just as a dream inevitably died with the morning light, neither could anything as commonplace as money buy that dream. Some said the price was the buyer's soul. Others, a year of one's life. Others still said that no matter what was purchased here, no matter what the price paid, it would not bring happiness. And now, this ancient merchant was telling me that I was actually standing in the Shop of Dreams? That this grimy, junk-filled place was a fable come to life? I would have laughed if the Hokusai painting hadn't been in my hands.

"I see," I said politely. "Yes, I realize now that have heard of this place. But I thought it was just a legend, that it didn't exist."

"As you see, it does." Ota smiled gently. "I wonder, have you also heard from those that believe in my shop that nothing here is ever given without cost?"

"That is so." I nodded and glanced at my painting, held tightly in my hands. Ota obviously understood my confusion.

"That trifle is truly a gift, I assure you. I said that I had something that would be of interest to you, and that is not it. Will you come through?"

He turned as he spoke and lifted the bead curtain aside. I desperately wanted to turn around and leave this place. Suddenly, the shadows were sinister rather than just gloomy. I was sure if it became necessary, I could push Ota aside easily, but I was reluctant to even think about touching him. He was so very old, I thought his skin might crumble to dust at the slightest touch. I rubbed my fingers on my robe with distaste at the thought. His hand was still apparent, holding the curtain back for me. I took a deep breath and told myself to be sensible. Ota was no more than an old man who owned an old shop. But if he truly traded in information, he might know something that would be of value to me.

This was not the Shop of Dreams. Such a place could not exist. It was no more than a foolish dream itself. Ota was obviously a very clever man. He traded on the superstitions of his customers, no doubt to his own profit. But in spite of my sensible thoughts, I was reluctant to go behind the counter. Even more reluctant to touch Ota's hand.

"Come through, samurai warrior woman." Ota's voice was the soothing sound of an evening breeze whispering through pines. I moved forward without realizing I had moved a single step. How did he know what I was? Come to that, how had he seen through my disguise and realized I was even a woman? I was still dressed as a kagema. Not even Adam had thought me anything different until I had revealed myself to him. The thought was a passing nuisance; suddenly, it didn't really matter. The only important thing was what Ota was going to show me.

The back room was so different from the shop, it made me gasp. Here, everything was spotless. There was no tatami on the gleaming woodblock floor. I automatically kicked off my zori in the doorway and noticed subconsciously that the wood was warm, as if it was still part of the living tree. The single piece of furniture was a tall, wide chest, made of some pale wood I did not recognize. It was perfectly beautiful, each joint fitting so very well that I found it difficult to believe any human craftsman could have created it. The walls were traditionally constructed of silk shoji with wooden laths, but unlike those in the shop, the silk was sheer and clean and allowed the sunlight to penetrate almost unimpeded.

"Please, sit." Ota held his hand out and I sat down silently. The air was scented with jasmine perfume. I looked around but could not find a source for it. The sweet scent was delicious, but at the same time, I thought I could detect something beneath the flower perfume that was...odd. Not corrupt exactly, but something that had nothing at all to do with jasmine blossoms. It made my chest tighten to the extent that it rapidly became difficult to breathe.

"That perfume..." I waved my hand languidly, lost for words to explain my interest.

"You like it?" Ota was smiling gently. "Jasmine, of course. And a little something else to enhance it. Just as in life, my dear Jun, nothing should exist in isolation."

I nodded and smiled. His words seemed to make perfect sense and I inhaled deeply, suddenly finding it not only easy to breathe the delicious perfume, but also very pleasant. A small, far away voice in my brain told me to be very careful here in the Shop of Dreams. I listened to it as if the words had been spoken aloud and decided it was right. I should be careful. I *would* be careful.

"What do you want from me?" I demanded.

"Surely it should be the other way around?" Ota's gentle smile didn't falter. "People come to the Shop of Dreams to purchase something they cannot get elsewhere. Often, they go away disappointed. They tell their friends that this place is not the Shop of Dreams at all. That I sell nothing they could possibly want. Occasionally, if I feel so inclined, I allow my customers to buy what they desire—if it amuses me to do so. And very, very rarely does it happen that a customer has something that I want and that I have something they desire in return."

"Yes," I said. That made sense. I was only courteous that I should sit for a while, and Ota and I would discuss matters. But the small voice in my head persisted and made me speak. "But what do I have that you want? For that matter, what do you have that I desire?"

"Please, be patient for a few moments and you will have answers to your questions. You do not know me, Jun. But I know of you. I know of the Jun who was taken by Hana-san and caused her great anger by escaping. I know also of Kamakiri the blind anma, the woman the clumsy gaijin was seeking so very urgently."

"If you know about Kamakiri the anma, why didn't you tell Adam she no longer existed?" I interrupted.

"Because that was not what he wanted to hear. If I had convinced him of the truth, he would have been deeply unhappy. He is a very loud young man, and he was drawing unwanted attention to my shop. If he thought that he had not only lost his anma, but that he had been fooled and she had never existed in the first place, he would have been very angry. Someone would have called the authorities to deal with him. I do not wish the whole world to know about this place. It is for the select few only. Besides, I had no need to hurt him. The gods sent you along at just the right moment to take him away." He nodded at the Hokusai print I still held in my hand. "That trifle is a small gift to express my thanks at your intervention."

In spite of the subtle enchantment of the jasmine, I was chilled by his words. How did he know that Kamakiri the anma had not just gone from the Floating World but had never even lived? I did my best to sound casual. "Thank you.

But I assure you it was pure coincidence that I happened to be passing when I heard Adam's voice."

"Coincidence?" Ota wheezed. It took me a moment to realize he was laughing softly. "You and I know there is no such thing. It was fate. Had it not been destined, you would not have passed at that moment. Have you noticed my shop when you passed this way before?" I shrugged. He was right, but I was unwilling to admit it. "You see? Karma led Jun here, just as karma led Kamakiri the anma to Adam the gaijin. And it is also karma that I have in my possession something that the samurai lady Keiko will willingly give me what I ask for it."

My head was reeling. Truly, Ota knew everything that happened in the Floating World. Somehow, he knew me not just as Kamakiri the anma and Jun the kagema, but also did he know I had once been Keiko, a samurai's daughter. There was only one link he had missed—Kamakiri the oiran. I was astonished. There was no point in pretending I didn't know what he was talking about.

I met his eyes firmly and said, "What? What do you have that I want? That I will give anything for?"

Ota didn't speak. He stood—surprisingly fluidly for such an old man—and walked across to the beautiful chest. He threw open the lid and folded back layers of silk. The faintest odor of jako—musk geranium—cut through the intense jasmine smell. It was the clean, subtle perfume of newly laundered clothes folded and ready for use, and I breathed deeply, feeling my senses coming back to me with the familiar, homely smell. I was alert, and deeply suspicious.

Ota walked back toward me with something cradled in his arms. I stared at it and held my breath. He bowed and presented it to me silently.

I took his offering and almost dropped it, my hands were shaking so violently. It was a scabbard for a sword—a traditional samurai saya. I knew it instantly. The whole saya had been beautifully lacquered in black, with a pattern of chrysanthemum flowers embossed in gold and silver on top. It lay across my outstretched arms balanced so well I knew it belonged there. I stared at it, hardly able to believe what my eyes were showing me.

Very slowly, very carefully, I took hold of the pommel of the sword that lay within the saya. The blade slid out as easily as if it had been oiled. Now, a traditional samurai sword—the long katana—was grasped in my hand. It was much lighter than it looked and perfectly balanced. The light caught the blade, skimming a rainbow across the steel. This was perfection. I knew that the blade had been made from traditional tamahagane metal—the name means "jewel steel," and once seen, it is obvious why the metal is referred to thusly. It was light because during the making of the sword the steel had been forged and folded and forged and folded sixteen times, each time increasing the strength and precision of the blade. The master craftsman Masamune had made this sword many centuries ago. It was unique.

I knew this beautiful weapon. The last time I had seen it, it laid beside the body of my father.

The horror of the moment when I found the bodies of my father and my brother came back to me. I felt tears crowd my eyes and I blinked furiously to stop them from falling. *This* sword had been there when I found them. Overcome with grief and exhaustion, I had laid on the ground at their sides and sleep had overcome me. When I was awoken the next morning by my lover, Yo, father's sword was no longer at his side. At the time, it had seemed a small thing compared to my family's death. I had assumed that one of the surviving peasants had come back whilst I slept and stolen it. In any event, I had never expected to see it again. And now, I cradled it in my arms tightly and knew that my father had once loved this sword as much as his own father and grandfather—as much as all his ancestors back to the samurai who had commissioned it from the great Masamune—had loved it.

As I also loved it now. It was mine by right. I grasped the pommel fiercely and glared at Ota. If he tried to take it away from me, I would use it to kill him.

"It is yours by right, onna-bugeisha," he said in answer to my unspoken thoughts. "I will not tell you how I came by it. It doesn't matter. It is in my power to restore it to you, and I do that freely."

"And in return?" I demanded. "It's beyond price. The emperor himself would give you anything you demanded for it. I don't believe you are handing it to me for nothing."

"As you say, it is beyond price," Ota agreed. I thought he was looking at my katana hungrily and I grasped it firmly. "There is not enough money in the whole of Edo to buy that sword. And if there were, I wouldn't part with it to anybody but you. But there is something you can give me in return for it. Something more important than money could ever be."

It was on my tongue to say *anything,* but the spell of the Shop of Dreams had left me now and I was cautious.

"What?" I asked simply.

Ota stared into space. He did not speak for a long time, and I was becoming impatient. I wanted to leave the Shop of Dreams and take my father's sword with me. When he did speak, I was puzzled. His words seemed to have nothing to do with me, and still less with my father's sword. *My sword.*

"There are great changes coming to the Floating World. To the whole of Japan. Not this year, nor perhaps the next. But the changes are coming, and old as I am, I think I will live to see them."

"So?" I shrugged. Was Ota so old that his wits were wandering? Then his bright eyes caught my gaze and I sat still.

"Japan has been sealed from the outside world for hundreds of years." He stared at me, as if making sure I was paying attention. I nodded, silently urging him to go on. "But recently, there have been more and more gaijin appearing in Edo. I believe that still more and more of them will come. Those that have returned to their own lands have taken back tales of this nation to their masters, and they in turn will become hungry to make us share our treasures with them. The world outside Japan is vast and mysterious to us. We have made no effort to change, content to believe that nobody can match us. This is not so. I rarely leave my shop, but the world comes to me, and I hear everything.

"I have heard that the gaijin have weapons that would leave us gasping in awe. I have heard that they have medicines that can cure anything." I frowned, remembering the morphine pills I had stolen from Adam. "Also have I heard that they have magical ships that can cross an ocean with no need for a favorable wind. If they come—*when* they come—we will be powerless against them. All our past will be as nothing. The gaijin's dreams are not our dreams. They will destroy my shop because although they won't understand it, they will fear it. If the Shop of Dreams falls, then the Floating World will fall with it. And if that happens, then I have betrayed the trust that has been placed in my hands by my ancestors."

I almost smiled at Ota's vehemence. True, everybody grumbled that there were more gaijin in Edo every year that went past. But as for the rest of it, that was pure nonsense. Japan had cut itself off from the contamination of the outside world centuries ago. No man alive could remember when it had been any different. I could not believe that it ever would be different. Let the gaijin come if they wanted to. Of course they were envious of us; that was only natural. Besides, what did Ota think I could do to help if things did happen as he forecast?

"I hear you, Ota-san," I said politely. "But surely the future is in the hands of the gods? I don't see how I can help you."

"*You* cannot help me." Ota put a curious emphasis on the word "you." I frowned at him suspiciously. "But I told you, you being here is karma. There is perhaps a single man in the whole of Edo who can defend the Shop of Dreams. He will keep the old traditions alive and keep those who would destroy the Shop of Dreams away. He will do that if you ask him to help me when I need him."

"And who is that?" I asked indulgently. "The shogun? The emperor himself? I'm sorry to disappoint you, but I don't know either of them."

"Akira-san. Akira the yakuza," Ota said simply. "He is a young man now. But already he has much power. In the years to come, I believe he will become even more powerful than his father was. The supremacy of the Floating World will hang from his obi like a netsuke. If you ask him to be here when I need him, he will do it."

I almost laughed. Akira the yakuza? How could this silly old man really believe that a mere gangster could ever wield such incredible power? There was, I acknowledged, something very seductive about Akira. Already, he had an aura of authority that went far beyond his years. But such dominance as Ota was talking about could surely only lie with the highest in the land. Besides, I could hardly claim to be very close to Akira. Had we been lovers, then perhaps I could approach him with Ota's request. But we were not. A thought occurred to me and I stiffened.

"How did you know I'm acquainted with Akira?" My voice was abrupt with surprise. Ota smiled and bowed his head, apparently not noticing my discourtesy.

"The news of the whole world comes to my door, onna-bugeisha. Just as you have."

I was shaken, but still refused to admit it. I spoke lightly. "I see. Well, I'm sorry, Ota-san. If things happen as you say, I don't believe a mere yakuza will ever be powerful enough to overturn it. And I certainly don't know him well enough to ask him for such a favor."

"No matter. If I give you the sword, all I ask is that you go to Akira and pass on my words. Nothing else."

"Yes. Yes, I will," I said quickly. If all Ota wanted from me was a promise to speak to Akira, then I would do it, even though in my heart I knew it was all nonsense.

Just as much as the Shop of Dreams was nonsense.

SIX

A butterfly seems
To look at me. I wonder
What it really sees

"Keep still," Hana hissed. "If you wriggle, your makeup will smudge and we'll be here all night waiting for you."

I hadn't moved at all. It was Fuku's hand that was shaking so much that she had blurred the line of my brows. The geisha glanced at me timidly and I crossed my eyes at Hana's back. Fuku giggled behind her hand and tried again. I could barely believe how long it was taking. To begin, Fuku had applied an oily lotion all over my face, right down to where my breasts disappeared into my chemise. I had watched, fascinated, as she mixed a white powder with water and then applied it over the same areas with a thick brush. It tickled, especially when she moved on to the nape of my neck, taking the paste almost between my shoulder blades in a "W" shape. By that time, I was desperate to move, but there was still more to come. My eyes and eyebrows were drawn in with a charcoal stick and my lips colored a bright, glossy red.

A drop of the same flower distillate I had used to blur my vision when I needed to make myself more convincing as Kamakiri the blind anma went into my eyes. The cold sting was comfortingly familiar. That was the finishing touch. Finally satisfied with her work, Fuku held a small mirror up so I could see myself.

This was really me? I blinked to focus my vision. I had been anxious that someone at the party might recognize Kamakiri the oiran despite her geisha disguise. I understood at once that I need not have worried. I had worn plenty of makeup when I was acting the part of an oiran, but it was nowhere near as stylized as the face Fuku had created for me. When she finally put my wig on for me, the transformation was complete. This wig was quite compact, with just three understated—but costly—ornamental pins inserted carefully. Kamakiri the oiran's wig had been huge and hung with so many vulgarly large ornaments that they jingled in the breeze like a horse's harness.

"Ready?" Hana snapped. She inspected me and finally nodded grudgingly. "You look the part, at least. Apart from you being so tall and slim, that is."

Hana sounded amused. She exchanged a glance with Fuku, who also smiled. I shrugged it off; I could hardly help my height and figure.

I stood carefully, fiddling with my obi. Hana slapped my hand away and wagged her finger silently at me. That I could understand. The elaborate knot had taken Fuku forever to get exactly right. I could never have hoped to fasten it myself. To make things even more complicated, it was worn at the back rather than at the front where Kamakiri the oiran had worn it.

"I'm used to wearing the knot at the front," I complained. "It's going to be uncomfortable at the back."

"Only yujo and oiran wear their obi with the knot at the front," Hana sneered. "For obvious reasons."

It took a moment for me to understand what she meant, and then I winced at my own naiveté. Still, I was finally ready. I took a deep breath and straightened my back. Instantly, Hana was snapping at me.

"No," she barked. "You're all wrong. You're supposed to be a geisha. Look at the way Fuku is standing. Keep your head down modestly. Look at the ground. Let your shoulders fall. Curve your back a little. Fold your hands in front of you, just above your obi. I have only allowed you to come tonight because Akira-chan asked it of me. I would have been very happy never to see you again. Do not bring disgrace on my house, Keiko."

"I will do my best, Hana-san," I said calmly. I heard real anxiety in Hana's voice, and suddenly I understood that she was not just angry that I was here. In fact, this occasion was almost as important for her as it was for me. If I behaved poorly, then I would shame Hana in front of one of her most important clients. A man to whom she already owed a debt of honor that she could never repay. Although even as the thought came to me, I wondered if perhaps Akira had his own ideas about that.

Akira. I squeezed my arms against my ribs to suppress a shiver of excitement as I thought of him. He was an enigma to me, and the more I saw of him, the more confusing I found him.

I had spent three long days waiting for him to tell me that the arrangements had been made for Endo's party. Every time I thought about it—and that was very often—I had resisted the urge to go to him, to demand if arrange-

ments were in place yet. I controlled my impatience, anticipating that he would come to me himself with the news
when everything was done. Instead, he sent one of his men
with a note. I was furious. I sent the man away with a cool
message of thanks. I went and thanked Akira myself, in
spite of the fact that I thought that was exactly what he had
planned. No doubt that was why he had sent his man in the
first place. He knew how much it would annoy me. Or at
least, I hoped that was what he was thinking. The
conflicting thoughts were beginning to give me a headache.
Damn the man; how dare he play games with me when
Niko was the stake?

He welcomed me politely, though I was sure I saw a
smile of pleasure cross his face, quickly concealed. In
contrast, Marika threw herself at my feet in an ecstasy of
pleasure. I scratched her belly, smiling as she threw back
her head and screamed loudly.

"The shiba scream." Akira sounded amused. He leaned
down and ruffled Marika's fur. "Do all animals like you,
Kamakiri?"

"I've never thought about it. They do seem to. But
that's probably because they sense I like them." He was
smiling, an infuriating, indulgent smile. I was instantly
annoyed. "Why do you still call me Kamakiri? Both
Kamakiri the anma and Kamakiri the oiran have gone
from my life."

"I see." He stroked Marika very gently. I watched his
fingers busy themselves in her neck. I felt a flash of deep
annoyance with myself as I envied the fact that he seemed
more interested in his dog than me. "Then what should I
call you? It seems that Jun the kagema has also vanished.
Shall we settle on Keiko?"

Akira lifted his head and stared at me. His grey eyes

were unreadable. Would anything ever get past his guard, I wondered. Anything, or anybody?

"Keiko will do very well," I said stiffly. "But that doesn't matter. I came to thank you for making arrangements for Endo-san's party. And also to show you this."

I had wrapped my father's katana—*my* katana—in silk. I pulled the cloth aside and held out the beautiful saya for Akira's inspection. I was strangely torn. At one moment, I wanted to keep it to myself, and a heartbeat later, I wanted to show my treasure to the world. Now, I had the pleasure of seeing deep awe in Akira's eyes.

"It's a samurai katana, isn't it? Is it very old?" he asked. I noticed with surprise that he didn't try and touch it. The saya was so beautifully lacquered, it invited the hand to caress it, but Akira seemed immune to its draw.

"Yes. It was made by the great master Masamune many centuries ago." I slid the blade from the saya. It glided out with the hiss of oiled silk, and it seemed to me that the gleaming steel rejoiced in the light. "It was my father's katana. There isn't another one like it anywhere. It has belonged to the men of my family for generations."

I laid the sword across my hands and held it out to him courteously. I was shocked when he almost flinched back.

"It's not for me to touch such a sword," he said. He raised his eyes from the gleaming blade and looked at me. "There are many legends about such katana. I've heard it said that they will obey only their rightful owner. That if anybody else tries to touch them, it will bring the greatest ill-fortune on them. If I dared to touch your katana, I don't doubt that it would turn in your hands and cut me for my disrespect."

I was amazed, and also rather amused. So, the feared Akira had a weakness, then. He was superstitious. I almost laughed out loud at him, then I looked at the gleaming blade that lay across my palms and any inclination to laugh died. This was my sword now, and instinctively I knew that the katana understood that. It would fight to protect me, but should anybody else try to use it, would they be as successful? Somehow, I doubted it. I slid it back in the saya reverently and wrapped the silk around it, hiding the whole from sight. Akira breathed a sigh of relief as it disappeared from view.

"It knows you," he said quietly. "It knows you are its mistress. It will obey you, just as Marika obeys me." The pretty dog wagged her tail at the sound of her name. She laid her head on my foot with a deep sigh of contentment and Akira laughed. I laughed with him, relieved that the tension had been broken. "It seems you have stolen my dog's soul, Keiko-chan. No matter. It has undoubtedly gone to safe hands. Tell me, how did you come to acquire your father's katana?"

Now that the moment had come, I felt incredibly foolish.

"I found it in a shop, deep in the Floating World. A funny, old fashioned place that seemed to sell everything but had nothing of any value on display." Oddly, I found myself extremely reluctant to tell Akira how I had been led to it by the sound of Adam's voice. "It was very strange. I had never been in that particular shop before, but the merchant knew me. He insisted he had something that would interest me. Something that belonged with me. I recognized the katana at once, but I have no idea how he knew it was mine by right."

Akira was leaning forward, his whole face alight with interest. "It must be worth a prince's ransom. Did the merchant say how he came by it?"

"No. We didn't discuss it. And he wouldn't accept any money for it either." Akira's eyebrows betrayed his amazement as they shot up. "He asked only for a single favor in exchange for it."

"How extraordinary!" he said. "And was it a very great favor?"

"No. It wasn't even something that I could do for him." I paused, ordering my thoughts, and then the words left my mouth in a rush, as if they were glad the moment had come to be released. "He insisted that *you* are the only person who can help him. The merchant—Ota—is sure that the gaijin are going to force Japan open in the future. That everything is going to change, especially in the Floating World. He asked only one thing in return for my precious katana. He wanted me to ask if you would protect him and his shop when the danger comes."

There. It was out. And spoken aloud my bargain no longer sounded at all silly. Akira stared at me. His face was unreadable, but his eyes were very bright, the pupils so big they almost drowned out his grey irises.

"This merchant—Ota you said his name was?" I nodded. "And the shop? Can you describe it for me?"

I closed my eyes, the better to remember every detail. Akira said nothing at all until I finished.

"Could you find the shop again?" he asked. I was about to say of course I could when I hesitated, first tracing the route I had taken in my mind. I had gone down the main street in the Floating World, Nakanocho, and branched off into Willow Street. Or had I? Was it Willow Street or Cherry Tree Avenue? The more I thought about it, the less certain I became.

"Actually, I'm not sure I could. I was so excited to find the katana, I can't remember how I got there," I said lamely.

"What was it called? This shop?" Akira leaned forward, pinning me with his gaze.

"Ota said it was the Shop of Dreams," I said. I expected Akira to laugh, to say that I had been deceived by the old merchant, but he did not.

"The Shop of Dreams," he whispered. His eyes were so bright, he looked as if he was in the grip of a fever. "And you say Ota-san told you that I was the only man who could help him when the time comes?"

"Yes. I don't understand how he had even found out we knew each other, but that's what he said. He gave me the katana in return for my promise that I would pass his words on to you."

"Ah. I am truly in your debt, Keiko. You have given me my future." Akira got to his feet. He was moving around as if his body was unable to contain some violent emotion. I stared at him in bewilderment.

"What do you mean? I've just passed on Ota's message, no more."

He paused and hunkered down in front of me. He was so excited that he forgot his manners entirely and held my wrists in his hands. His grip was firm. Had it been anybody else who was holding me imprisoned—even Yo—I would have jerked away angrily. But Akira's hands were cool and strong. I found his touch pleasurable.

"You have given me my future," he repeated. "They say that the Shop of Dreams cannot be found unless it desires one to find it. It led you to its door and gave you your heart's desire."

I was about to protest that I had not spared a thought for my father's katana since his death, but I did not. The moment I had seen it in the Shop of Dreams, I knew it belonged with me. Me, and nobody else. Possessing it satisfied a need that had been buried deep inside my soul. Now that I had it, I was complete. I would never allow it to be taken from me. I was a warrior woman of the samurai, and I had a samurai's weapon.

"Perhaps," I said cautiously. "But why does Ota's message mean so much to you?"

"I don't know Ota-san," Akira said respectfully. "I have never been to the Shop of Dreams. But Ota knows of me. Better still, he knows my future. Do you understand, Keiko? He told you that in the time to come I will be the only man in the whole of Edo who has enough power to keep him safe from the gaijin. Don't underestimate the foreign barbarians, Keiko. Their ways are strange to us, but I believe that they have very great and terrible strength. A strength that will grow with every year that passes. But thanks to you, I now know that they will never be my master. That I will triumph over them. If Ota-san has asked for my help, I am deeply honored. I will do all I can to help him with great joy."

I took a deep breath. My encounter with Ota and the Shop of Dreams had become blurred in my mind. If I were not holding my katana in my hands, I would have thought I had slept and dreamed of the Shop of Dreams. But Akira was clearly overjoyed by Ota's request. A sudden insight gave me understanding; it would not have mattered in the least if I had lied about my encounter with Ota. Akira clearly believed it was all true. As far as he was concerned, his future was clear. He was destined to become the most powerful man in Edo. He believed it, so it would happen.

"Then on behalf of Ota, I thank you." I rubbed my wrists where Akira's grip had left the impressions of his fingers. "But that is all in the future. Tell me, your message said the party was arranged for Endo-san and his friends. Will you be present at Endo-san's party?"

Akira laughed. "No. I hardly think a noble such as Endo-san would welcome the presence of a mere yakuza at a party given in his honor. Hana has agreed that you can attend—" I could tell from his tone what Hana thought about *that* idea. "—along with all of her most sought after geisha. She has told Endo that he is most welcome to bring along as many of his friends as he wishes. The event will bring him great face, and I'm sure he will invite as many of his friends as he can to show off the honor. I hope Ikeda will be amongst them. If he is, Hana will introduce you to him and then it's up to you to find out all you need to know. If he doesn't come for some reason, it will be more difficult. But I'm sure that Hana will think of some way of getting the information out of Endo."

"If she doesn't, I will," I said firmly.

Akira nodded. "I cannot imagine that any man would be able to withstand you once you have your mind set."

We smiled at each other, both understanding perfectly what he actually meant.

SEVEN

How strange. My words will
Echo from a mountaintop
and inside a cave

*N*ow that the moment had arrived, I found myself extremely nervous. Fuku had assured me that all I had to do was watch what she did and follow her lead. She seemed to find it amusing that I was worried. But of course, she had no idea how much depended on this evening. I took a moment to myself, seeing my katana in my mind, trying to draw courage from its shining blade, but it did little to help. I felt as if the ancient blade was bewildered why I had left it behind and that it did not understand my need. Had I asked it to support me in battle, I felt it would have been as eager as a faithful dog. This evening *would* be one of strife, but not one my blade had ever experienced. I felt not in the least foolish as I mentally assured my katana that the time for real action would come. And soon.

I put the thought to one side, confident that when the time arrived I would be ready.

I had expected that we would be waiting to greet Hana's patrons when they entered the tea house, but instead, I huddled in an ante-room with the rest of the geisha. They chattered like birds, glancing at me occasionally and tittering behind their fans. After a while, I became irritated with their silliness. How could they not understand that this was an important night? At a signal I missed entirely, Fuku beckoned me forward and I walked behind her into the large, beautifully appointed reception room. Hana, I thought grudgingly, had excellent taste.

The guests were already seated. Three maiko were circulating with flasks of sake, stopping frequently to fill raised cups. The men had already eaten; the tatami was littered with dishes and chopsticks. As we entered, maids scurried in from the opposite side of the room and cleared the remains of the feast away briskly. I was relieved. My stomach was churning so badly I knew I could never have eaten a morsel. I glanced around from behind my fan and my spirits plummeted.

Ikeda was not here.

Very well. This would be more difficult than I had hoped. No matter. Somehow, I would find the information I needed. I would not let Niko down.

Hana rose to her feet as we entered. She waved her hand graciously, and my fellow geisha dispersed themselves with the grace of petals floating on a gentle wind. I hovered, waiting for my signal.

"Keiko-chan," she cooed. I blinked in surprise, wondering for a moment if she was talking to somebody else. "I have told Endo-san all about my newest jewel, and he is burning to meet you. Do come and sit next to him."

I bowed deeply and did my best to imitate Fuku's submissive glide. I was surprised when Endo rose to his feet to greet me. I kept my foolish smile plastered on my lips as I understood at once why Fuku and Hana had seemed amused when they commented on my height. The top of Endo's head barely reached my chin. And I saw from his fatuous expression of delight that—like many small men— he adored tall women. Particularly those who were happy to kowtow deeply to him as I did now. Unfortunately, he was not only short, but portly as well. When he smiled at me, his eyes almost vanished in folds of fat.

"Keiko-san," he murmured, "I am delighted to meet you. Please, do sit beside me."

Endo must have had short legs and a reasonably long back. He was built rather like a duck, I thought. Seated, we were much of a height, especially as I took care to keep my head bowed at an attentive angle. The posture gave me a backache very quickly, and I began to feel a certain respect for the geisha around me who not only did this every day, but even managed to look as if they were enjoying them-selves. Grudgingly, I admitted that there was more than one sort of courage in this world.

At least my patron was easy to amuse. I was deeply on edge for the first few minutes, worried that I would run out of conversation. I needn't have bothered. As long as I tittered politely at his every witticism and constantly looked adoringly at him, Endo was obviously delighted with me. In any event, he talked non-stop—exclusively about himself.

As the evening wore on, I became increasingly desper-ate. I had barely been able to squeeze a word into the conversation. If this went on, it would be time for Endo and his friends to move on to a house of assignation and I would not have had a chance to steer the conversation round to Ikeda.

"Endo-san." Hana kneeled at his side and held out a flask of sake temptingly. "I do hope that this foolish girl is not boring you too greatly?" I hid my indignation behind my fan. Hana flashed me the quickest of warning looks and then turned her full attention back on Endo. "I wonder if you would like to try a little of this sake? It is rather special and is reserved for only my most honored patrons."

She poured with a generous hand. Endo emptied his cup in a single swig and held it out for more.

"That is excellent sake, Hana-chan." He beamed. "And I assure you, Keiko-chan here is a delightful companion." He leered at me and I lowered my eyes as I managed a delighted smile.

"I am most grateful that you are enjoying the evening," Hana purred. I kept the smile painted on my lips as she hunched her shoulders and drew her brows together in an expression of concern so exaggerated it was theatrical. "I hope that all is perfection for you, Endo-san. But I must apologize for bothering you with one tiny thing. I had hoped that your friend Ikeda-san would have accompanied you this evening. I am afraid that I owe him an apology regarding a certain business matter, and I was looking forward to speaking to him about it."

Endo chuckled, a ripe grin splitting his face. He was obviously drunk, and I wondered about the sake Hana had given to him.

"Oh, I know all about that!" he said happily. "Ikeda was most distressed about it at the time." He leered at me and I made my expression appear fascinated. "My friend Ikeda-san has a certain problem that can only be resolved by the intimate attentions of an untouched flower. I suppose it's understandable that he came to the Floating World to find his heart's desire. Unfortunately, Hana here managed to let his prize slip through her fingers." He wagged his own finger roguishly at Hana. She bared her teeth in a smile and I guessed she would have enjoyed biting that finger clean off. "I daresay if he'd gone looking for such a thing in a backwater like Hakone, where he lives and is an important man, everybody would know about his problem and gossip behind his back. Here in the Floating World, Ikeda-san is nothing special, so nobody cares. But in his own little town, he's the wealthiest man in the place and a big landowner. Shame you lost the lady in question, Hana-san. He would have paid you very well for her. But there, spilled water cannot be coaxed back in the tray. If it bothers you, I'll make sure to give him your apologies next time I see him."

And that was it. As simple as that. Hana filled his cup yet again and murmured her apologies for disturbing us. She slipped away like a shadow, but I was sure I could feel the triumph radiating from her turned back. I might have gotten the better of her once, but now she was surely showing me that she was the superior of the two of us here on her own territory.

I was almost shaking with relief. Suddenly, I was very relieved that the evening was far advanced. I was so full with nervous excitement, I could barely keep still. My responses to Endo became automatic; I barely noticed what I was doing or saying. Perhaps he was even drunker than I had thought, as he still seemed delighted with my company. So delighted that he was reluctant to leave even when his friends began to rise and make polite leave-taking noises.

I was grudgingly grateful when Hana came back to us, bowing deeply.

"Endo-san." She smiled. "I am deeply honored that you

and your friends have enjoyed our company this evening. As you can see—" She waved her hands at the other men, who were on their feet. "—your friends wish to move on to other pleasures. I do hope that I have anticipated your wishes correctly. I have arranged for you all to move on to Miko's house. It is at your sole disposal. At my cost, of course."

"Miko's, eh?" Endo pursed his lips. I could read the indecision on his fat, sweating face. Had he been hoping that the Hidden House would have been made available to him? Finally, greed and lust obviously combined and won. "That is most kind of you, Hana. One could wish for no finer house of assignation to end a most enjoyable evening. Perhaps you might like to say your farewells to my friends? I'm sure they will wish to give you their thanks. I would like a quiet word with Keiko-chan."

The hint was heavy and ungracious. It was also unforgivably rude. Even Hana's polite mask slipped for a second, and I saw naked loathing in her eyes for this vulgar man who had her in his power. I found myself sympathizing with her. Akira had hinted that he would pay Endo a visit when this evening was over. I hoped he would.

"But of course, lord." Although her voice was smooth, the irritation shone through clearly. Endo appeared not to notice. "I will leave you to enjoy Keiko-san's undoubted pleasures for a moment more."

"Dear Keiko-chan." As soon as Hana was out of earshot, he bent close to me. There was no need at all to whisper as there was nobody else left anywhere near. The room was very warm, and Endo was beginning to smell unpleasantly sweaty. It was an effort to keep my smile in place. "I cannot tell you how much I have enjoyed this evening. I do hope it will be the first of many for us."

He was making an assignation with me. I struggled not to laugh.

"You honor me, Endo-san," I managed to murmur. His fat face creased into a wide grin.

"As my friends are clearly anxious to move on to Miko's house, I must join them. But I promise I will send a message to you tomorrow. I can find you here, I trust?"

"Certainly," I murmured.

Endo produced an envelope from his obi and slid it into my hand. He took the opportunity to touch my breast as he did so. I remained seated, my head bowed as he rose and strutted off. I expected him to throw back his head and crow like a dung-hill cockerel.

"How much did he give you?" Hana asked.

I opened the envelope and showed her. She flushed with anger.

"The cheap rat!" she snarled. "How dare he dishonor one of my geisha with such a trivial amount."

"I'm not one of your geisha," I pointed out.

Hana shrugged. "He didn't know that." She glared at the envelope, and suddenly we were both grinning.

"You have my admiration, Hana-san," I said genuinely. "You and all your geisha. I could never manage to pretend to please these vain, ignorant men night after night."

"*Pretend* is the right word," she said quietly. "That's all it is—play-acting. But not one of the fools sees that. They all think my girls kowtow to them for pleasure. Most men are stupid. If you are fortunate to find one who is not, I suggest you keep him very carefully, if it is possible for you to do so."

We stared at each other in full understanding. Akira's name was not mentioned. But I understood the implicit warning in her words. I held her glance for a moment, and then looked at my envelope with its miserable contents.

"I would not enjoy this money," I said. "But I think the kannushi at Jokan-Ji Temple will be able to make good use of it."

I thought even Hana approved of that.

EIGHT

If you wish to see
Yourself, you must look in a
Mirror, not at me

*I*f I had not owed Akira a huge debt of gratitude for arranging the meeting with Endo, I would simply have gone to Hakone immediately and left a message for him. But I could not. No matter how much I wanted to go—*now*—the courtesy that had been ingrained in me since I could first speak demanded that I thank him and tell him my plans.

"I'm deeply grateful to you for making it possible for me to meet with Endo-san." I spoke to Akira formally, hiding my excitement. "And to Hana for persuading him to tell me where I can find Ikeda. Now that I know where Ikeda lives, I intend to set out for Hakone at once."

"You're planning on entering the tiger's lair alone?" He sounded so amused, I was immediately on my guard.

"Most certainly," I said stiffly. "I am deeply grateful for the help you have already given to me. But Niko is my problem. Besides, what else would work? If I took an army of men with me and marched on his house, if he is as rich and well-connected as Endo said, he would simply send for the magistrate and have us all imprisoned. For all I know, he may even be the magistrate."

I saw reluctant admiration in Akira's eyes. "You may well be right. But what other way is there? We must assume Niko is in his house. And she is no doubt well-guarded. How do you intend to get to her and get her out?"

I had a sudden memory of Yo flitting past the guard at my family's house. The man never knew he had been there. True, Yo was shinobi; it was his tradition to be unseen and unheard. But I was onna-bugeisha; what was easy for a mere paid mercenary should surely be achievable for a warrior woman of the samurai? The thought of Yo made my mind still for a moment.

My life had been so very full since he had left me to take care of his own business, it had not been so very difficult to push thoughts of him away. Besides, I was determined that I would not miss him too much. Naturally, I would be happy when he returned to the Floating World. But I refused to devote my life to wondering and worrying about him.

Akira was staring at me curiously. His eyes were cool; I had never seen anybody with eyes as light as his before. Was it natural for them to show no expression? It annoyed me. I had always taken particular pride in my ability to read a person's inner thoughts from their expression. In Akira's case, I perceived nothing beyond his words. I snapped my concentration back to Niko and spoke firmly.

"My plans are in place. I will go to Ikeda as Kamakiri the blind anma. Once I arrive in Hakone, I will seek an audience with Ikeda. Very properly and politely, of course. I intend to tell him that one has told me about his problem and that I have in my possession some magical gaijin pills that are guaranteed to cure his condition. Once he has those, he will have no further need for Niko."

I knew I sounded smug. And why not? I was pleased with my plan. It seemed to me to fulfill all my desires. Niko would be released. At the same time, I would have my revenge on Ikeda. My pills would be useless, no more than an herbal remedy that could be found in any apothecary shop. They would have no effect on his baidoku. I would win, no matter what. If fortune smiled on Ikeda, he would remain disgusting and disfigured, forced to stay a recluse until death claimed him. At best, his disease would overtake him and he would die quickly, which would probably be a merciful end for the wretched man, and far better than he deserved.

"So easy?" Akira's face was serious, but I was sure he was mocking me. I stared at him coolly.

"I believe so," I said loftily.

"It's not going to work," he said bluntly. I was immediately annoyed, but I hid it, staring at him silently, my eyebrows raised in question. "To begin with, he would wonder how an anma from the Floating World had found out about his condition. You know yourself how he has tried to keep to the shadows. He'll demand to know who told you. The only person you know who is acquainted with him is Endo, and you can hardly name him. It would be far too easy for Ikeda to check to see if he had sent you. You would have to pretend you had just heard some gossip. And even if he were foolish enough to accept that an unknown anma had found out he needed her services, he would be deeply suspicious that she had walked so far out of Edo just on the chance that he would grant her an audience."

Although I said nothing, Akira raised his hand as if to

ask me to wait until he had finished. "Listen to me for a moment. The man is far from a fool. I have found out a little about our friend Ikeda. He started with almost nothing and worked his way almost to the top echelons of society in his province by a combination of intelligence and ruthlessness.

"His first wife was said to be remarkably ugly, but fortunately for Ikeda, she came from a good family and carried with her an immense dowry. His father-in-law died very soon after the marriage. His wife and son were so distraught at his death that they both conveniently committed suicide shortly after, leaving Ikeda the sole heir. Then he once again he married well.

"His second wife—the wife he has now—is the daughter of a very minor noble. Her father had fallen on hard times and it was rumored that Ikeda was given his daughter in exchange for the purchase of his debts. Of course, for the marriage to be acceptable to society, Ikeda had to be adopted into the noble family. Once that was done, Ikeda became noble himself. I believe that's the way these things are arranged in polite society." Akira smiled gently at me, and I nodded briskly. He was amusing himself at my expense; he knew perfectly well that he was right. "The second wife is still alive, but hasn't been seen in public for many years. It may well be that Ikeda has infected the poor woman with his loathsome disease. In any event, he has no living children. I have heard that that is one of the reasons he is so anxious to obtain a cure. He wants an heir. A man-child to carry on his newly noble line after his death."

Akira paused, looking at me with his head on one side as if I was a bright child and he was hoping for an intelligent answer. He irritated me deeply.

"I hear what you say. But your point is?" I asked arrogantly. "I knew he was a deeply unpleasant man, and I assumed that if he had enough money to bid for me, he was rich. You may be right when you say my plans for Kamakiri the anma to visit him are flawed. But how else am I going to get close to him? He's obviously seen me in the streets of the Floating World dressed as Kamakiri the oiran when he was hiding in the shadows. I could hardly turn up at his home as her. There would be no reason at all for an oiran to venture into the provinces unless she had received a specific invitation from a patron." My mind was working furiously. I spoke eagerly as a solution came to me. "I agree I can't confront him as either Kamakiri the anma or Kamakiri the oiran. But there is another way. Ikeda wouldn't know anything at all about Keiko the noble samurai lady. In spite of his marriage, Ikeda's never gained access to samurai society. If he had, I would have known of him. So if he doesn't know me, what's to stop me turning myself into a newly widowed noblewoman, traveling to take her mind away from her sad bereavement? I'm sure Hakone must have something worth visiting—a decent temple, at the least. If I arrived there all alone and grieving, surely it would only be polite for the most important man in Hakone to get in touch with me to offer his condolences?"

I heard the rising excitement in my voice as I elaborated my new plan. It felt right. It would work, I was sure of it. If I had never come across Ikeda in samurai society, neither would he have heard of me. And surely a newly widowed and apparently rich samurai lady, alone and friendless in a town that was strange to her, would be enticing bait for an ambitious man like Ikeda.

Judging by his expression, Akira failed to share my enthusiasm.

"Have you gone deaf, Keiko?" He asked so rudely he

made me gasp. "Didn't you hear me tell you not a moment ago that Ikeda was completely ruthless? I have no proof that he actually murdered his family, but my guess is that he did. If he's prepared to murder even those who are close to him for his own gain, he's a very dangerous man. I'm not going to allow you to get anywhere near him on your own."

My mouth opened and closed in amazement as I repeated his words silently to myself. *He* was not going to allow *me* to do what I thought fit? I made sure I had control of my temper before I spoke.

"Thank you for your concern, Akira-san," I said icily. "But what makes you think you have any right to dictate to me what I will or will not do? You are not my husband. Not even my lover. We have repaid any debts that lay between us. You cannot stop me doing what I want to do. *I* will not allow *you* to tell me what I'm going to do."

I got to my feet and bowed formally to him. I was so furious I felt I had to get out of his presence at once before my temper betrayed my manners. I had taken perhaps two steps toward the door when Akira laid his hand on my arm, his fingers biting through my robe and holding me like bonds of iron.

"You will not go, Keiko. You will not go to Hakone. Still less will you leave me until I'm satisfied you've seen sense."

Pure fury made me flush with heat. Akira had gone too far. He had not only touched me, he had actually held on to me, against my will. Perhaps he was only a riverbed beggar of a yakuza, but that was no excuse. What was going to happen to him was entirely his fault.

I swiveled, ducking under his arm and twisting so he was forced to let me go or sprain his wrist by hanging on. Before he had time to get over the first shock, I pivoted around and drove my elbow into his ribs. Or at least that had been my plan. But Akira was no longer standing there. He had moved with incredible speed, and my elbow gave nothing but a glancing blow to his upper arm. I had a moment to hope it had hurt anyway, then he snaked forward and his arms were around my waist, lifting me against his chest and off my feet.

That worried me not at all. The essence of bodily combat is to use the strength of one's opponent against them. Unless a small man—or woman—is facing an opponent the size of a sumo wrestler, it is a strategy that invariably works. I moaned softly and allowed my body to go limp as if Akira had hurt me. He hesitated, and I put my hands together just like my former namesake the praying mantis and forced them quickly between his arms, at the same time bringing my foot around to kick his knee. He gave a grunt of pain and relaxed his grip sufficiently for me to dart away from him.

I could, I knew, have escaped at that moment. But I was having far too much fun to even consider it. We circled each other warily, assessing strengths and weaknesses.

"Keiko-chan," Akira said softly. He was smiling, and I knew he was enjoying our contest every bit as much as I was. "You took me by surprise. You should know that it is many years since that happened to me. And I promise you will not be able to do it again."

"Akira-san," I mocked, my head tilted to one side. "How can that be? You know I am onna-bugeisha. How did you come to let your guard down in my presence?"

Akira didn't answer. Instead, he glanced to my left and looked annoyed. I almost laughed. Did he really think I would fall for that? I pretended to follow his gaze. When he lunged for me, I put my foot out and tripped him up. I was surprised when he gathered himself and recovered his balance with the grace of a dancer.

"One has to try the obvious." He shrugged. "Most men would have fallen for that trick. But of course, you are not a man. I must try and remember that."

"Do," I said cordially. "And I will try and remember that you are not samurai and could not be expected to understand the code of bushido, so you think it's only fair to do anything to win out over a poor, defenseless woman."

He gave a great shout of laughter, but I could see his eyes were cold. For a moment, I felt deeply guilty. Of course he would care nothing for the samurai code, and I should never have sneered at him in that way. I was angry with myself and distracted by that anger. Akira chose his moment well; before I could speak, he feinted to one side. I expected the move to be corrected and tensed, ready to go in the other direction. But it was all a bluff; Akira stood his ground and caught me slightly off balance. He had learned his lesson well. He did not attempt to put his arms around my waist, but instead grabbed my hair, tugging my head back fiercely. A second later, a dagger was at my throat, the sharp point just breaking the skin. I felt a bead of blood run down my neck.

"As you pointed out, I know nothing about the code of bushido. I am nothing but a lowly yakuza. One so beneath notice that any samurai wouldn't think twice about testing the sharpness of his blade against my unworthy neck."

He sounded genuinely bitter. His breath was hot against my ear, and it was the words as well as his breath that were angry. He let go of my hair and put his free arm around my shoulders, hugging me tightly in an embrace that had nothing to do with affection. I had insulted him carelessly. I lowered my head with genuine regret.

"I spoke with no thought at all. My words were unforgivable. I deserve to be punished for it. But tell me, Akira-san, how can it be punishment if I have no fear of whatever you might do to me?"

I felt his body tense with uncertainty. The dagger was removed slowly, but I thought more out of caution that it wouldn't tear my skin than with any intention to hurt. Akira's arm still kept me pinioned and I wondered if he had any idea how much I had enjoyed our contest.

"You have more weapons in your armory than I realized," he said huskily. "If I hurt you now, the dishonor would be mine. My apologies, samurai woman. I underestimated you. It will never happen again."

He dropped his hands to his sides and I turned to face him. We were both panting. I was astonished when I understood that my breathlessness had little to do with our fight.

"Then shall we say we are equal?" I said cautiously. What felt like a long time ago, I had said the same thing to Yo. And he had respected that, as had I. If that had not been so, then he would not be in Kyoto now, carrying out his own business just as he had left me to carry out mine. And the separation had been made with no promises on either side, I reminded myself.

"Can a mere yakuza ever be equal to a samurai warrior woman?" Akira mocked. "If you had passed me on the street when your life was that of a samurai lady, would you even have seen me?"

I almost laughed aloud. I doubted that any woman, no matter how high-born she was, could ever see Akira and fail to notice him. He was attractive, but also he carried with him an aura of power that was almost magnetic.

"I would have seen you, Akira," I said simply. "But the

question I ask myself is, would you have seen me? And perhaps remembered me in your thoughts?"

His reply shocked me.

"Yes. If I had seen the samurai lady Keiko, I would have wondered about her. I think I would have seen sadness in her for a life that was wrapped in traditions she didn't care for. A life that held nothing at all for her. And in my turn, I would have felt very sad for her, as I would have had no way of knowing then that she would blossom into a woman the likes of which I had never dreamed might exist."

I was so amazed by the perception of Akira's response that I could do nothing but stare at him. Very occasionally —and I was sure out of nothing but politeness—some of my father's guests had written haiku to me, praising my grace and nobility. Unlike them, Akira's speech had the ring of truth. I glanced at the bloodied dagger in his fingers.

"Would you really have hurt me with that?" I asked.

"Would you ever have allowed me to hurt you with it?" he countered.

I smiled and shook my head. "No. Of course not."

He stared at me as if I puzzled him. "There is no one in the Floating World who would dare to insult me to my face. To be sure, many men—and women for that matter— would be happy to stab me in the back if they thought they could get away with it. But to take me on openly and honestly? Not a single one. Except you."

"I do not cheat. I would never deceive you. But neither would I ever let you tell me what to do," I said firmly.

"You are a remarkable woman, Keiko." Akira smiled slowly.

"Thank you. But I'm not what matters," I pointed out.

Akira licked his lips and nodded. "We have a truce,

then? You'll accept my help to find Niko and get her back safely?"

"There is peace between us," I said neutrally.

"You will let me go to Hakone with you?" Akira persisted.

I felt like beating my hands against his chest. Would this damned man never understand that I meant what I said?

"No," I snapped. "I will go alone. I told you that."

"You might at least give me the chance to explain to you," Akira said wearily. "You now intend to go to Hakone as a widowed noblewoman. Have you given any thought to how dangerous it will be for you?"

"I think you forget that I truly am samurai." I closed my eyes in exasperation. How often did I have to repeat this to him? "Ikeda is one man, not an army. I'm more than capable of looking after myself."

"If it came to a fair fight, I don't doubt you would be in no danger at all. But Ikeda isn't honorable. He doesn't fight fairly. From what I've heard of him, I believe he's capable of doing anything, no matter how terrible. He may well have murdered his own family. I don't doubt he's infected his second wife with the plum blossom disease. And now he's abducted Niko because he believes that she can offer him a cure. If nothing else, doesn't that tell you what kind of a man he is?"

I stared at him stonily. Did he think I was stupid? Of course I understood the danger I was facing. And there was nothing he could say that would change my mind. I knew Akira hadn't listened to me when he carried on speaking.

"Keiko, think, I beg of you. If Ikeda truly believes he's going to be cured of his disease, what use does he have for a wife who is going to die anyway? It can only make the situation worse for her if he believes that the gods have smiled on him and allowed a rich, noble, and available widow to arrive on his doorstep. You may be signing her death warrant."

I met Akira's gaze calmly. "I hear what you say. But it just makes me all the more determined. I promise you, I will not allow his wife to be hurt by anything I do. If I'm going to be enticing to Ikeda, that must be a good thing? Won't it distract his attention from his wife? Besides," I added practically, "I still don't see why I need you to accompany me."

"Be sensible, woman. You need me to provide an escort for you precisely because you are traveling as a rich samurai widow." Akira spoke slowly, as if he was trying to reason with a drunk. "You—or rather, she—would never travel alone. You must have an armed guard to protect you. Would a samurai lady ever travel with any less?"

I bit my lip in frustration. He was right, of course.

"I suppose you're right about the escort," I said grudgingly. "I should have a maid with me as well, but I can always say my maid was taken ill on the journey and had to be left behind. How many men?" I added abruptly.

"Three, including me."

I stared at Akira silently. The great yakuza was willing to venture outside his stronghold in Edo to protect a mere woman? A woman who was neither kin to him nor a permanent part of his life?

"You? You will put everything aside to accompany me?" I asked softly. "Why?"

NINE

> I do not need to
> See my breath smoke on the air
> To know it is cold

"I could lie to you." Akira smiled. I thought that smiling did not come naturally to his face. In repose he was handsome, but his expression fell into serious lines. When he did smile—naturally, with no thought behind it, as he was doing now—he seemed much younger, almost mischievous, as if an imp of amusement was looking out of his eyes.

"You could lie, but you're not going to." It was a statement, not a question.

"No, I will not lie to you. I will never lie to you, I promise. Generally, I would never hesitate to lie or cheat to get what I want. I am, after all, nothing but a low-caste yakuza." Suddenly, his smile was oddly gentle. "But you are a beautiful woman, Keiko-chan. And both rare and precious as well. I hope that you will value my honesty, just as I value yours."

I had no idea how to respond. Nobody had ever called me—Keiko—a rare and precious woman before. Kamakiri the oiran had been much sought after, but she was not *me*. She was an illusion; men looked at her and saw what they expected to see and nothing at all of the real woman beneath the paint and sumptuous clothes. Akira's words had given me great pleasure—for a moment at least. Until I understood that he was amusing himself at my expense and my delight curled and died.

Unbidden, a memory of my lovely sister flashed through my mind and lodged there. The words she had spoken—often—were so clear she might have been sitting next to me. *It's not your fault you're so very unattractive. Obviously you did something very terrible in a past life and this is your punishment. Nothing you can do about it except hope for something better in the next life.*

Akira was making fun of me. And I had believed him. Anger at my own naïve stupidity—and even more, the knowledge that I had wanted to believe him—made me speak brutally. I wanted to punish him very badly for allowing me to make a fool of myself.

"I always value honesty, Akira-san, no matter how unlikely the source. But I doubt that I could ever trust you to follow my orders immediately and without question. If you can't do that, then you're no use to me."

I stared him straight in the face as I spoke, watching for his reaction. I was deeply disappointed when I saw nothing at all. His expression was polite, his head on one side, as if he expected me to say more.

"I see," he said thoughtfully. "You're quite right. I'm afraid I'm not used to being given orders. And certainly not by a woman. But perhaps it might be fun to try. One should always try everything in this life at least once."

His voice mocked me. I had been right, then. He was amusing himself at my expense. Fury made my vision waver. I clicked my fingers and pointed to the floor at my feet.

"You think so? I'm afraid I don't find the situation in the least bit amusing. But shall we at least try and see how good you really are at taking orders from a mere woman? On your knees and beg forgiveness, yakuza, before you taste the anger of a true samurai."

Oh, but he was quick! Even though I expected some retaliation, I was amazed by how fast his reactions were. He was a blur as he crossed the space between us, his arm snaking around my neck. His lips trailed down toward my shoulders until they found the puncture left by his dagger. He bit—hard enough to hurt—and blood oozed out of the wound. He licked it with the tip of his tongue and then kissed my skin softly.

"You let me do that." His words buzzed against my neck.

"Of course I did," I answered coldly. "If I hadn't wanted you close, you would have been on the floor now, moaning for mercy."

"Why? Why put me in my place and then entice me forward? Are you really a woman, Keiko, or are you a demon sent to pay me back for my sins?"

"Your sins must be small indeed if a mere woman can punish you for them. Although it would give me very great pleasure to put you in your place, yakuza." I snarled into his face.

"Thank you." His voice had become harsh. "For a moment, I had forgotten the great gulf that existed between us. You understand, in my life, many women have said they have wanted me, Keiko-chan. Some of them were courtesans, who were practiced in saying one thing and meaning another. Some of them thought themselves in love with me. Others confused fear with lust. Still others wanted to capture me with the spell of love, not knowing that it can never be a one-sided gift." I was suspicious; what had this talk of lust and love to do with me? "But until karma brought us together, I never thought twice about any woman. I'm sorry if you think I'm insulting you by speaking like this. I said I would be honest, and I shall be."

I had no words. I was no longer sure of anything. Was he mocking me? If he was, was I prepared to forget it for the pleasure of this moment? His tongue licked my earlobe so softly it felt like the caress of a night breeze. His words, too, were very soft.

"I have never met a woman like you, Keiko. I doubt if there is another woman in the whole of Edo who is your equal. I understand your tradition tells you it's impossible that you could lower yourself to take a mere nobody into your heart, but I tell you, I'm going to change your mind. I will not let you go."

"Really? And I have no say in the matter, I suppose?"

He stiffened, and I sensed he was annoyed. "Must you always have the last word?"

I didn't bother to think about it. "Yes."

He laughed and shook his head in obvious exasperation. I would have said more, but Akira gave me no chance. He moved his mouth from my ear to my neck and his tongue flicked at my skin. I tensed, still unsure, then my body defied my mind and I shivered with desire. Perhaps he was amusing himself at my expense, but I was beginning to doubt it. I could feel the need in his body. He was almost trembling as he caressed me. Suddenly, I wanted to take pleasure as well as give it. Remembering how much Adam had enjoyed the caress of my tongue, I maneuvered my head so my lips were pressed against his mouth.

I felt his surprise and pushed harder still in response. Japanese men rarely kiss their women on the lips. Wives, of course, are not meant for the pleasures of the flesh. But concubines and yujo are expected to kiss a man's body and their tree of flesh. I had seen shunga—erotic woodcuts— where the male was using his tongue to explore his woman's sex. But to kiss on the lips is generally seen by men as something distasteful rather than arousing. Given Akira's obvious amazement now, I found myself wondering if men thought a kiss was an attempt to steal their breath or their essential being. I was wrong. After a startled moment, Akira's tongue rolled against mine and his mouth opened wide enough to allow him to bite and suck at my lips.

Still, I was reluctant to let myself go completely. Akira bewildered me. I was not in control of myself with him, and that frightened me.

He sank to his knees and pulled me down with him. I became aware of a strange noise, something like the hum of angry bees, and I gasped as I realized it was the sound of my hunger, moaning from deep within my throat.

Akira yanked at my obi until the knot finally gave way. His parted my kimono and his hand ran down my body, lingering between my breasts. It was not the hand of a gentleman, unused to greater work than flicking characters on to paper. His palm was lightly calloused and the joints of his strong fingers were wide and thick. It was the hand of a warrior. A man who practiced with the sword and the bow every day. I knew his reputation, knew that this same hand had undoubtedly bestowed hurt and even death on his enemies. But at that moment, I cared nothing for it. Akira would do what he had to do to survive. Was I so different from him? Our lips mashed hard against each other, and I knew the answer to my own question. We were the same. We were omyodo—the two halves that make a whole. In and yo. My sensei—the ancient priest who had taught me the mental and physical arts needed to be an onna-bugeisha—had spoken reverently of omyodo. But to him, it had meant the two halves of a warrior's character. Thought and action; anticipation and response.

I had thought I understood the concept of omyodo. Now, I knew I had missed the vital understanding that lay at its heart. Neither was in or yo assigned to one or the other of us. One moment and Akira was grabbing my hair, pulling my head back so he could bite and chew at my exposed throat. The next, I had my fingers thrust between his lips, forcing his mouth wide open so I could scratch his tongue with my nails. One on top, one below. One commanding, one giving. Yet at each movement, one knowing what would delight the other. Sometimes in dreams, I would not even admit to myself on awakening that I had felt this oneness with an unknown somebody. But come daylight, I was always left with only the shadow of what had been.

Akira rolled over on top of me and parted my thighs with his knee. Hissing with pleasure, I threw my legs as wide as I could, mocking his action and at the same time inviting him inside me. His robe had been flung open by our movements and I ran my hands down his chest and belly.

"Ah, if there is ever a time of famine in the Floating World, then you will be the first to starve, Akira!" I laughed in his face. His body was muscular, but so lacking in any fat that he seemed slender.

"Then I shall have to steal some of your flesh, woman!"

he responded, squeezing my breast so hard my flesh oozed between his fingers.

We stared at each other, our faces barely a finger's width apart, and Akira raised his eyebrows.

"Now?" he asked. My mouth was so dry I had no words. I nodded.

He leaned into me, his tree of flesh sliding into my depths with subtle power. He fit me exactly, or perhaps it was my flesh that molded to his contours. I had no way of knowing. Nor did I care. In and yo; together, we found perfection.

Since Yo had first made love to me, I had become curious as to what it felt like for a man. I had asked, and Yo had shrugged, assuring me it was very good. When I probed further, he had become annoyed, telling me simply that it was different for a man and to let it alone. I would never understand, he insisted. Now, I knew.

Our rhythms matched each other with no hesitation, no awkward need for adjustments. As Akira moved away from me, my sex pulled him back in, holding him as securely as an oyster welds itself to the seabed. It did not matter that he was lying on top of my body; had it been the other way around, we would have adjusted ourselves instinctively. My body became no more substantial than early morning mist. I had no consciousness of flesh and blood. I was elemental, knowing nothing but the feelings Akira was summoning into life within me.

We were neither man nor woman but pure feeling. Pure pleasure. I stared into his eyes and saw my face reflected there. He kissed my lips and I tasted his mouth.

I felt my yonaki begin to build. Slowly, so very slowly. It seemed to me that I hovered on the cliff edge of fulfillment for a lifetime. I wanted to scream, to cry out, to tell Akira to plunge *harder, harder, harder*. Yet he knew me as well as I knew myself. His rhythm slowed fractionally, but at the same time, he lingered longer when his thrust pushed him deeper into my body. I felt the slow itch of orgasm begin to blossom and I wrapped my arms around his waist, hanging on to him. At the same moment, his lips parted in a feral snarl and I felt his seed spurt hot into my womb. I may have cried out loud; I had no way of knowing. All my senses were focused within me, and I was deaf and blind and dumb to anything but the burning heat of the wave that enveloped my body from my sex up into my belly.

We lay together silently when we were both spent. Akira pulled his robe across us, and I put my hand on his chest, enjoying the feeling of his breath giving his body life. I had a flash of pure pleasure as I felt certain that I had been wrong. Akira had been serious all along. Any doubts had only been the shadows of my own insecurity. The joy was short-lived; it was chased away by an intense guilt. I had had no business taking my own pleasure when I should have been concentrating all my thoughts and efforts on Niko. Yet still, my body betrayed me. I was so satiated, I could do nothing but close my eyes and feel relaxation take me.

After a while, I roused myself and leaned forward to rub my face against Akira's chest. A lazy thought came to me and I scratched his breast bone with my fingernails.

"Why don't you have irezumi tattoos? That horrible man Hara was covered in them. I thought all yakuza had them to show reverence for their leaders."

"I have no leader," Akira said superbly.

I tickled him and he gasped. I exulted in knowing that it had been me who had caused his skin to be so sensitive.

"In that case, shouldn't you have them to show respect for your father? For your ancestors?"

I realized I had hit a sore point. Akira's skin tightened beneath my touch. I waited for him to respond. I waited so long, it became a battle of wills between us as to who would speak first. I won.

"I have no need to show respect for my father in my body. I feel it here, in my heart." I waited. There was more, I knew. "Besides, one day I will be greater than any of my ancestors. I am different from them." Once started, the words seemed to flow of their own will. "My father and my grandfather were both great yakuza. My father told me that my great-grandfather began as a humble member of an unimportant yakuza gang. He worked his way up to become second in command to his leader. I respect each of them for what they achieved. But I am going to do more, Keiko. I am not just going to be a yakuza. I am going to have power and influence. I am going to hold the whole of the Floating World in my palm. And when that happens, I do not want people who think themselves my better looking at me and seeing irezumi tattoos and nothing else."

I felt oddly sorry for this powerful, ambitious man. I—who had been born samurai—knew that no matter how wealthy he became, no matter how much the gentleman he appeared to be, he would never be accepted by the aristocracy. To them, he would always be scum and beneath contempt. It was a dream that would never become reality. Knowing he would hate my pity, I chose to speak lightly to hide it.

"Well, whatever your reason is, I'm pleased. I like your skin as it is, unblemished."

"Thank you. I was considering getting some tattoos to show my solidarity with my own men, but if you dislike them, then I will not."

I rubbed my face on his chest. I hoped Akira would

think it was with pleasure at his words rather than to hide my expression from him. There was so very much I didn't know about this man. Instinct told me it was better that I did not know, but I couldn't help being curious. How, I wondered, could he be so very open and even tender with me when everybody else in the Floating World shuddered when his name was spoken? I told myself it was because they knew only his reputation, not the man. A disturbing thought came to me as I considered his words. Once obtained, tattoos were there for life. Did Akira's also think that I was going to be a permanent part of his life from now on?

"You may feel free to get as many tattoos as you like once I have gone."

I spoke cheerfully, as if our conversation had meant nothing to me. I forced my body to appear relaxed as I waited for his response.

"I don't believe I am ever going to be free of you, Keiko." Akira's voice was calm, so very certain, it gave me a flash of concern.

I shrugged my doubts aside, telling myself that I had nothing to worry about. After all, my life was in my own hands. Or at least it would be as soon as Niko was back with me safely.

With or without Akira's help.

TEN

I do not know the
Way of the path when it bends.
Neither do I care

*T*hat good man Aisha agreed readily to take care of Matsuo for me while I was gone. Even more, he asked me no questions at all about where I was going or how long I would be gone for. But I had a question for him.

"Still no word from Yo?" My voice sounded odd. Far too casual. I thought Aisha hadn't noticed anything when he shrugged and smiled.

"Nothing. If I had had word from him, you would have been the first to know. Shinobi matters can be very delicate. I'm not surprised we haven't heard from him. It may well be that the first message I get is to say he is on his way home. It will be a pity if you are not here to greet him."

I swallowed dryly at his words. Was there just a hint of disapproval in that last sentence? Or was it just my guilty conscience at work? No matter. I had to go. Niko was my responsibility and I hoped that Aisha would understand that. And just as I had an obligation to Niko, now I also owed Akira a considerable debt of gratitude for all he was doing to help me recover my younger sister.

I thought I had made myself perfectly at home in the Floating World. That I understood the ways of Edo outside the protected walls of samurai society. Now, thanks to Akira, I was learning I knew nothing at all.

Until my brother Isamu had taken to me to the Floating World—and to get there from the family estate, we had traveled on back roads that were little more than cart tracks —I had never left home except to visit our estates. I knew, vaguely, that travelers had to have certain permits from the authorities. But as to how these were obtained, or from where, I had no idea. Neither did I understand how important they were.

Akira had taken care of all that, and so much more that I had never given a thought to. I cringed at my arrogant naiveté; I was nothing but a green fool who had thought herself capable of taking on the world. I tried not to look at him as he held my horse steady while I mounted in case he was laughing at my clumsiness. I was hampered by a tight kimono and high geta, so it was not easy.

In my intense anxiety to make a beginning, it had not occurred to me to give any thought at all as to how I would travel to Hakone. My father and brother had often traveled the Tokaido Highway from Edo to Kyoto on business, and I remembered with a heart-stopping surge of nostalgia Isamu talking about breaking their journey at Hakone. And of course, Yo would also have traveled this same road. But until this moment, all my thoughts had been with Niko, and I had given not a moment to the practicalities of the journey. I tried to shrug off my embarrassment, telling myself it was only natural. When would a samurai lady ever have to concern herself with practical matters?

"It's not going to seem odd, me traveling by horseback?" I asked with belated caution. "Would it have been better for me to hire a palanquin?"

Akira busied himself adjusting my harness. I knew he was smiling from his voice.

"It's more usual for ladies to travel by palanquin, but it's far from unknown for them to go on horseback," he said. "It will be much quicker for you to go by horse, so I thought you would prefer it. I have your travel documents here." He patted a bulge beneath his robe. "Everything is in order."

"Good," I said stiffly. Every word, every action, added to my debt, and I resented it deeply. I added sulkily, "Are they very important?"

"They're essential," Akira said crisply. "If you tried to travel the Tokaido Highway without the correct papers, at best you would be turned back. It's more likely you would be arrested and held until somebody came forward to vouch for you. And in your case, that might take a long time. Even if you had all the correct papers, if you traveled without an escort, it would appear so strange that you would be detained, even if only on suspicion of impersonating an aristocrat."

"Thank you," I said in a very small voice. But there was worse to come. I was mounted on a very fine horse. I glanced around, expecting to find other—no doubt less well-bred—horses waiting for Akira and his two men. There was nothing. Before I could ask, Akira grasped my horse's bridle and pulled the mare gently forward. His two men fell into place behind me.

Of course, I was once again a samurai lady. As Akira had pointed out, it was to be expected that I would travel with an escort. But for the great yakuza Akira to humble himself by walking in front of me as my humble servant! If his enemies saw him, the loss of face would surely be enough to destroy him. He turned his head as if I had spoken out loud and smiled as if he was amused.

"You see? Isn't it a good thing I have no irezumi tattoos? An honorable samurai lady would hardly employ a low-life yakuza as a personal groom."

I nodded, but already he was looking in front of us, taking care to lead my horse over the smoothest ground. Our progress kicked up dust, and I glanced back to see if the men behind me were comfortable. They immediately stared down at the ground humbly, hunching their shoulders to avoid my gaze.

So very much had happened to me in such a short time, I had forgotten that this had once been a normal life for me. Lady Keiko might have been no more than a disregarded youngest sister, but she was born of a noble house, and all of my menfolk would never have hesitated to take a peasant's head off their shoulders if they had dared to look at me in an insolent way. I had simply accepted that as how things should be.

But that was then. Before my brother had decided it would amuse him to teach me the ways of onna-bugeisha. Before I ventured into the Floating World and came to understand that all men had a life to live, no matter how far removed it was from the life of a samurai. And also before Yo had stolen into my life and I had taken him for my lover. Guilt flared in my guts at the thought of him.

I had not forgotten him, I thought fiercely. Each day when I had awoken, I had thought, "Will it be today? Will this be the day he returns to me?" And I had hoped that it would be so. Now, I felt deeply unhappy as I prayed that his return would be delayed, at least for as long as it took me to return to the Floating World.

Quietly, I acknowledged to myself for the first time that when both of us returned, nothing would be the same as it had been. While Yo had been gone, I had learned to look after myself. At least I thought I had; wryly I acknowledged that I still had much to learn. And, of course, now there was Akira. I watched the back of his head bobbing to the movement of his brisk footfall.

Lady Keiko would have been appalled at the thought that an unmarried lady could contemplate taking not one lover, but two. I bit my lip as I remembered my gaijin, Adam. Worse and worse. Not two lovers, but three! One of them a despised foreign barbarian, and the other two no more than riverbed beggars. But of course, had I still been the innocent samurai lady Keiko, none of this would have happened. I would have gone to marry my old man as a virgin and lived out my life never knowing all I had missed. I took a deep breath and sat tall in my saddle.

Did I regret that I was no longer the protected daughter of a samurai family? Even though I had forsaken a life of sure and certain luxury for one where I lived on my wits and had nothing that I did not obtain for myself, I knew instantly that I had no regret at all. I was onna-bugeisha. My life and everything that happened in it was up to me. I sighed deeply and happily, and as if in response, Akira quickened his pace.

An army patrol stopped us late in the morning. Akira bowed his head to them and produced our papers quickly.

"Your mistress is going to Hakone? No further?" the patrol leader demanded. Akira nodded and spoke humbly, his voice soft.

"Yes, sir. My mistress's husband died not long ago. She is

stricken with grief and wishes to be away from the family estate for a while so she can compose herself. A particular onsen in Hakone has been recommended as being good for restoring the balance of mind and body, so she is hoping to find comfort there."

I was deeply grateful the soldier spoke only to Akira. I suddenly realized I had no idea what my new identity was, not even the name of my poor, dead husband. But Akira obviously had no concerns; I guessed he knew that a properly accompanied lady would never be addressed directly by a mere soldier. I was deeply grateful for Akira's thorough preparations, and even more annoyed with myself for not thinking about it.

The man nodded, his lips pursed as he stared at our permit closely. I had to choke back amusement as I wondered if he could actually read it or was just impressed with the huge seal. To hide my thoughts, I raised my eyebrows and glared frostily over his head. The permit was handed back quickly, and the patrol stood to one side to let us pass. I gave the officer such a frigid stare of anger that he bowed deeply, and all his men followed his example.

My triumphant smile died away when I saw Akira's shoulders slump and heard his sigh.

"That could have been difficult," he murmured. "I had no time to get our papers through the correct channels. The ones I have are excellent forgeries, but if that oaf had looked closely enough, he might have been suspicious. Well done, you distracted him beautifully."

I accepted his praise, thankful that I had known no better. When we finally approached Hakone, Akira reined my mare to a halt at an impressive-looking military building. He spoke quickly and softly.

"This is the first official checkpoint on the road from

Edo," he said. "Our papers will be checked again here. Because they've already been seen and passed on the road, and we're going to turn off to Hakone, I don't anticipate any problems."

I sat rigidly, the picture of a bored aristocratic lady who cannot understand why she was being delayed by mere peasants. Akira showed our papers to the man who strolled out of the checkpoint. I saw a silver coin change hands and the man was immediately friendly. He bowed us through and Akira tugged my horse down a side road shortly after the checkpoint building.

The discreet sign on our ryokan proclaimed it to be the Kansuiro. Akira helped me down and I stretched the stiffness out of my limbs as he bustled ahead of me to strike the bell outside the ryokan's door.

"Lady Keiko has arrived, as arranged," I heard him call arrogantly as the shoji was slid back. He must have sent a message ahead of us. Something else I had not even considered necessary. Still, I was grateful for Akira's consideration as I found that my room was light and airy and superbly clean. It also opened straight to a pretty garden, which pleased me. Everything was in delicious contrast to the Tokaido Highway. Our road had been well paved with large, smooth cobbles, kept in good order. But for much of our way the route had been overhung with tree branches that almost met overhead, blocking out the light and making the air cold and dank.

The innkeeper bowed anxiously. "Everything is to your liking, mistress?"

I nodded. The futon looked inviting, as did the feast that was already spread out waiting for me on a low table. My stomach rumbled, reminding me that I had eaten nothing since early this morning.

"Should you require anything, please clap for the maid. She will be awaiting your pleasure."

"Thank you," I said briskly, though all I wanted was for him to go away so I could eat and sleep. My bones ached from my day in the saddle. I would have liked to take a long, hot bath, but I was too tired to make the effort. Tonight, I would sleep in my stink. But the innkeeper was determined for me to know everything about his establishment, and no matter how stonily I looked at him, he babbled on.

"We have a large and very excellent bathhouse, just down the corridor, mistress." He gestured with his hand. I nodded. Tomorrow, I would be delighted to try it. "And your servant tells me that you wish to visit the onsen here. It is just beyond the garden, merely a very short stroll. It is covered over for your greater pleasure, and it is widely agreed to be one of the very finest in Hakone. All of our best local families prefer to use our onsen over the rest of those to be found here in Hakone."

He was rubbing his hands together as if he was washing them and looked so very eager to please that I relented and inclined my head graciously. Besides, his words had caught my attention.

"I shall try your onsen," I said languidly, and the innkeeper was so overwhelmed by my words that he literally hopped from foot to foot with delight. "I have never been here before. I do not believe that I am aware of anybody who lives in Hakone. You have some great families here, do you? Apart from the onsen, I thought the town was just a checkpoint for the military."

The contempt was so obvious, I felt like apologizing for my arrogance. But I did not, and the innkeeper was obviously delighted by my aristocratic disdain.

"We are not a samurai town, mistress." His voice

suggested that the lack was entirely his fault and he was deeply sorry for it. "But we have a number of families hereabouts who are very great landowners, and most certainly at least one of our local gentlemen is a frequent visitor to Edo. I believe Ikeda-san has many friends who are very highly placed, even some who are well known at the shogun's court."

My thoughts crowed, triumphant as a cock greeting the morning. Ikeda-san! Of course he would be the type of man who would ensure that those beneath him were impressed by his status. And—although it was a bitter thing for me to acknowledge—I believed that his friend Endo-san was known at the shogun's court. Not that he would be a habitué of the shogun, of course. I had no doubt that Endo-san attended only on ceremonial occasions and for the great festivals, just as my father had done. Although in Father's case, it was because he grudged every coin of the expense a court visit caused. I rejoiced in the knowledge that Ikeda was no doubt the type of wretch who thought that he would gain class by association with his betters. An idea occurred to me at the thought.

"I do not know Ikeda-san. Of course, my own late husband spent a great deal of time at the court, but the shogun's affairs were not something he would discuss with his wife." I glanced at the innkeeper's face, hoping he understood the subtle hint that my husband's business at court had been so important that he would never disclose it to a mere wife. Judging by his awed expression, he believed me. "But even so, I think perhaps it would be polite if I sent a note to Ikeda-san's wife. One would hardly wish to be discourteous."

I was delighted with myself, envisaging a prompt invitation to take tea with Ikeda's wife, and it was a bitter disappointment when the innkeeper's face sagged into lines of sorrow and he shook his head.

"I am so sorry, mistress. I am afraid that cannot be done." I had worked myself so far back into the role of the aristocratic lady Keiko that I found myself glaring at him with genuinely astonished disbelief. He spoke quickly. "Ikeda-san has only the one wife, and she has been very ill for a long time. It is said that the poor lady is very near death now. In fact, we have been expecting to hear of her demise for some weeks now."

"I see. In that case, I would not wish to disturb the poor lady." I shuddered inwardly. Akira had been right, then. Ikeda had infected his wife with his terrible disease. And surely it could not be a coincidence that she was now expected to die just when he was confident he had found a cure for himself. I bared my teeth in what the innkeeper could take to be a smile, if he chose. It felt wolfish on my lips, but he seemed not to notice.

"Lady Keiko is most thoughtful," he gushed. "Ikeda-san often makes use of our onsen. If it pleases you, I could send a message to him and let him know that you are honoring my poor establishment with your illustrious presence. I'm sure he would be most unhappy if you thought him so lacking in courtesy that he missed the opportunity to visit with you."

The thought of Ikeda, with his rotted nose and blotched, diseased body, using the same bathwater as me made me feel sick. I waved my hand languidly.

"No, no. I am certain Ikeda-san would not wish to leave his wife at this difficult time. By all means, send a message to say that I am here. One would hardly wish to be lacking in courtesy. Should Ikeda-san feel it is appropriate for him to receive a visitor, though..." I shrugged and raised my hands as if to say I had done all that politeness dictated.

Gleefully, I wondered how long it would take for the message to get to Ikeda.

The food set out for me was tempting, but I had lost my appetite. I paused hopefully at every sound, wondering if it was Akira come to bring me some news. The attentive maid had taken my almost untouched supper away before there was finally a polite scratch on my screen door.

"Mistress, I trust all the arrangements are in order? Is this humble room acceptable? If it is not, I will speak to the innkeeper immediately."

Akira had stopped at least ten paces away from me. His hands were clasped in front of him, his head bowed. I almost laughed and asked him what game he was playing? I only stopped when he looked up at me from beneath his eyelashes and gave a quick sideways flick of his eyes to the outer shoji. I followed his glance and was sure I could see the faintest of shadows outside. Suddenly, I was cautious. This was a border town, where people came and went every day. If a widow visiting alone disappeared, who would notice?

"The room is adequate," I said briskly. "The innkeeper tells me that the ryokan's spa is the best in the town. I may try it tomorrow. He has also told me that a certain gentleman lives in the area who may have been acquainted with my husband. It is possible that they both knew a noble who attends the shogun's court." I paused, trying to decide myself whether my words had made sense. Apparently they had; Akira dipped his head, an expression of satisfaction flickering over his face.

"That is excellent news, mistress." He spoke to the

tatami. "If all is well with you, then I will leave. I wish to make sure your other servants are comfortable."

I nodded. Although I appeared to be watching Akira, my eyes were on that mysterious shadow. As he spoke, I saw the shade move and blend with the weaving silhouettes of the garden shrubs. I waited for a moment and then spoke softly.

"He's gone. Is everything all right?"

"I think so." Akira rolled his shoulders. I guessed the humble posture he had assumed all day was irksome to him. "How did you find out about our friend?"

Such caution! I fell in with it all the same. Better to get into the habit of taking care than making a mistake.

"The innkeeper was keen to impress me with talk of the local gentry. He told me that our friend was well known in Edo society. And it seems that you were right about his wife. Do you know any more than that?"

"A little." A quirky smile crinkled Akira's eyes. "One of the kitchen maids had finished her work for the day just after we arrived. She was most helpful in getting me and the men nicely settled. And the dear creature was delighted to be served with sake herself—in another ryokan, of course—in company with a man who is a personal servant to a wealthy samurai widow. She was delighted when I showed an interest in all the local gossip."

I flinched inwardly. Not so long ago, I—just like the rest of my family—had spoken freely in front of the servants. To us, they were beneath notice. And had our servants gossiped about us? I supposed they must have. I would remember that in the future.

"So, what did your kitchen maid tell you?" I asked.

"Her name's Miki." Akira grinned. "She's proud of working in the best ryokan in Hakone. I think she wanted to impress me as she told me seriously that the innkeeper likes to keep it exclusive. He prefers to encourage patrons who are on a pilgrimage to the temple, and other than them, only the wealthiest locals are welcomed. After a couple of cups of sake, I asked her if she did well earning flower money from the guests."

"And does she?" I interrupted.

"She says so." Akira smiled slowly. "She also said the only trouble is that some of the locals in particular seem to think they're buying more than just good service for their money. Especially one of them. She says she can't stand him being near her as he terrifies her with his horrible looks. But the innkeeper thinks he's a particularly valued client, so she has to smile and pretend she likes it when he rubs up against her. She also said he was such a fool he really believes she likes him touching her."

"Ikeda," I said flatly.

Akira nodded. "It has to be him. Miki says it's well known that he's riddled with baidoku, and that the reason his wife is so ill is that he's passed it on to her. That's another reason she hates being touched by him."

"Ah." I spared a moment of sympathy for the maid who was forced to endure Ikeda's touch. "Anything else?"

"I told you this was his second wife?" I nodded impatiently. "Miki thinks that once this one is dead, our friend will be on the hunt for a third wife. In fact, she says he'll have to find a rich wife, and quickly. He's a gambler, and an unlucky one. He's deeply in debt, according to Miki. She says the innkeeper is the only one around here who gets paid, and that's because our friend likes to show off. He entertains here regularly."

That made perfect sense to me. Hana had borrowed money off Endo-san, who was also Ikeda's friend. Did Ikeda owe the wealthy nobleman money as well? With rising excitement I wondered if that was yet another reason why he needed to find a cure for his baidoku so urgently. I grabbed Akira's sleeve and tugged it to get his attention.

"Didn't you say that if a man survives the later stages of the disease, it often burns itself out and doesn't actually kill him?" Akira nodded. He was smiling slightly, as if he was encouraging a clever child. I was so excited by my thoughts, I wasn't even annoyed. "He must know that, surely. And if he does, the main reason he's so desperate to cure himself is because he hopes to reverse the way the disease has made him look. After all, no woman is ever going to want to marry him looking like he does. And if he's desperate for money, the only way he's going to get it is by marrying a rich woman."

"I think you're right," Akira agreed. "If he's superstitious enough to believe that intercourse with a virgin is the only real cure for the plum poison disease, then he's also stupid enough to think that a cure means a cure, and that his appearance can also get back to normal. And if that happens, he can marry again to his advantage. Don't forget, his second wife is a minor noble, and he was adopted into the family. There's plenty of rich merchant families who would find that an enticement, but I doubt even the most ambitious merchant would allow his daughter to marry a man who looks like Ikeda does at present. And of course, his wife has to be out of the way. There's no prestige in being a mere number two wife."

I shuddered. What a vile man Ikeda was! I grabbed Akira's arm, tugging urgently.

"Akira, we have to get Niko out of there. Even if he can't infect her, I can't bear the thought of him touching her." I recalled the times Niko's own father had sold her casually to any man who was interested. My poor younger sister had used her wits to escape from the predators of the Floating World, but this time she was helpless. And it was my fault. Guilt made my stomach hurt.

"Can we act tonight? We know the direction of his estate. Now that I've established myself as a silly, rich widow, nobody is going to suspect me. If we wait until the middle of the night, you could get your men together and we can go to Ikeda's house and take her back. We could be well back on the road to Edo by morning. With a little bit of luck, nobody would know anything had ever happened until we were well away from here."

"No." Akira spoke so calmly I was infuriated. Didn't he understand my urgency? "We have to plan things very carefully, and it's not going to be easy. Ikeda may have gambled away most of his wealth, but that's made no difference to his status here in Hakone. When his name came up in conversation, it was obvious that the locals are terrified of him. To make matters worse, he's the local magistrate, and he has a great deal of power. When I pretended to be drunk and made a silly comment about how he must be a prime target for all the peasant rebellions that are going on, everybody stared at me as if I had lost my mind.

"It appears that Ikeda is well known for handing out fierce punishments to keep people in order. I was told he'll have somebody beheaded for stealing a bowl of rice just to warn everybody else not to try it. And he knows how much he's hated. He has his own guards, armed with bows and swords, who patrol his estate day and night. If we took the risk of just walking in there and trying to grab Niko without knowing a thing about the place, we would be taken, I have no doubt. We would all find ourselves publicly executed as an example to anybody else who might try and be so foolish."

My hopes had been soaring high, but they crashed to earth as I understood he was right.

"Then what are we going to do?" I asked. My frustration rang in my voice. "We've come this far, we can't back away now. Akira, we must get Niko out of there somehow. And when we do, I intend to make sure that Ikeda understands the errors of his ways."

"I don't doubt you will," Akira said quietly.

ELEVEN

The deepest river
Is low in the summer's heat.
My love will not dry

I considered our position silently. I had been sure that all was going well. I had had no doubts that we would succeed. But that was before I had known how powerful Ikeda was in his own jurisdiction. Now, I could think of no way ahead. I was not only frustrated, I was angry. It seemed to me that the samurai code had no meaning here, a world where honor had no place. And without the code of bushido to give me direction, I was lost.

"It was never going to be easy," Akira pointed out. "But problems are intended to sharpen the mind. We came here with the intention of rescuing Niko and to allow you to get your revenge on Ikeda. We will do both. I promise you."

I stared at him. I longed to ask, "How?" But I was so afraid that, just like me, he had no answer, that I kept the words behind my lips. Instead, I managed a tired smile.

"If there's nothing we can do now, perhaps we should just sleep on it and maybe things will look better in the morning," I suggested with false cheerfulness. I thought he wanted to say more to comfort me, but he did not.

"I'll sleep with my men, in the stables," he said. "Don't worry about me, it's comfortable enough there. I've slept in far worse places. I'll be back tomorrow morning, early. Get a good night's sleep. It would be good for you to be seen by the locals, to get yourself established. A nice long walk so you can see and be seen, perhaps?"

"Tomorrow," I said. I knew I sounded abrupt. Akira closed his eyes and spoke so softly I barely heard him.

"Keiko-chan, I know you are angry with me, and I know you want to move quickly. But please, listen to me. This is not a game. Nobody here cares about your honorable code of bushido." I was startled; had he read my thoughts earlier? "If Ikeda finds out why you are here, or if he somehow makes the connection between you and Kamakiri the oiran, then we are done for. If we rush things and make a mistake, we are dead.

"I want to get Niko back. And I want to see Ikeda punished for what he was going to do to you even more. But you have to remember, I'm nothing here. I'm just your servant, not Akira, the feared yakuza. And as for you—the world thinks that Lady Keiko is already dead and buried in Jokan-Ji Temple in the Floating World. You no longer exist. Ikeda has nothing to lose by killing both of us. He's a desperate, ruthless man. We have to tread very, very carefully."

I shrugged, hiding my surprise at his perception. I watched him walk out silently. His words were sensible, I knew, but I was in no mood for sense. I was angry and frustrated. I slapped my pillow into shape and huddled beneath my kakebuton. My futon was so wide, and so very empty, I was certain I would never find sleep. But I did. And when I did, I dreamed.

I was walking along Tokaido Highway again. Oddly, although I knew where I was, this was not the part of the highway I had traveled. *This* was the road that led to Kyoto, beyond the checkpoint at Hakone. It seemed perfectly natural that my brother Isamu was at my side. In front of us, our father strode along, glancing to neither left nor right. And although I could not see her, I knew my elder sister, Emiko, was pattering behind me. She was wearing high geta; I could hear the slap of the soles as she tried to keep up. She was panting with the effort of trying to catch us. I wanted to slow down, to wait for her, but Isamu took my arm and tugged me along briskly.

"You can't help her, you know. Not until she wants to be helped," Isamu told me. I frowned in confusion, not understanding his words.

"We could slow down," I suggested.

"*You* could slow down," Isamu agreed. "But Father and I have to hurry. We are going on a very long journey together, Keiko-chan. We didn't want to leave you and Emiko, but we had no choice in the matter. Now, there's only the two of you left. I'm glad we had this chance to talk. I'm proud of you, little sister. And so is Father, although, of course, he's not going to tell you that. Emiko is going to need your help, you know. She doesn't think she does at the moment, but she will. Emiko never had a thought that wasn't about anything but herself, but you'll forgive her that because you're far stronger than she is. When she needs you, you will be there for her."

I turned to glance back at Emiko and found I was staring at an empty road. When I turned to look forward again, Isamu and Father had somehow advanced into the far distance. They were so very far that had I not known who they were, I would not have recognized them. I was completely alone, but lying on the road was Father's katana. I bent down and picked it up. It felt warm and almost alive in my hands, as if it awaited only my command to spring into action. I buckled the strap around my waist and the katana hung down against my leg, as comfortable and consoling as the hand of a lover.

"It's yours now, onna-bugeisha." Isamu's distant voice was a whisper on the breeze. "Use it well and the honor of the family will be in safe hands."

When I awoke, it was the deepest hour of the night. I threw back my kakebuton—and I could have sworn that it wrapped itself around me, trying to tie me to my futon—and ran my hands to the very bottom of the packages that carried my clothes. When I found it, the katana's scabbard was silken beneath my fingers. I took the sword from its sheath and held it against my face. Then I turned it deliberately so the edge ran along the base of my throat, following the line where my head joined my shoulders.

I held the katana in place for a long time, waiting.

I had to know. Isamu had said the katana was mine by right. But Isamu was dead. He had spoken to me in a dream, and this was reality. Every samurai knew the myths about the ancient blades. It was said that they would never cut the righteous, but only those who deserved to be punished. If they were wielded by a hand that did not deserve them, then they would turn on the one who would be their master and taste their blood.

I left it there until the blade grew warm against my skin. Finally, I sighed and lowered my head, pressing my lips against the steel before I slid it back into its saya. When I laid back on my futon, the katana lay at my side—where it belonged.

TWELVE

Moonlight upon your
Face is beautiful. Yet it
Makes you a stranger

"If the innkeeper doesn't let Ikeda know a newly-widowed and wealthy samurai lady is staying at his inn, then we'll have to contrive an invitation for you to visit his house some other way," Akira said quietly.

He was walking behind me, as was only correct for a groom escorting his mistress. I looked straight ahead, barely moving my lips as I spoke. I understood the need for caution instinctively. The countryside around the ryokan was very pretty, but it was also very closed in. Hedges and copses ran along each side of our path. It would have been very easy for somebody to be hidden close enough to see and hear us. We were strangers in these parts, and in these present, uncertain times, it would have been far from surprising if the citizens of Hakone wanted to be sure we were as innocent as we appeared.

"Yes. Perhaps I should pretend to be bored, ask about the local residents?"

"Worth a try if Ikeda doesn't visit the ryokan to use the onsen. Didn't the innkeeper say he was a frequent visitor? I've heard the waters at this particular onsen are supposed to be excellent to beautify the skin. Who knows, perhaps he's hoping it might help him. If he does come to bathe, you could contrive to be there at the same time. And then it would only be natural for you to chat with him."

I shivered at the thought of sharing the onsen with Ikeda. His appearance had been the stuff of nightmares when I had seen him in the shadows when I had been Hana's prisoner in the Hidden House. How much worse would it be to see him not only naked, but to know I was bathing in the same water? I swallowed nausea at the thought.

"I can only pray not," I muttered. "I have no desire at all to share a bath with him. If he doesn't show any interest in inviting me to his house, then I will have to entice him somehow. As his wife is so ill, I can't do the correct thing and send her a note. But we have one thing in our favor. He might know noblemen, but he wasn't born into noble society. He isn't going to know all the complex intricacies of polite behavior. If there's no word from him by the time we get back to the ryokan, I'm going to send him a little note anyway. All very formal, just expressing my regret at not being able to meet his wife while I'm here. With perhaps just the tiniest hint that we might have acquaintances in common and how barbaric and boring I find the countryside after Edo. If he truly were a noble, he would be appalled by such forward behavior. But as it is, I think we could get away with it."

"I'm sure *you* could," Akira murmured.

A bird broke cover in the hedge just in front of us and Akira reached for his sword instantly. I had no need to be told that there was somebody there. I could feel their presence, smell the faint odor of tobacco. I turned my head slowly, as if I was astonished by Akira's behavior, and spoke icily. And far too loudly.

"Really, my good man. What are you doing? I know neither of us is used to the quiet of the countryside, but if you're going to draw your sword every time a bird takes flight I'll be a nervous wreck in days."

Akira took his cue instantly. He was the picture of embarrassment as he stood with his head down, his whole posture meek.

"I'm so sorry, mistress. I thought it might have been a bandit. The peasants are very bold these days, and a lady as noble and wealthy as you are would be ripe for ransom."

I started to laugh and managed to change it to a cough. "Really, Akira. How dare you speak of such things? You forget yourself," I scolded. "You know perfectly well that's why I wanted to get out of Edo, to get away from my would-be suitors. I daresay I may wish to marry again, in the fullness of time, but not unless and until the right sort of cultured and well-connected gentleman presents himself. Whilst we are here in Hakone, I wish to be seen as no more than a moderately well-off widow, and I'll thank you to remember that. My poor husband's spirit would find no rest if he thought I was going to be pursued for his fortune."

I could feel Akira's surprise. I had spoken in just the right tone of voice, I knew, to reprimand a wayward servant. How often had I heard ladies who never dared to raise their voice above an adoring whisper in their husband's presence lash their servants stridently for some imagined error.

"Yes, mistress. I am sorry, mistress," he said humbly.

Suddenly, I felt the time was right to move on. I pretended to stumble on the uneven ground and shrieked loudly.

"Oh, my ankle. I am in such agony! We will go back to the ryokan at once. I have had enough of this fresh air. Take my arm, you wretch. Can't you see I can barely walk for the pain?"

Akira held out his arm and I slid my hand through, gripping him tightly. I was vibrating with muffled laughter and I felt him relax as we walked back.

"It's all right," he said softly after perhaps ten paces. "He's gone. Slipped down the other side of the hedge and doubled behind it to come out in front of us, around the next bend. What a shame you're not a man. You could have made a wonderful career as an actor, Keiko-chan. You were so realistic you had me trembling for a moment!"

"My apologies," I whispered. "Do you think whoever was watching us will report back to the innkeeper?"

"Possibly. But better still he might have been sent to take a look at you by Ikeda himself." Akira paused to pretend to help me navigate a muddy patch of path. "I caught a glimpse of the man. He doesn't belong to the ryokan. I saw all the ryokan's servants last night when I let them beat me at dice. It's amazing how easily it is to be accepted when one appears to be drunk enough to lose heavily to those who belong here."

"And did you find anything interesting?" I asked.

"Most certainly," Akira said promptly. "I found that Miki-san's affections are easily lost. Once she thought my purse was empty, it seemed I no longer had any charm at all for her."

"Such a shame!" I grinned. "Let that be a lesson to you. Never trust a woman."

"Except for one," Akira spoke quietly. "There is one woman I know would never betray me."

I hesitated. I didn't know how to answer him and so put the moment off. We had reached Hakone, and I decided quickly that I would take tea. Akira, of course, was forced to remain alert on duty outside while I sipped my tea and pretended to enjoy a daifuku cake. Akira simply fell into place behind me when I left the tea house, and I wondered if he regretted his words earlier. I couldn't decide if I did or not.

The innkeeper was waiting for us at the front door, practically hopping from foot to foot with eagerness.

"Lady Keiko." He bowed, holding out a folded piece of paper to me. "I do hope you had a pleasant walk in our lovely countryside?"

I kept my expression calm, even as I realized that our caution had truly been more important than I had realized. We had set off in the direction of Hakone before turning aside. How had he known I had been walking rather than tasting the limited pleasures of the town?

"What is this?" I didn't bother to answer his question but plucked the paper from his fingers as if it was grubby.

"My lady, a message for you. From Ikeda-san. His servant is awaiting your reply, if it pleases you."

My heart exulted. I opened the folded paper and scanned the note within. Ikeda-san had, it appeared, heard of the presence of the noble lady from Edo who was honoring Hakone's most humble ryokan with her presence. He hoped I would forgive his insolence in addressing me without introduction. He deeply regretted that his wife was unable to welcome me to his humble house, but unfortunately, she was rather unwell and unable to write to me herself at this moment. But perhaps I could bring myself to overlook this terrible impoliteness and do them both the honor of dining with them this evening?

I was so surprised, I almost gave myself away. As it was, I spoke sharply to the innkeeper.

"Ikeda-san says his wife is only a little unwell. How is it that you told me that she is extremely ill and not expected to live?"

"Ah." The innkeeper did not hesitate. I wondered cynically how much Ikeda had paid to bribe him? "I understand that Ikeda-san's wife, Waka-san, has made an amazing recovery very recently, the gods be praised. The poor lady is still rather fragile, but it is hoped that she will be fully well again very soon. I am sure that a visit from a lady such as you who can bring news of the world outside Hakone would be of very great benefit to her recovery."

He was smiling at me hopefully. The calligraphy of the note was less than stylish, and I guessed that Ikeda had written it himself. I wanted to hand it back and wipe my fingers on my robe. Reluctantly, I wondered if I had underestimated Ikeda. I had no option but to pretend to believe that his wife was recovering and that she would be delighted to meet with me. And if I believed that, then politeness dictated that I had to respond favorably to Ikeda's request. But I felt instinctively that there was something very wrong here. I would have been much happier to have met Ikeda for the first time somewhere far more public than his own home, but it appeared that I was not going to get the chance.

I bowed my head very slightly to the innkeeper. His fat face immediately broke into a delighted grin.

I spoke in a bored drawl. "You may tell Ikeda-san's messenger that I will be pleased to visit him and his wife this evening. Will you arrange a palanquin for me? My groom and the other men will accompany me," I added grandly. I could hardly take my katana out to a dinner appointment; without it, I would feel much safer with my guard of yakuza close by.

I should, I suppose, have been thrilled by the turn of events. But something felt very wrong to me, and I was deeply anxious. I did not believe for a moment that Ikeda's wife had made a miraculous recovery. If he had infected her with the plum poison, the poor woman was never going to recover. But if she was still very ill, how was Ikeda going to explain her absence tonight? Or did he intend to make the dying woman get up and somehow make polite conversation with me? Surely even a man as ruthless as Ikeda would not do such a thing. And apart from anything else, the invitation had come too soon. I had to assume that Akira was correct and that the innkeeper was watching me carefully. In that case, I would have no opportunity to get Akira to one side, to speak to him privately to discuss in detail what our roles would be this evening.

I thought that once we arrived at Ikeda's house Akira would try to look around the outside areas of the estate to make our escape plans. For myself, I would try and persuade Ikeda to show me around his house. If he was as little of a gentleman as I thought he was, that should be relatively easy. Just like Hara, I hoped he would want to impress me with his supposed wealth. I doubted I would actually see Niko, but locked doors would tell their own stories.

I took a deep, steadying breath. Such a great pity I could not find an excuse to take my katana with me. I would have known I was safe with it to hand. As soon as my shoji was shut to prying eyes, I took it out of its hiding place and ran my hand down the blade carefully. *Soon*, I promised it silently, *very soon indeed if I had anything to do with it, it would once again be used to right the unrighteous.*

The blade glowed softly in the daylight. I felt that it was reluctant to slide back in the saya. The thought gave me courage. Then I remembered Ikeda's dreadful skin and the hole in his face where his nose should have been and I wanted to pack my things and walk away, go back to the Floating World and find another plan.

I stroked the silken lacquer of the saya and remembered Niko telling me earnestly to take care while I was away from her. My eyes filled with tears and I cursed my weakness. I was a warrior woman of the samurai. I should be above mere womanly emotions. Oddly, I rather thought that my katana understood and forgave my failings. Niko would, I knew.

The knowledge made me feel desperately sad.

THIRTEEN

On a very clear
Night, if I stand on tiptoe
I can reach the stars

I paused uncertainly before Ikeda's open shoji. My hand clutched the frame for support as I wondered in disbelief how it was possible that we could have been so very wrong. I could barely begin to disentangle the surge of emotions that left me wordless. Anger, certainly, and deep embarrassment. And perhaps above all, total and utter despair. It was only the fact that my feet were rooted to the ground with shock that stopped me turning and walking—no, running—away.

Impossibly, the man who stood inside the shoji, bowing deeply in welcome, was not the Ikeda who had tried to buy me from Hana. The gods had been laughing at us all along. By some bizarre coincidence, the name was the same. But the man was not.

The Ikeda I had expected to meet had a rotting pit in the center of his face where his nose had been eaten by the baidoku. The hole had run constantly with mucous; I had a sudden memory of the slug-trail of snot that was obviously so ever-present that he often forgot to wipe it away. His skin had been severely disfigured as well, pitted with pustules that were worse than those left by smallpox. The man who stood in the subtly lighted room before me had a nose. And his skin, although muddy and rather coarse, was unmarked.

In spite of my horror, I moved forward stiffly as he stood back to allow me to enter. It was instinctive. From my first steps, I had been taught to be polite. Courtesy was instilled into me until it was as unthinking as breathing. I had been invited to this man's house. I had accepted his invitation, so now that I was here nothing—short of a heart seizure—would prevent me from spending the evening in his company.

Whoever he was.

I was distracted for a moment by movement barely seen in my peripheral vision, shadows melting away into the deeper shadows around the house. Akira had been right yet again. The place was well guarded. If Akira had not convinced me that we had to plan carefully, we would have been taken easily. And for nothing.

My host straightened and smiled at me.

"My dear Keiko-san, I am delighted to welcome you to my humble home. Please, do come inside."

He stepped back and my heart began beating faster and faster still. I had been shocked and deeply disappointed; now, I was confused as well. The man's voice sounded as if he was speaking through a mouthful of food. Akira had told me that it was common in baidoku for the roof of the mouth to rot through just like the nose. Ikeda's voice had sounded exactly like this man's.

I entered with cautious, teetering footsteps and bowed

in my turn. All my senses were on alert; I could hear a bat screaming to frighten its prey in the garden. Ikeda's robes rustled as he moved back to allow me to enter and I knew without looking what colors he wore. And that smell that trembled on the air...I took a deep breath and instantly wished I hadn't. The odor was very faint, but it was also very terrible. Was it coming from my host? I inclined toward him slightly, as if I was adjusting my balance from the uneven path to the smoother tatami within. No, there was the faintest tang of nervous sweat seeping from his clean skin, but the smell I was seeking was different again.

This odor was so faint and far away that it was barely a smell, but rather something that I sensed. It was the lingering reek of flesh that was very close to death. Of a body that had already given up the struggle to live. Dirty hair and dirtier skin. Breath that exhaled sickness. I held my own breath for a moment in pity as I understood it was a womanly smell. I knew instinctively that I was sensing the last of a life that had been abandoned to die alone and unmourned. What had the innkeeper called this man's wife? Waka-san, that was it.

My heart cried out to the poor woman, and I almost wept as I knew that she had somehow felt my pity and, so very faintly, was reaching out to grasp it with the dim gratitude of those who had no hope left. *I will help you,* I shouted silently. *Whatever is going on here, whatever happens, I will help you. You will not die alone. You will have justice.* The thought burned so fiercely in my mind that I thought the man in front of me must have heard it. I was surprised when I saw he was smiling at me, waiting for me to speak. I bowed my head and managed to control my voice so that it was no more than a polite drawl.

"Ikeda-san, thank you for inviting me to your home.

How fortunate for me that a man who is more accustomed to the pace of life in Edo is here in the country and has also been so kind as to invite me into his home for the evening."

My smile was gracious. I stood just a little closer to him than was polite, my gaze fastened on his face as if I found him fascinating. It was worth it. A tidal wave of relief made me tremble.

Akira and I had not been wrong. This was the Ikeda I had been seeking. The light in the ante-room was provided by a single oil lamp. Its flame was subtle, but my vision was sharp. Even so, if I hadn't been suspicious, Ikeda would probably have gotten away with it. He was wearing makeup. It had been applied with very great skill, but it was thick—it had to be to cover the pustules on his skin. The nose, also, was false. It was an excellently contrived prosthesis. I lowered my eyes politely and stared from beneath my lowered eyelashes. I could just make out how it had been done; there was the faintest irregularity where the false material overlapped his skin. Probably a still thicker layer of the cosmetic had been used to glue the prosthesis in place.

A sudden thought came to me and I swallowed bile. Was it possible that the false nose was not false at all but was a genuine nose? Not Ikeda's own nose that had long rotted away, but could this be a nose stolen from a corpse and preserved by some terrible alchemy? My mind swerved away from the idea instinctively. Of course not. It must be made of fine leather. The same sort of leather that Ikeda's tobacco pouch had been made of. The feel of that had made me cringe as well.

I was grateful for the dim light. If the light had been brighter, Ikeda would have seen my sickly smile and known there was something wrong. I concentrated on practicalities to focus my mind away from his face. The makeup must have taken a long time for him to apply, but still I doubted that it would have been successful in daylight. Ikeda hadn't bothered with it in the Floating World. It would hardly have been worth the time and effort. He was not known there, and the plum poison disease was so prevalent in the Floating World that unless he had drawn attention to himself, his bizarre appearance would have been barely worthy of notice. But he would have expected that the aristocratic Lady Keiko would have run shrieking from his unexpected and bizarre appearance.

I was thankful I had taken such care with my own makeup. Nothing as elaborate as Kamakiri the oiran had worn, of course. But still, such an excess of paint as I had used would have raised surprised eyebrows if I had been in truly noble company. And my wig had far too many discreet but obviously expensive ornaments pinned to it. I had aimed for the contradiction of appearing to be a woman older than I really was, who in her turn was trying to pass for someone younger. Altogether, my appearance was completely different from any other time Ikeda had seen me. I hoped it was enough.

I was relieved when Ikeda stood aside politely to allow me to pass into the main room. He held his hands out to indicate that I should sit and I folded to the tatami with as much grace as I could manage. I glanced around the room —anything to put off the moment when I had to look directly at him—and finally rested my gaze on his forehead. I fixed a smile to my lips and spoke through it.

"Ikeda-san, so very kind of you to invite me to your home. I trust your wife is fully recovered? I was expecting to meet her."

"Ah. I am afraid my poor wife has relapsed into her illness and will be unable to join us this evening." My face betrayed my genuine sorrow, but Ikeda read something else into my expression and spoke hurriedly. "I assure you, it is nothing contagious. I have had all the best surgeons in the area to attend to her, but none of them can hold out any hope. As you know, she rallied somewhat recently, but it seems that was the last gasp of her spirit."

I thought flatly what a horrible man he was. Not only was he happy to entertain another woman when his wife was dying beneath his roof, but he was worried that I might think she would infect me with her illness. And this monster had my Niko in his possession and had been very close to having me also. I was suddenly cold, wondering if we were too late and he had already taken Niko. Whether he had or he hadn't, in the matter of his fate, it made no difference. I *was* his fate. I gave thanks to the gods for allowing me to be the instrument of revenge for all of the women he had mistreated so badly. For his wife. For Niko. For me. And also for the unknown first wife who had been disposed of casually in the interests of his advancement.

"I am so sorry to hear that, Ikeda-san," I said smoothly. "Had I known, I would have sent my apologies. Naturally, you will not wish to be distracted by a visitor at such a difficult time. Perhaps I should call my escort and return to the ryokan?"

I expected him to agree instantly. Had he been a gentleman, he would have been loud in his apologies, but he would also have understood how improper the situation was. But then again, had he truly been a gentleman, he would never have invited me—an unknown but presumably high-caste lady—to his house when he was effectively here alone. The thoughts passed through my head rapidly and I was barely surprised when he smirked and rubbed his hands together in an oily manner.

"Please, Keiko-san. Think nothing of it. I would be devastated if you left after sparing the time to honor my house. As would my poor wife, if she thought that her indisposition was an irritation to you. Your beauty illuminates my humble home. Would you like some sake, perhaps, before we enjoy a light repast? I'm sure the ryokan does its best, but I always think there's nothing to beat good home cooking."

Before I could answer, Ikeda clapped his hands and a maid came in with a tray bearing sake in a warming flask and cups. Ikeda gestured for her to put the tray down and he poured the sake himself, passing a brimming cup to me. He raised his own cup in salute.

He was staring at me with such open interest, I became nervous. His gaze flitted over my wig, sparkling with expensive pins, and greedily inspected my remarkably fine kimono. I realized with a sigh of relief that he didn't remember me at all. He was simply taking note of the worth of everything I was wearing and obviously approving of it. I had worried when I dressed that I had perhaps gone too far in my vulgar display of riches. Now, I understood that as far as Ikeda was concerned, more would always be welcome.

I kept my eyes cast down politely as the food arrived. The thought of eating with Ikeda made me feel ill. I doubted I would be able to swallow a morsel. But there was no way around it. If food was served to me, politeness demanded that I at least pretend to eat and enjoy it. I prayed it would be no more than a very light dish or two, which could be consumed quickly.

Once the food was out of the way, I had decided that the way forward would be to praise what I had already seen of Ikeda's home in the most extravagant terms. Courtesy would demand that he promptly offer to show me around the rest of the house. Under normal circumstances, it would have been unthinkable for me, a single lady alone with an unknown host, to accept the invitation. I guessed shrewdly that Ikeda would have no idea of that and would be delighted to show off what remained of his wealth. I had little hope of finding a trace of Niko, but knowledge of the layout of the house would be invaluable when Akira and I came back later.

I was suddenly full and overflowing with anger. If I hated every moment I had to spend in this man's company, what must my poor Niko be enduring as his prisoner? I could walk away; she could not. I bared my teeth in a sweet smile as I thought how exquisitely Ikeda was going to suffer for what he had done to my younger sister.

The "light repast" was actually an overblown *kaiseki* feast. The ostentatious display of luxurious food should have been a subtle melding of taste, texture, appearance, and colors that tempted all the senses. Instead, over-filled dishes smothered the tatami. Even if I had been hungry, the sight of so much food would have dimmed my appetite. Ikeda seemed not to notice my reluctance. He picked up a dish of sashimi and began to help himself, stuffing the food into his mouth. His manners were disgusting. Even though I guessed the collapsed roof of his mouth made it difficult for him to eat, I had to work to hide my distaste. He spoke with his mouth full, spraying the delicate seafood in a mist down his robe.

"I do hope you enjoy fish, Keiko-chan."

I kept a smile on my face with considerable effort. How dare this uncouth man think we were so well acquainted that he could call me by such a familiar endearment? Enough! Even for Niko's sake, this was hard to bear.

"I normally enjoy it, Ikeda-san." I put a heavy emphasis

on the formal "san." Ikeda appeared not to notice he had been reproved. He swigged sake to wash down his sashimi and cleared his throat loudly before he spoke.

"Excellent. I knew you would be a woman of the most refined tastes. Now, would you like to try some of this lobster? It's excellent."

He poked out a fillet of the succulent shellfish with his chopsticks and popped it into his mouth before holding the dish out to me. Those same chopsticks had already traveled from various dishes into his mouth; nothing could have enticed me to eat from any dish that they had touched.

"Perhaps just a little rice. And some vegetables," I murmured, helping myself from untouched dishes.

Ikeda shrugged. "As you wish. All you ladies are the same!" He leered at me, and guessing some witticism was about to follow, I composed my face carefully. "All worried about getting fat! Although, I very much doubt that you need have any concerns about that."

His glance wandered down my kimono, lingering on my breasts approvingly. For one horrifying moment, I thought he was about to reach out and touch me. I grabbed a dish of flame-grilled bass and held it out to him enticingly. His gaze flickered greedily from my body to the fish, and finally the fish won. He dug his chopsticks in and took half of the fish at one go.

"Delicious," he muttered. "I've left the head for you, Keiko-chan. I always think the brain is the most delicate part of the fish."

"Absolutely," I murmured. "So kind. But I think I'll try the sea urchin. It's always been a favorite of mine."

I picked up the untouched dish of thinly sliced raw urchin and began to pick at it. In any other company, it would have been truly appetizing. I watched Ikeda guzzling his food, and gradually I began to relax. The man was so sure of himself, he appeared to think he had captivated me. I barely had to speak. It was sufficient to smile and agree with him—and make sure his sake cup was constantly full.

He put down the final rice dish with a satisfied burp. "Pardon!" He patted his mouth with a napkin. The room had become very warm as we ate, and I stared at the napkin in fascinated repulsion. Ikeda's makeup had begun to run with the heat. The cloth was stained olive where he had dabbed his lips. I had to fight to keep my face still as I wondered if his nose would begin to peel off. What would I do if it fell into his dish? The idea was so appalling I nearly erupted into hysterical laughter.

"That was delicious, Ikeda-san," I gushed hurriedly. "But of course, anything eaten in such lovely surroundings would always taste wonderful." I glanced around the room admiringly. Very grudgingly, I had to admit it was furnished in quite good taste, although there was too much furniture for my liking. "I had heard that your house was the most beautiful in Hakone. If this room is anything to go by, I can see that is true."

I paused, waiting for him to take the hint. He was clearly pleased with my words, but simply nodded in agreement. I was at my wit's end. What else did I have to say to get him to show me the rest of the house?

"You are very kind, Keiko-chan." He shrugged, pretending modesty. "Although, I'm sure after the style and luxury of Edo, it must appear very provincial to you."

"Not at all!" I exclaimed. "I find your home to be quite lovely. I notice you have some particularly beautiful Hirado items." I nodded toward a stunning pierced incense burner in white, painted with cobalt blue. I had no need to pretend to sound envious that he owned such a piece; I was. "Hirado ware was a great favorite of my late husband. He particularly treasured one delightful brush rest that was given to him by the shogun himself." I lied casually, hoping the less than subtle boast would not be wasted on Ikeda.

"Really? That incense burner was also a gift from a friend of mine. By coincidence, he is also well acquainted with the shogun, so it may well be that this item was also once owned by the shogun." He was trying to impress me. Trying far too hard. I smiled even as I frantically searched for something—anything—that would make Ikeda offer to show me the rest of his house. He smirked and added complacently, "I have several more Hirado pieces. Also some Nabeshima ware."

Such an ostentatious reckoning of his wealth was so vulgar I could barely believe I was hearing it. But I had to take my chance. I spoke quickly.

"How wonderful!" I added pointedly, with a glance at the half-burned down candles, "I would love to see them before I leave."

"But of course!"

FOURTEEN

It is difficult
To tell if it is raindrops
On your face or tears

*A*s easy as that. Subtlety was clearly wasted on this man. I thought sourly that I could have saved myself the discomfort of spending an evening in his presence. If I had simply demanded to be shown around his house earlier, he probably would have been delighted.

He insisted on helping me to my feet. I could barely believe he didn't feel my flesh trying to creep away from his touch.

"Now, you will like these," he instructed. He paused in the hallway. "As you can see, I have the whole series, depicting the passing of the seasons. They cost a fortune, but one must always pay for the very best."

I murmured my agreement, barely glancing at the plinths topped with Imari porcelain plates. I assumed that they were expensive, but they were painted in red, gold, and black on a blue background and were far too gaudy for my taste. But I nodded and smiled my admiration and took the chance to orientate myself as Ikeda pointed out the finer points of the Imari. We were in the central corridor. The reception room was to my right. I guessed from the lingering cooking odors that the kitchen was straight ahead.

"May I show you the rest of my poor house?" Ikeda asked.

"Most certainly," I agreed promptly. "I would like that very much."

He took my elbow to steer me down the corridor. I managed not to flinch.

"The bathhouse." He threw back a shoji and I poked my head through the door, making appreciative noises. It was huge, easily as big as the communal bath at the ryokan. Did Ikeda entertain guests frequently, I wondered? It was far too big for just a couple to use. Or was it simply that he felt that bigger must be better? "It's fed by the same mineral springs as the onsen. But of course, this bathhouse is completely private. If you would like to take the waters here, away from the rabble that uses the onsen, I would be delighted to welcome you as my guest."

His tongue flicked out from his mouth and licked his lips very deliberately. I had to fight the temptation to reach out and yank his false nose off to teach him a lesson. Only the knowledge of what lay beneath stopped me.

"Thank you," I said coolly. "But I can assure you I find the onsen perfectly comfortable."

Perhaps even Ikeda realized he had gone too far. He stepped out of the bathhouse and guided me quickly back into the main part of the house.

"My own apartment." He waved his hand to indicate that I was welcome to look. I hesitated, expecting to find his wife inside, then common sense told me I was being silly.

Even a man like Ikeda would hardly want me to see a woman on her sickbed.

Still, I was relieved to find the room empty. It was also unlit, and I struggled to find something flattering to say about the almost unseen space.

"What a large room!" I said desperately. I was running short of compliments. "So very pleasant!"

"I am so glad you like it." Ikeda was far too close to me again. I decided enough was enough.

"Such a pity your wife was unable to join us," I remarked pointedly. Ikeda glanced instinctively to his left, where a shoji partitioned this room. I hid a smile of triumph; his wife's apartment must be through there.

"Indeed. She was most disappointed that she was unable to be with us tonight." He stepped back quickly and we were once again in the main corridor. My senses were alert for the smallest of noises. I heard nothing, but I noticed that the odor I had sensed earlier was much stronger here. I understood instinctively that it was the smell of flesh corrupted by illness. Of breath that emanated from a body that was near death. I almost cried aloud with pity for Ikeda's wife. I spoke quickly to hide my distress.

"And these rooms?" I gestured to the other side of the corridor. Ikeda barely glanced across. "Are they as lovely as the rest of the house?"

"Oh, nothing but a guest room and a small storeroom," he said dismissively. I waited for a heartbeat before following him, still concentrating on trying to hear anything from behind the doors that were closed to me. Was Niko there? I searched for her presence, but felt nothing. Still, I sensed Ikeda's strong desire to steer me away, and I guessed that this was indeed where he was keeping my younger sister imprisoned. Probably she was drugged to keep her silent. I almost smiled; it would take a strong sleeping draught to keep Niko quiet!

"Yours is such a delightful house, Ikeda-san," I gushed. "And filled with so many beautiful things."

I was actually slightly puzzled. If Ikeda owed a great deal of money in gambling debts, how had he managed to hold on to so many treasures? As if he read my thoughts, he answered my unasked question cheerfully.

"I am so glad you like it. Actually, I have changed things a great deal recently. My very good friend Lord Endo has spent years telling me I should adhere to Zen principles and that simplicity is everything." He glanced at me and paused. I guessed I was expected to exclaim at Lord Endo's name, but I did not. Ikeda sighed his disappointment. "In the end, I decided that I would follow his advice. I used to have far more ornaments and prints and furniture and so on than you have seen tonight. Oh, much more! But Endo-san was insistent, so I gifted many things to the local temple. It's quite famous. Have you visited it yet?"

"No. I really must see it before I return to Edo," I murmured. What a liar the man was! I had no doubt at all that he had parted with his treasures, but for cash to pay his debts rather than as a gift to the temple. His hand brushed against me as we reached the ante-room. With a deliberate effort, I did not snatch my arm away from him.

"Do you have to go so soon, Keiko-chan?" He leaned toward me and smiled. "In fact, do you have to go at all? It's a cold night, and I do believe it may rain. I would hate for you to catch a chill on your journey back to the ryokan. It would be no trouble at all for me to have a futon laid in the guest bedroom for you."

I patted my lips with my finger as if I was really considering his ludicrous offer. Inwardly, I exulted. Niko was not in the guest room, then. That left either the storeroom next to it or a storeroom in the kitchen. The latter was unlikely; even the best trained and fearful servants would be unable to resist gossiping about something so openly outrageous. But Ikeda could simply give orders for the servants to keep out of the storeroom. If, as I suspected, Niko was drugged, there was no reason for them to know she was there.

"My thanks, Ikeda-san. But I really think I must be on my way back to the ryokan." A glint of anger deep in his eyes made me cautious. "People do gossip so. They can make something out of nothing." I tittered as if I was deeply amused. "But perhaps on another occasion? When we have come to know each other a little better?"

I was sliding the shoji open as I spoke. Even then, I sensed that Ikeda was going to try and detain me. I wanted desperately to get away from him, from him and also from this house with its lingering aura of sadness and imminent death. But neither did I want to anger him. Until we actually had Niko, there was far too much at stake to risk anything at all.

"Mistress, I have your palanquin ready."

Akira loomed out of the shadows. I wondered how long he had been waiting. His height was diminished by his hunched shoulders. His hands were balled into fists. I swallowed laughter; his whole appearance was so overdone, he might have been the villain in a kabuki play. He was barely managed anger personified. He smoldered. Ikeda gave a small gasp that he turned into a cough and stepped back from me hurriedly.

"Akira, thank you. Are the men ready to go?" I asked as if it didn't matter at all to me. Akira nodded sulkily. I turned to Ikeda and bowed politely. "Such an interesting evening, Ikeda-san. Please, do give my compliments to your wife and be sure to tell her how much I regretted not being able to see her."

"Of course." Ikeda was still staring at Akira. I tried not to giggle as I saw his expression change from something that was close to fear to surprise. I suddenly guessed that he thought my bodyguard was also my lover and that Akira was jealous of him. As I stepped out of the doorway, Ikeda leaned forward into the light and I saw he was smirking. "I hope to see you again very soon, Keiko-chan. This evening has been a very great pleasure. I'm sure we have much still to talk about."

I climbed into the palanquin and waved languidly at him from between the curtains.

"Keiko-*chan?*" Akira growled. "You seem to have got very well acquainted with Ikeda."

I shook my head in amazement as I realized that Akira had not been pretending to be angry at all. He *was* furious. And jealous.

Well, well. Who would have thought it?

FIVETEEN

When I take my hand
Out of water, how is it
There is no hole left?

*A*kira remained stubbornly silent on the journey home. I was tempted to speak, to try and coax him out of his bad temper, but I decided against it. Let him stew in his ridiculous jealousy for a little longer. It would do him no harm.

The ryokan was closed fast when we finally arrived. I had forgotten that provincial inns would bolt their doors far earlier than in Edo. But even so, I was surprised. The innkeeper knew where I had gone. He should have waited up to let his distinguished guest back in. Or did he—like Ikeda—think I was not going to return to my own futon tonight? Akira pounded on the shoji frame until it rattled, and the innkeeper came at a run, his sleeping robe clutched around him as he babbled his apologies.

I nodded at him icily, too furious to speak.

I lay down on my futon and pulled the kakebuton over me as soon as I was alone. I was deeply grateful for its warmth as the charcoal-burner had not been lit and the room was cold and felt damp. I thought cynically that I was right; the innkeeper had obviously been instructed that I would not return tonight. Even when I was warmly bundled in my bedding, sleep would not come to me. My thoughts were far too anxious to allow the blessing of oblivion.

The shoji slid back silently. If I hadn't been alert, I would have missed it. Akira loomed over me, blocking out the moonlight.

"You took your time at Ikeda's place. I was beginning to think something had happened to you," Akira said sulkily. "In fact, if you hadn't come out when you did, I was going to come in and get you."

"I was perfectly fine," I snapped. "You should have known that. What are you doing here, anyway? I thought you said that while we were here it must be clear that you are nothing but my servant. That nobody suspect anything else."

We glared at each other like two sumo wrestlers squaring up in the dojo. I was determined not to be the one who gave in. Then the memory of the awful sorrow I had felt in Ikeda's house slid around me like mist and I closed my eyes in distress. What did our trivial differences matter compared to what I had left behind?

Akira's voice broke in on my thoughts. "The innkeeper works his servants so hard, they must sleep like the dead. In any event, they don't matter too much as their quarters are well away from your room, at the back of the ryokan. And their master is back in his room snoring. I checked it was safe before I came to you. I'm sorry I was angry. I was worried about you," Akira added apologetically. My thoughts were still with Niko and Ikeda's poor wife, and it took me a moment to catch up with his words.

"I'm sorry as well," I said contritely. Although whether I was sorry for arguing over nothing or for both of the poor women imprisoned in Ikeda's house, I wasn't sure myself.

Akira hesitated for a moment and then sat down cross-legged at the side of my futon. Although he was close enough to touch me and be touched in his turn, bundled in my kakebuton I felt as if I was imprisoned in armor and was unable to move even if I wanted to.

"Is everything all right?" he asked softly. "I wasn't really angry with you at all. When I heard that slimy Ikeda calling you Keiko-chan, I wanted to rip his head off. Did he behave himself?"

"More or less. Nothing I couldn't take care of," I assured him. I had never expected jealousy from Akira. I found it both shocking and oddly interesting.

"Was there any trace of Niko?" he asked.

I shook my head. "None. But I think I know where he's holding her. I had him show me around the house. I didn't see the kitchen or the servant's quarters, but I can't believe he would have her in either of those. I saw everything else, apart from a guestroom and what he said was a storeroom. He offered to have the guestroom made up so I could stay the night." Akira growled angrily. I nudged him to silence. "That being so, I can't believe he would have had Niko in there, so she must be in the storeroom. I think he must have drugged her. I made sure I spoke loudly in the corridor outside. If Niko had been able to hear me, she would have called out. If I'm wrong about her being in the storeroom, is there anywhere on the grounds of the house where he might be holding her? What about the outside? Are there guards?"

"He has guards, alright." Akira nodded. "He must be a very worried man. He's quite protected. I was tempted to take a good look around the estate, but I decided to take my men straight to the guardroom instead. Just as well I did. We were expected. The guards were very hospitable, especially when I handed over the flasks of the best Edo sake I happened to have with me. They told me that there are four guards on duty, night and day. Two of them patrol the grounds constantly while the others keep the house in sight. The two that patrol the estate split up and walk around the perimeter, meeting up outside the guardhouse to report. I pretended to be impressed and said Ikeda-san must be a very important man to need so much protection."

"Is it possible for us to get back in unseen, then?" I interrupted anxiously. "I suppose I'll be welcome back there anytime I choose to go, but I can hardly demand that my escorts be allowed inside as well. And even if I could get Niko out on my own, how would I get her past the guards?"

Akira tapped his finger against his lips to silence my flood of words. "I haven't finished," he said reprovingly. "The guards said that Ikeda is hated by the local people. All magistrates are severe, but he's worse than most. And they hinted that he's corrupt as well. It's only recently, since all the civil unrest, that he's employed the men. They don't like him either. Apparently he's neglected to pay them the full amount he owes for their services for months. But what can they do about it? If they go, they'll never get their full money. At least if they stay, they're fed and they have somewhere to sleep. They were very interested in *you,* Keiko-chan. In fact, they told me that Ikeda was so intent on attracting the wealthy widow who's come to visit that he'd gone to the trouble of trying to hide his disfigurement."

"I noticed. If I hadn't known he didn't have a nose, it was so well done he might have gotten away with it. When he first greeted me, I thought we'd made a mistake and he was the wrong man." I grimaced at the memory. "What else did the guards say?"

"They were quite blunt. They said if I could, I should try and warn you off Ikeda. They seemed to think he has a habit of losing wives when they become inconvenient. And they also told me he was riddled with baidoku. I did my best to look shocked, but as I explained to them, I'm a mere servant. How could I possibly tell my noble mistress something like that?"

He sounded amused and I glared at him reprovingly. "No mention of Niko?"

"None at all. Which makes me think that you're right. She is inside the house, probably in the storeroom. If he were keeping her in the stables or an outbuilding in the grounds, he would have instructed the guards to pay special attention to the area. And she can't be in a storeroom in the kitchen. Even though his servants are terrified of him, they wouldn't be able to resist gossiping about something like that."

I nodded in agreement. "Good. But if he's so well guarded, how are we going to get back in the house? And more importantly, out again with Niko safe?"

Akira was smiling. "It's not as bad as you think," he said. "I suggested to the guards that as Ikeda was obviously occupied and it was a cold night, they might prefer to stay in the guardhouse and we could finish off the sake together. It took no persuasion at all. They jumped at the idea. I daresay the patrols were resumed when you left, but for the time you were there the house and grounds were wide open." He added grimly, "If they were my men, they would have been punished severely for their lack of discipline."

"You mean I could have gotten Niko out tonight after all?" I cried out loud in distress. I had missed what might have been the only chance I would get to rescue her. I was horrified.

"No, you couldn't," he said calmly. "What were you going to do? Demand that Ikeda let you into the storeroom and then pick Niko up and run out with her? Even if you'd done that, he could have just shouted for his guards. You were unarmed. My men and I had taken only short swords with us, and the guards insisted we take those off as soon as we got into the guardroom. We had no option but to agree. It would have been suspicious if we had argued. They were locked away until the moment we were ready to leave. You may be onna-bugeisha, and my men know how to fight, but do you really think we would have gotten out of there, with you carrying Niko and all of us facing four trained soldiers armed with good swords? Not to mention a furious Ikeda."

"I suppose we couldn't have done it," I admitted. "But I must get back in there. If it means I have to put up with that dreadful man thinking I'm madly in love with him, I'll do it."

"No, you won't." Akira's voice was ice. "There's no need. We will go back tomorrow night, as soon as we're sure that the innkeeper and all the servants are asleep. I have a last flask of sake. It has something very special in it. I'll send it over with one of my men early in the evening with my compliments. Now that I've met them, I'm certain the guards will be happy to neglect their duties in favor of something better."

I heard what he said, but rather than calming me, I was

flooded with the need to act. I scrambled to my feet at once, energy flooding my limbs. Akira put his hand on my arm. I resented him stopping me.

"Why do we have to wait?" I said angrily. "Why did we leave in the first place? You could have taken the drugged sake with you and used it when you saw what kind of men they were. We could have waited outside the estate wall and gone back when you were sure they were asleep. Why are we sitting here doing nothing now? Can't you go back immediately and tell the guards some tale or other? Say I was angry with you and dismissed you on the spot, so you've come back to drown your sorrows with them. They'll believe you."

"Keiko, listen to me." Akira stood and put his hands on my shoulders. He spoke slowly, emphasizing every word. "It's inviting trouble if we go back tonight. No matter what tale I told them, the guards would never let me back into the estate in the middle of the night. And they would be deeply suspicious as well. They'd probably overpower me and hand me over to Ikeda in the morning. And don't forget, Ikeda's the magistrate for Hakone. Here, he's supremely powerful. I would simply disappear. And Ikeda knows I'm your servant. If he were suspicious of me, he would be suspicious of you as well. At the very best, Lady Keiko would no longer find herself welcome in his house. At worse, you would vanish alongside me." I shook my head angrily. He was wrong. He *had* to be wrong. He ignored me and carried on speaking softly. "If you don't care about me or yourself, think about Niko. If he thought he was in danger, he would kill her without a second thought."

I acknowledged wearily that Akira's words made sense. "You're right. I'm sorry I was too impatient. It was just the thought of Niko, being kept in his house with him and not knowing if he's already had her..." My voice trailed off with the horror of it. "Tell me, then. What are your plans? If it means that we stand a chance of getting Niko out safely, I'll wait. Somehow..." I added ruefully.

"Before we do anything, you need some different clothes." I frowned at the apparent irrelevance. Akira hissed with amusement. "What? Did you think you were going to sneak in wearing your fine kimono? Even with the guards asleep, the gate will be closed and barred. We'll have to climb over the wall. My man Asahi is about your height. He can go into Hakone tomorrow morning and buy a short yukata robe and some breeches for himself and pass them on to you. When the time comes, tie your hair up firmly so it's out of the way. And we'll all blacken our faces and hands with soot from the lamps. It'll take longer than riding, but we'll have to walk there. We can't take the horses. Our innkeeper would be bound to hear them being taken from the stables. He'd think they were being stolen and raise the alarm for the militia. We'd be caught before we could even make a start."

There was a flaw in his argument. I pointed it out quickly.

"Doesn't that mean it will be impossible for us to get away afterward? If we leave the horses here, we can hardly come back for them. As you said, the innkeeper would hear us. But we have to get well away quickly, and we're not going to be able to do that on foot. Especially if Niko has been drugged and has to be carried."

"True enough." Akira shrugged. "But I've thought of that. We have to leave our own horses here. They're fine animals, and I'm sorry to do it, but there's no option. When

Asahi has finished buying clothes for you, he will also buy some horses. He's not known in Hakone. If anybody's interested, he can explain that he needs some pack animals to await his master, who is on his way to Hakone on pilgrimage to the temple. He can let it be known that his master has traveled a long distance and will need fresh horses to take him on to the next stage in his journey. He'll say the tired horses will be stabled in Hakone and picked up later to be driven back in easy stages once they're rested. It'll work and nobody will think it's suspicious."

"And once Asahi has our fresh horses? Where's he going to keep them?" I wanted to know every detail. My mind would never rest if I thought anything was wrong. It sounded right to me, though. My father had occasionally traveled long distances, and he had taken Isamu and many of the servants with him when he did. He had also broken his journeys into stages, with fresh horses at each stop. Isamu had told me that he grumbled endlessly about the cost involved.

"Asahi will pick the new horses up late tomorrow afternoon. Or rather today—it's well past midnight," Akira said patiently. "We can tether them quite close to Ikeda's house. From what Ikeda's guards said, they never go outside the estate. They don't get paid enough to go looking for trouble. I noticed there was a stream close by with good pasture. It's hidden from the house by a hill and should be safe enough. Asahi can come with us. My other man will stay with the horses to keep an eye on them. It would be ironic if they were stolen while we were gone."

"I think it would be better to leave both of the men with the horses," I said thoughtfully."

"Why?" Akira asked simply. I was faintly surprised that he was taking me seriously.

"Ikeda's house isn't that large, but it's cluttered with all sorts of furniture and bits and pieces. If we all go in, there's a good chance somebody will knock a pot or something over. Or we could trip each other up. Besides, with Ikeda's guards out of the way, there's only going to be Ikeda there to cause us any trouble. Surely we wouldn't need two armed men to take him."

I raised my eyebrows casually in question. I could feel a pulse beating beneath my eye, and I wondered if Akira would believe me. He had an irritating habit of under-standing what I meant rather than what I said. This time, it was vital that he took my word.

If I told him the truth, that I needed it to be me who was the one who gave Ikeda the justice he deserved, how would Akira react? I knew the answer as soon the thought came to me. He would listen carefully and then explain to me carefully and clearly that there was an advantage in numbers. That it mattered not at all who dealt with Ikeda, as long as it happened. Of course he would. Because he was a yakuza, a gangster who lived by his wits, not a samurai who was bound to follow the honorable code of bushido. His solution would make perfect sense to him. Mine would not.

I stared at Akira, keeping my face neutral as I willed him to believe me. Finally, he blew out a deep breath. It was obvious he was excited by the thought of our raid. Perhaps that overcame his natural instincts. In any event, I was relieved when he shrugged.

"You may be right." He nodded. "We'll have surprise on our side. Between the two of us, we should be able to deal with that wretch Ikeda if necessary."

He believed me. The thing was settled. All at once, I felt an overpowering need to be alone. Akira's surprise showed plainly when I stood and walked toward the shoji, sliding it open silently in invitation for him to leave me.

"It was you who said we couldn't risk being seen together," I pointed out reasonably. "It's nearly dawn. The servants will be stirring soon."

"You'll wait? You promise not to do anything silly?"

I shook my head meekly. "Trust me," I said.

SIXTEEN

If I sow my rice in
Winter, do I expect to
Harvest in summer?

I awoke after a short, not at all refreshing sleep
with the instinctive knowledge that I needed to
go to the temple. I had to meditate, to calm mind and body
both. I knew intuitively that it was only there that I would
be able to find the peace I needed. I left the ryokan
midmorning, casually telling Akira that I was going to
spend some time at the famous temple. I was sure the
innkeeper was eavesdropping on our conversation. I did not
trust the man at all; I was certain that everything I said and
did would be passed back to Ikeda.

No matter. Very soon, that particular dog would be
lacking his master.

Choan-Ji Temple was very beautiful, and also very busy.
This was not at all what I wanted. I stayed in the main
building only briefly and then went to stroll the grounds. As
the weather was overcast and rather cold, most visitors had

elected to stay inside. The more steps I took away from the temple, the quieter it became. The countryside of the temple grounds was quite hilly, and my tight kimono was not at all suitable for walking up the steep hills. I put the discomfort out of my mind, but still I was pleased when I came to the shore of a small lake.

I sat down on a stone and watched the surface of the water. I guessed pilgrims must have sat on this spot for centuries, as the stone was hollowed to a comfortable shape. Koi carp—immense, rounded fish—broke the surface with flashes of color. I knew that these treasured fish could live longer than most men, and probably also had greater wisdom than many people. I bowed my head in veneration of their longevity.

"I am sorry," I murmured. "If I'd known you were here, I would have brought food for you."

I thought the koi must have forgiven me. In spite of the lack of grain thrown to them, they continued to mill about just beneath the surface of the water. Their bright colors reminded me of Ikeda's flashy Imari ware. But on the lovely, supple fish, the colors were infinitely pleasing and *right*.

Other than an occasional plop as a fish broke the surface, there was no sound at all. I relaxed, pleased that my mind and body were both without fear. I opened my mind to the elements, feeling the still air linger softly on my face, the clouds casting shadows on my eyes. Gradually, my thoughts became one with the world around me. I swam with the koi, enjoying the feel of the water against my skin. I was the sky, kissing the earth lovingly. My body no longer held me. My consciousness was not mine but was dissipated into the very air.

I had no idea how much time passed. I blinked and stretched and came back to my body, feeling as if I had just awoken from a long, dreamless sleep. I took a deep breath and found the simple action very pleasurable. After a while, I felt cold. I stood and glanced around. I wasn't surprised to find that the shadows had lengthened. The koi had swum out to the center of the lake, searching for the last of the sun's warmth. A leaf fell from the tree I had been sitting beneath and stroked my cheek tenderly. It was a reminder that I was within my own flesh again, and that time was passing.

The innkeeper must have been waiting for me. He opened the shoji before I could touch it. I watched him bow and waited silently for him to speak whatever was on his mind.

"Mistress, I was becoming anxious when you did not return. Your manservant said you had gone to the temple, so I sent one of my own servants to look for you, but he said he could not find you." He waited, obviously expecting a response. My silence seemed to unnerve him as he went on quickly. "Ikeda-san has sent a gift for you. His messenger waited for a reply for a long time, but eventually said he had to go back. If it pleases you, mistress, Lord Ikeda sent this for you."

He held a silk-wrapped parcel out to me, clasped carefully in his podgy fingers. I knew what it was from the shape, the incense burner I had admired last night. I couldn't bring myself to touch it. Any beauty it once held had been tainted forever by Ikeda's touch.

"So kind of Ikeda-san," I murmured. "I'm sure it's lovely. Please, put it somewhere safe for me until I leave the ryokan. I will take tea."

The innkeeper looked bewildered. His mouth moved but no words came out as his eyes swiveled from the package in his hands to my face. He looked so hurt, it was as if it were his gift I was rejecting. I was tempted to explain to him that I had no intention of ever touching anything that had been possessed by Ikeda, still less owning something. But I smiled instead and turned away serenely. When I was safely away from Hakone, the incense burner could go as a gift to the kannushi of Choan-Ji Temple. If he sold it and used the cash to do good, then it would surely be unique amongst Ikeda's possessions.

I moved past the innkeeper into the ryokan and then paused casually as if a thought had struck me.

"Please, ask my servant, Akira, to come through to me."

I sipped my tea with pleasure. My hands were chilled and the warmth of the cup was almost as welcome as the tea. Akira stood to attention in front of me, the portrait of a well-trained servant.

"Did you enjoy the temple, mistress?" he asked icily. Every muscle in his body was tense. He was angry. Angry that I had been gone so long. Angry that he had been forced to worry about me.

"I did. It allowed me time and space to meditate. Sit down, Akira-chan," I said quietly. "Take tea with me. The innkeeper must have foreseen that I would have company. Look, he has left me two cups."

Akira's brows snapped together in astonishment. His cool, gray eyes narrowed—I could not tell with anger or disbelief. They were very beautiful eyes, I thought. Any woman would have been delighted had they been set like jewels in her face.

He did not sit, but remained standing rigidly. He spoke so softly that I—who sat no more than a body's depth away from him—could only just make out his words.

"Have you suddenly lost all your wits, Keiko? Or did you stop at a tea house on the way back and drink too much sake? Have you forgotten I am supposed to be no more than a humble retainer? A servant does not take tea with his mistress."

"Akira, sit down." I thought I spoke reasonably, but perhaps I had not. He jerked back as if I had shouted at him. "Nobody is watching us. Nobody is listening to us. We can speak freely."

A curious expression passed over Akira's face. It was as if all his assurance, all his belief in himself had been stripped away for the moment. Was this how he had looked when he was very much younger, I wondered. Before the world had stolen his innocence and plated his body with the hard layer of invincibility he now chose to wear. It was a deeply disturbing insight.

"How do you know it's safe?" he demanded. He glanced around as he spoke, clearly suspicious still.

"It's just past the time of the afternoon meal for the patrons of the inn. The innkeeper and the servants will be busy with their own food. He probably makes the servants eat the scraps the guests leave," I said grimly. "Besides, it's only natural that I should want to speak to my trusted servant after I've been gone all morning. I promise you, if anybody was close, I would hear them. I'm sure we are alone. If anybody does come, I'll know about it in good time. Please, sit and take tea with me."

He sat, but carefully. He accepted a teacup from me and sipped, all the while sliding his gaze around the room, searching for a hidden peephole that could betray us.

"So." He cleared his throat and spoke firmly. "Do you want to know what I've been doing while you spent the day sightseeing?"

I could have told him how I had really spent my time, I supposed. But I guessed he would not understand the need to make sure that body and mind were completely aligned. My way was strange to him, and he was uncertain. Wary of what he could not comprehend. I understood that.

"Everything is arranged," I said. It was not a question. I knew that nothing had gone wrong. Akira would have told me at once if there had been problems.

"Yes. The horses are pastured near to Ikeda's estate." As Akira spoke Ikeda's name, he glanced around yet again. I supposed his extreme caution was no bad thing and stayed silent. "As we discussed, both of my men will stay with them. Your clothes are there." He nodded toward the chest in my room. "Together with some straw waraji sandals. They may be a little large. Asahi had to guess the size."

"Thank you. Everything is ready, then."

"Is it?" He sounded so astonished that I found it difficult not to smile. "Perhaps my memory is at fault. Did we discuss the detail of what is actually going to happen? Have I aged so much overnight that my wits have become addled and I forgot that conversation?"

His sarcasm was so heavy it almost hid his genuine worry.

"No, of course not. But everything is clear to me. We will go to Ikeda's estate," I said. "The two of us. I suggest we wait to set off until the bells have sounded for the hour of the rat. In a place as quiet and provincial as Hakone, everybody should be asleep by then. That will give us most of the night to carry out what needs to be done."

I sipped my tea. Akira stared at me as if he was waiting for me to go on. Finally his patience gave way and he spoke angrily.

"That's it? We walk out there—presumably without being stopped by a patrol looking for insurgents—stroll into the house, grab Niko, and walk out again? Woman, you have no idea what you're talking about. I'll tell you what's going to happen. What the plan is."

I listened courteously as he spoke confidently, watching him ticking off points on his fingers.

"We will set off immediately after the bells chime the hour of the rat. I agree that's sensible. Once we reach the estate, I'll get over the wall and make my way to the guard-room to check that the guards are unconscious. If all's well, I'll come back and help you over the wall. If there is a problem—which I doubt—and the guards are still awake, we wait until they pass our part of the wall on their patrol. Then I help you over the wall. I'll lead the way to the house. You follow close behind and do as I tell you. Once we get there, you wait in the shadows until I do a final check. The servants are housed in an outbuilding some way from the house, so they shouldn't be a problem. I'll use my dagger to cut the outside shoji. Once inside the house, you wait in the ante-room. I'll find the storeroom, break in, and grab Niko. If Ikeda shows his face, I'll deal with him. You just take care of Niko. Is all that clear? Is there anything you don't under-stand?" he asked finally. "Trust me, Keiko. I have led many raids in my time. I have thought of everything."

Akira was so obviously delighted with his plan that it made me sad to know that I was about to hurt him. I stood and crossed to the clothes' chest. I delved to the bottom and brought out my precious katana. As I carried it back across my outstretched arms, I saw Akira's eyes widen. His hand jerked out and he pointed his index finger at the sword, wagging his finger frantically from side to side. I knew then that the katana filled him with such superstitious dread that it had driven everything else out of his mind. My gaijin, Adam, had pointed to some-thing in his room once. Even though he thought I was blind, he was still deeply embarrassed by his mistake. He had snapped his fingers closed at once and put his hand to his mouth to cover his confusion. Japanese people never point a finger, not even at inanimate objects. To do so is grossly rude. Even the naughtiest child would never do it.

I stared at Akira. He had gone white, his eyes bulging as he stared at the katana. I almost laughed as I wondered if he thought I was about to threaten him with it. I would have liked to explain that the feel of the weapon in my hands gave me confidence. That once I was touching it I knew that nothing could go wrong. I did not; he was too superstitious about my sword already.

"I hear what you say," I said softly. His gaze was still fixed on the katana, and I wondered if he had heard me. I waited until he tore his glance from the sword and focused on my face before I went on. "I hear you, but it is not going to happen like that, Akira. You're right, but only up to a point. We will go to the estate and we will get over the wall. We will go to Ikeda's house. Together. But once we get inside, I will show you where Niko is being held. You're the one that will get her out and take her to safety. When I have done what I need to do, I will follow you. That is what is going to happen." I slid the katana from its saya and held it out in front of me with a two-handed grip, the traditional samurai way of wielding a sword. The katana felt so very right in my hands, it filled me with a wild joy. "I know I will be safe with my ancestor's weapon in my hands."

"No." Akira choked the words out. "No, that cannot be. You have no idea what might happen. You don't understand how dangerous this is going to be."

His words trailed off as he stared at me miserably. I lifted my sword so that the mellow afternoon light reflected from the blade. Akira stared at it with all the intensity of a rabbit hypnotized by a snake.

"It's you who doesn't understand, Akira-chan," I said gently. "This katana was my father's, and all his ancestors' back to the day it was forged. And now it is mine. It fits my hand just as it fit theirs. And you know the legends that surround the old samurai katana. It's said that they will only hurt those who deserve it. And that once drawn, they must taste the blood of the unrighteous or they will twist and cut those that wield them. I have drawn my sword. It must and will be used tonight. By me, and nobody else."

"Take it with you, then. Use it if you need to." Akira's face was cunning. He shrugged, as though my words were nothing that mattered. "But that doesn't alter the plan. I go first, you follow. And you do as you're told."

"No," I said flatly. "This is my problem, not yours. If it weren't for me, Niko wouldn't be in danger in the first place. But I still need your help, Akira. I can't do it alone. I don't have the strength to carry Niko and get her over the wall. I need you to do that. I need to know you're there if anything goes wrong. And I also need your men ready with the horses to get us away. I need you to be there with me. But if you don't feel you can do it, if the idea of following a woman into danger is too much for you, I understand that. I'll do it alone."

I had spoken no more than the truth. I did need Akira to be with me. I was pleased that I had not been forced to lie to him. I was trained in martial arts. I could wield a sword or a staff as well as any man. Far better than most, in fact. But the essence of all the martial arts is skill, not strength. If Niko had been drugged, she would be a dead weight. I knew my own limitations, and I knew that carrying her and getting her over a high wall was beyond my strength. And I would be very happy to know that he would be there if I needed him. But also I had spoken truly when I said I would understand if he felt he could not carry out the part I had cast him in. To a man like Akira, my words must have sounded like an insult.

I hoped that I had said enough to soothe his male pride so that he would be able to give in gracefully. We stared at each other, and then Akira's gaze fell back to my sword. He saw my knuckles, white where they gripped the hilt. Saw the way the sword balanced perfectly in my hands. And I saw in his eyes that he knew I was lying to him. Knew that there was much I wasn't telling him. He was deeply hurt by the knowledge. I longed to explain everything to him, but caution made me silent. Our worlds were so very different. How could I ever hope to make him understand that this was not just about Niko, but that it was also a matter of honor? It was perfectly clear to me that the responsibility to avenge not just Niko and me, but also all the women that Ikeda had hurt so casually, was mine. And I had accepted it. I would do it or die rejoicing in the attempt.

And if I told Akira that? Explained that I was grateful for his help but that it was I who must lead and he who would follow, and do as he was told? If I explained that he need not be hurt by my actions? That I was worried for his safety? Would he laugh at me? Or would he be appalled that I—a mere woman—dared to think that he needed my protection? I knew the answer. His dignity would take it as an intentional insult. And even worse, he would be ashamed that a mere woman—little more than a girl— could laugh at his plans and think she had to protect him.

The loss of face would be too much for him to take. Even if nobody else ever knew, Akira would remember. And if his feelings for me—and I was certain in a moment of supreme clarity that he did care for me—forced him to agree, he would hate himself for what he perceived as his intolerable weakness every day that the gods spared him to live.

I felt a sudden spasm of pity for him. I had put him in an impossible situation. If he agreed, he would hate himself for his weakness. If he refused, his every waking moment would be filled with shame and remorse. Either way, he would think of himself as a coward. I was deeply sorry, but I could not back down. I was onna-bugeisha, and the code of bushido was far greater than my personal feelings. I slid the katana back in its saya and put it aside.

Akira got to his feet without looking at me and walked away. He paused at the shoji and spoke quietly.

"I am afraid of nothing that lives, Keiko." His voice trembled. I saw his lips compress into a tight line as he tried and failed to keep his words steady. "If it came to it, I would die for you. Gladly. But you don't want that. You don't need me. You have your katana and your code of bushido. I hope they are enough for you."

SEVENTEEN

My thoughts are not your
Thoughts. How then will we ever
Know each other's mind?

I heard the bell begin to chime the hour of the rat
and stretched, tilting my head back and hearing
my spine creak. I had sat on the tatami without moving
since Akira had left me. From time to time, I stroked the
saya that protected my katana. I would not withdraw the
katana again until it was time to use it. I understood Akira's
fear of my sword. If karma had not allowed it to fit my hand,
I guessed that I, too, would fear it.

It was far more than mere metal. It had been used for
centuries to avenge wrongs. Although it belonged to me
now, I knew that I was only taking care of it for the generations to come. That it was far greater than I, or my father, or
any samurai who had ever lived.

If it hadn't been for his superstitious fear of my beautiful
sword, I thought I would have been able to talk Akira
around. I would have managed to convince him that he was

not showing weakness by allowing me to lead. If all else failed, I would have used the enchantment of my body to do it. I would not have hesitated to use my sexuality as a weapon, just as much a weapon as my katana. Equal, but different. I sighed. There was nothing I could do now. I would not go without my sword. Perhaps in my own way I was as superstitious as Akira, but I felt that without it, I would not succeed. I rose and rolled my neck, listening. The inn was deathly quiet. I slid my screen door open confidently.

I controlled my surprise as Akira stepped out of the shadows when I slid the outer shoji closed. In spite of my belief in my own ability to succeed, I sighed softly with relief that he was there. The two of us would be far greater than if I had been alone. As I had thought on another occasion entirely, together we were omyodo. Akira put his hand on my shoulder and turned me to face him. The night was dark, and I could barely make out his features. It didn't matter. He nodded once but did not speak. After a moment, he took his hand away. When I moved, he fell into step with me and both our shadows blended with the dark. As we left the last houses of Hakone behind, I held my hand up. Akira stopped at once, then we both took a step nearer to the wall.

"Cold tonight." The cheerful voice was in the distance, as was the voice that replied.

"You're right there. The sooner we get back to the guard-room, the better. If there are any insurgents stupid enough to be up to no good in this weather, then the best of fortune to them!"

Both men laughed as they passed by the entrance to the street where we huddled. One of them paused, and Akira put his hand on the hilt of his sword.

"Hang on a minute. I need to take a piss."

We both sighed as we heard the sound of water splashing on the cobbles. When the men were gone, Akira spoke very close to my ear.

"By all the gods, I thought he would never finish! May he be blessed with a stronger bladder in the future."

I smiled, joyful that the animosity had gone from between us. I would have liked to have spoken, to have told him that I understood how much it must have cost him to conquer both his pride and his fears to be with me now. But this was neither the time nor the place. Instead, I touched his hand lightly, hoping that he would understand.

We were as silent as the shadows, Akira perhaps even more so as he was truly my shadow. When the path allowed, he walked at my side. When it was too narrow, he walked behind me. Either way, I noticed that he was careful to avoid coming into any contact with my saya. I wanted to explain to him that the katana would never hurt him, but I did not. I had caused him too much loss of face already this evening. Far better to pretend that I did not see his fear of my beautiful blade.

Akira made stirrups with his hands when we reached the wall around Ikeda's estate. He had chosen a spot well away from the gate, and I guessed that—should the guards still be awake—this would be the farthest point from where they would be at this hour.

He threw me up as if I was weightless and then followed me at once, running at the wall and gripping the top to haul himself up. A moment later, we were inside. Akira inclined his head. There was enough moonlight for me to see he had raised his eyebrows questioningly. I nodded. He knew where the guardhouse was. I did not, so I fell behind him.

The guardhouse was completely dark. I inched my face against the shoji—no silk for the poor guards; these were made of coarse paper and coarser wood—and peered through cautiously. Although the paper was thick, I could make out four bodies. Two were lying with their heads on the table. One appeared to have toppled off a stool and was lying on the floor. The other seemed to be comfortably asleep on a rough palette. To be absolutely sure, I tapped cautiously on the paper, my touch as light as bird pecking for crumbs, yet loud enough for an alert man to hear and respond to. When nobody moved, I tapped again, harder. Satisfied, I drew back and nodded at Akira.

I was quite surprised when he didn't check for himself —and pleased.

Akira's dagger made short work of the shoji into the house. He opened a square large enough for us to slide through and then put his hand on my sleeve, stopping me as I stooped to enter.

"Nightingale floor?" he whispered. I shook my head. I had walked without any particular care when I had last entered the house and the floor had remained silent with none of the squeaks and groans a nightingale floor would have given off.

"Ikeda must be very sure of his guards," I said softly. My mouth was so close to Akira's ear that I felt his hair tickle my lips.

We entered carefully, all the same. Our vision had become accustomed to the dark. Neither of us found it difficult to see. Akira stood back and I put my hand on his sleeve, both to guide him to Niko's prison and to make sure his pace matched mine. I paused outside the storeroom, and he unsheathed his dagger again and cut the fine silk swiftly. Halfway through the first cut, we both thought we heard something. Akira stopped, his head up and alert. It seemed to me that we were still for half the night, yet when

I released my breath, I realized it had been mere heartbeats. Nothing more dangerous than the house settling in the cold night air. I nodded, and Akira swiftly enlarged the hole. He snapped one of the wooden laths with huge care, muffling any possible sound by leaning his body across it.

I could barely wait for him to finish. I jostled him aside and slipped through in a half-crouch. I caught my breath as I saw Niko lying on a futon in the middle of the small room. There was nothing else there except a bucket. It stank of stale urine and I wrinkled my nose as I understood that Ikeda had not even allowed her out to use the toilet. I controlled my breathing and stooped, putting my hand on Niko's forehead.

A huge bruise covered half her face, and her lip had been cut. She was freezing! I thought that she was dead at first, and my own heartbeat almost stopped behind my ribs. Then her skin warmed slightly beneath my hand and I saw with a joy that almost made me cry that her chest was rising and falling slightly. Akira took my arm and tugged me to one side. I shook my head at him, nodding toward Niko. I had to attend to her; why didn't he understand that I had to make sure she did not have other, much greater hurts than the ones I could see?

"I need to get her out of here," he whispered.

I relaxed as I understood. He was right. No matter how badly hurt Niko was, the priority was to get her as far away as possible. I stepped back silently, and Akira lifted her in his arms. He moved swiftly, but with obvious concern for Niko. At the hole in the shoji, he paused and stared at me. I shook my head.

For a moment, I thought he would refuse to go without me. I put my hand on the hilt of my katana and stared back at him, willing him to leave, to take Niko to safety. I could just make out that Akira's grey eyes were shining and I stared in silent amazement as I guessed that he was holding back tears. Tears for me? Nobody had ever wept for me before, and I found his concern intensely moving. I shook my head, and he turned and ducked through the hole in the shoji.

I waited until I heard nothing but complete silence before I moved.

I knew he had gone, and that Niko was safe with him. Perhaps it was a reaction to the intensity I had felt until that moment, but suddenly I was blanketed by overwhelming sadness. I wondered if anything would ever be right between Akira and me ever again. I had robbed him of everything that mattered to him; in his eyes, I had taken his manhood and trampled on it. I had not wanted to do it, but it had been necessary. By choosing to embrace the code of bushido, I had lost something that could have been very precious in my life.

"Enough." I breathed the word to myself and stood erect. I hovered by the tear in the shoji, listening but hearing nothing. This was the most dangerous moment. The time had come when I had my chance to avenge my sisters in adversity and take my own revenge on the monster who had wanted to use me to save himself. I took a moment to consider my own emotions. Only when I was sure that I was without distraction and entirely focused on the task I had set myself did I move.

I eased silently through the torn shoji and stepped on ghost-like feet to Ikeda's apartment. I paused at his screen, listening intently. I heard the horrid sound of him breathing; with his lack of nose and caved in mouth, his every breath sounded like a man gargling with a mouthful of mud. I swallowed disgust and took the few steps needed to bring me back to the adjacent apartment.

The shoji slid back silently under my fingers. I stepped inside and stopped as if I had hit a physical barrier, unable to take a single step further. The terrible stench I had smelled so faintly last night wrapped itself around me. I breathed through my mouth, knowing that I would retch if I could smell it fully. It was the odor of death, waiting impatiently to claim a living soul. The stench of prolonged illness and pain and the decay of living flesh. No living being should be forced to experience such degradation. Especially not at the hands of her husband. I heard the tiniest of sounds from the futon; not even a word, rather just a sigh. Yet I felt the desperate hope that it carried.

"I know. I'm sorry I've taken so long. But I'm here now."

I breathed the words almost silently. It didn't matter if she could hear me. She knew I was there. I felt it. I moved softly toward the futon and crouched down beside her.

In spite of the chill of the night, she had thrown her kakebuton aside. She was dressed only in a thin sleeping robe, and I felt pity shake my body as I saw how terribly thin she was. Her skin seemed clear, bearing none of the marks of the plum poison disease. For a moment, I wondered if I had misjudged Ikeda; surely, no man could intentionally infect his own wife with the deadly disease? Then I saw the deep cankers around her mouth that would never heal and I knew that I was wrong. Had she refused food, I wondered, trying to hasten her own death, or had Ikeda left her to starve deliberately? Hatred for the horrible man made me tremble.

Only once had I seen anybody as appallingly emaciated as this, and the experience had lived on in my unquiet sleep for years after.

When I was a very small child, a Buddhist monk in one of the monasteries Father supported had brought great honor on himself—and his monastery—by deciding he would undertake sokushinbutsu—living mummification. It was thought that by dying in this way, his soul would live on and linger in the monastery without being reincarnated anew and he would be able to guide others to the path of enlightenment.

Father had insisted that both my sister Emiko and I should visit the monastery with a suitable donation and pay our respects to the monk. Emiko had been unconcerned and couldn't understand my horror. "He's only doing it to make himself important," she had said cynically. "Don't go getting upset about it. Nobody's forcing him to do it. It's his choice."

But I was upset. Very much so. The monk had sat cross-legged, not so much as opening his eyes when we murmured our greetings and bowed before him. I glanced at Emiko; she rolled her eyes at me.

He was so thin! I could see the blood in his veins, the bones almost poking through his skin. His flesh had shrunk back so far on his face that it was like staring at a skull. I was very grateful that his eyes were closed, as I found it difficult to believe there could be anything in his eye sockets. I was terrified that those almost translucent lids would suddenly roll back, showing nothing but black, gaping holes behind. And he stank. The smell was an odd amalgam of bodily decay and something resinous. I learned later that the monk's diet was based on only things that came from trees. Pine needles and seeds, bark and roots. That and just enough water to sustain life until death finally claimed him.

I was deeply relieved when Emiko decided we had stayed long enough to pay our respects and pulled me away.

In spite of being horrified by the dying monk, I found I was morbidly curious and pestered my brother Isamu with questions.

"Why's he doing it?" I asked. Isamu whistled through his teeth and shrugged. In spite of his apparent unconcern, I sensed he was respectful.

"If his body doesn't decompose after he finally dies, it's a sign that he's particularly holy and then he'll become a Buddha himself. Quite a few monks try it, but very few are successful."

"He already looked dead to me." I shuddered at the memory. "Nobody could be as thin as that and be alive!"

"He is, though," Isamu told me. "He's still ringing his bell to let the other monks know he's alive. He could be there for years yet. It often takes around ten years for the process to be complete."

I stared at him in disbelief. Like all children, the idea of death was beyond my comprehension. And as for taking ten years to die—that was longer than I had been alive! It was impossible, all of it.

But being sure of that did nothing to stop the nightmares; dreams where the starving monk *did* open his eyes, and seeing my smooth, well-fed body, reached his hand out greedily toward me...

The memory was still so vivid that I shuddered as I forced my unwilling feet in their outsized waraji sandals to shuffle toward the futon. Waka-san was still, and her eyes were wide open. For a hopeful moment, I thought I was too late to help her. That she was already dead and I had imagined the sound I thought she had made. Then I saw that those wide eyes were filled with quiet courage and I dropped to my knees beside her.

"I'm here," I breathed softly. "I'm here for you. No more pain, Waka-san. Only peace. That is my gift to you."

Tears welled in her eyes and trickled down her cheeks. She blinked and her lips parted. "Thank you," she whispered. Her voice was the sound of paper being turned by careful fingers.

I leaned forward and lifted her up as gently as I possibly could. I wrapped my arms around her cold, thin body and pressed her head against my breasts as lovingly as if I was giving suck to a newborn. So close, her dreadful smell seemed to matter not at all and I felt no repulsion at all for the bodily decay of the poor lady, but rather an upwelling of love that made me shake. I had never met her before, but already she was precious to me. And because of that, I was going to give her the gift I was sure that she craved.

Death.

I held her tenderly, her head buried in my breasts. I sat for a very long time, until I was sure that her poor clay had breathed its last. When I finally laid her down and pulled the kakebuton over her—as if she could still feel the cold— I felt a puff of air flit past me in the still room, so subtle it barely touched my skin. Was it her spirit, finally released from suffering? I hoped so. Her unseeing eyes were wide open, and I closed them carefully, smoothing her face with my hand in a last gesture of tenderness. I had no means of giving her the water of the last moment, but I did the best I could. I wet my lips with my tongue and pressed my mouth against hers. I hoped she would understand.

I sat back on my heels and watched as her earthly flesh relaxed. I felt no remorse. Nothing but a deep happiness that I had helped to end a life that must have been at best intolerable and at worst something that I could not even begin to imagine.

When I stood, I made no attempt at all to be quiet. I stretched my cramped limbs and sighed deeply. My katana felt eager at my side. I was not at all surprised when the saya seemed to swing out on its own and struck the shoji briskly with a sound not unlike a handbell ringing, just as the monk undergoing sokushinbutsu had rung his bell to let the other monks know he was not dead.

If Ikeda were not awake, then he soon would be. I wanted him to know that I was here—and that his death was imminent. Also did I want him to fear that death.

He deserved it.

"Ikeda-san," I crooned into the silence. "Ikeda-san. Are you awake? Are you ready to receive me? I'm waiting for you. Hurry, I'm getting impatient."

EIGHTEEN

The pebble beneath
My heel. Your skin touching me.
All things were once one

*T*ook no care at all to be silent as I slid back the shoji that divided Ikeda's apartment from his wife's. There was no need. I had no wish to sneak into his presence like a thief in the night come to steal his treasures. I wanted him to be aware of me. To be aware and ready.

The code of bushido insisted that there must be fairness in all things. Where would the honor lie in slaughtering Ikeda in his bed like the festering animal he was? A single oil lamp illuminated the room. I bared my teeth with satisfaction as I saw that his kakebuton had been thrown back. The room appeared to be empty of any physical presence. I stayed perfectly still with my eyes closed, searching for any life with my other senses. My ears and nose told me the room was empty, yet still I sensed a certain warmth that lingered here. Was the room truly empty? Was I sensing the presence of a living body that had gone less than a heartbeat ago, leaving its aura behind? Or was there a chance that Ikeda was still here?

The room was quite sparsely furnished. A quick glance showed nothing but a chest, a lacquered table, and a byobu screen decorated with cranes in flight on a gilded background. Thoughts flashed through my head quickly. Byobu screens were usually used as room dividers or to give privacy for something or somebody. This one simply stood, sectioning off a corner of the room. It guarded no privacy at all, as far as I could see. I swiveled my gaze from side to side and hunched my shoulders, as if in an agony of indecision. Then I moved so rapidly that even an alert man could not have anticipated my movement and darted behind the byobu with my katana drawn and raised. I relaxed my muscles as I realized I had been right. Ikeda was not hiding here. The lovely screen hid the house shrine and nothing else. It was odd to find a shrine located in a bedroom, and I wondered if Ikeda was ashamed to display what to him would appear a weakness. Did the arrogant fool not understand that the gods would see his contempt of them as an insult and take action accordingly? It was fated, then. I was nothing more than the instrument of the gods.

I bowed my head and gave thanks to them for the great favor they had shown to me.

It would have been a great shame to have damaged the lovely byobu. Nor did I think it fitting to spill blood right in front of the house shrine. I lowered my katana and strolled out into the central corridor as easily as if there was nothing at all on my mind. I heard the faintest of sounds—a sigh? A murmur of surprise?—that I thought came from Waka-san's apartment. Ikeda was there, then. I guessed that he must have heard me and slipped out of his own apartment while I was with Waka-san. Had he waited, pleased I was doing his work for him while I gave her gift of death? The thought made me hiss with anger. I walked across quickly and stood in the open shoji.

His wife's bedroom appeared to be as empty of life as Ikeda's own apartment. But I knew he had been here, and not long ago. I could smell him and feel the warmth in the space left by his body. Suddenly, I understood from the almost unheard hiss of indrawn breath that came from beside the shoji that I was wrong. Ikeda was still here, standing completely still. Waiting in the deepest shadows. His katana cleaved the air a hand's breadth away from where I had been standing and he danced away from me with surprising agility, his katana upraised for another blow. I backed into the corridor. Even though I knew his wife no longer lived, I was deeply reluctant to kill her husband where her spirit might linger.

"Ikeda-san," I said eagerly. "I was beginning to think you had run away from me. So glad to find you still here!"

"Keiko? It's you? I would never have recognized you if you hadn't spoken." He was shocked. I could hear it in his voice. But it didn't give me as much advantage as I had hoped. I saw him glance at the ripped door of Niko's prison. "I see. I suppose you've snatched the girl already?"

"Most certainly." I bowed my head and smiled. "I couldn't bear to think she was going to be violated by something as vile as you."

I spoke lightly, with a politeness that belied my words. It took a moment for Ikeda to realize what I had said. When he did, he bared his teeth in a snarl of fury. I noticed almost absently that he had discarded his false nose. The hole in the center of his face shone black and corrupt in the moonlight. If any man deserved death, then surely it was him!

"So, that's what this is about, is it? I suppose that bitch of an oiran sent you to get her back. The pair of you got this up between you, did you? I should have known my luck couldn't have turned so much that a prize like Lady Keiko was going to fall into my hands. Well, all credit to the pair of you. You had me fooled with her." His lips peeled back from his teeth. "And my dear wife? It appears that she has finally given up her spirit in this world. You helped her passage into the next life, I assume." He sounded completely uncon-cerned. I felt a surge of gratitude that it was I who was going to kill him. And so very shortly.

"Yes. I gave the poor lady her release, and I was glad to do it. But it was you who killed her spirit. I hope your karma is a suitable one."

"You have my gratitude. I would have hastened her end myself if I thought it wouldn't have caused trouble. Now, it will be assumed that my wife either died at the hands of the bandits who broke in or passed away from shock at their intrusion. I will, of course, be devastated by her passing. By the way, what have you done with my guards? They should have been here by now. They're dead, I suppose?"

"Of course not. Merely sound asleep."

We circled in what to an onlooker must have appeared to be a ritual dance, our swords threatening each other but not making contact.

"Really? You might have saved me the bother of having them executed for misconduct." I shook my head. I had no worry for the guards. Come morning, their master would be dead and they would have the chance to get far away before he was discovered by the authorities. Ikeda went on cheer-fully, as if our bizarre conversation was perfectly normal. "No matter, Keiko, or whatever your real name is. Such a shame for you to come all this way for nothing. I had Niko as soon as I got her here. By now, my cure should be beginning. But don't worry about letting that fancy oiran know you failed. I'll send a message to her. Attached to your body."

Was he bluffing about Niko? I had no idea. But his bragging voice sounded genuine, and I felt a hatred deeper than anything I had ever thought possible chill my body. I wanted to kill him then, but forced myself to speak coolly. There were things I needed to know first.

"Tell me. How did you come to be expecting me?" I asked.

I watched his sword rather than his face. I was going to take him, I knew that. But still, no sense in allowing him any advantage. It seemed to amuse him to talk. Very well, I would encourage that. I needed to lure him out of the passage and into the reception room. There was more space to maneuver there.

He darted forward and slashed with the katana. His blade met air; I was already well back. I raised my own katana and the silver moonlight turned the blade into light. Did Ikeda flinch? It was difficult to tell. He feinted left and I slowed my reactions to allow him to think he had fooled me. This time, his blade barely missed. I could have parried the blow easily, but I was reluctant to allow my own katana to be tainted by the touch of anything that belonged to him. Apart from his flesh, of course, and there was time enough for that.

I scurried backward, glancing over my shoulder as if with fear. Ikeda pursued me; I moved quicker still, dancing into the reception room. He was grinning broadly as I pretended to pant with the exertion.

"Why bother to fight, Keiko? You don't stand a chance, you know that. That's a lovely katana you have, but it still needs great skill to use it properly. You must remember, you're just a girl. You don't have my strength and you haven't been trained to fight. You can't win. Give in gracefully, and I promise I'll let you live. If you tell me where you've hidden the girl, I'll even let you go back to Edo."

I glanced around wildly. Ikeda could think I was searching for an escape route if he liked. I doubted he would realize that I was making sure that I knew exactly where each item of furniture stood. He was clever, I had to admit. If I really had been no more than a green girl, his confident words would have planted the seeds of doubt in my mind. I waved my katana around wildly, allowing the point to just slash the front of his robe. I exhaled loudly, as if I was amazed and delighted that I had come so close to hurting him. If only he knew how much skill it had taken to allow the blade to cut silk and not flesh!

"How did you know I was going to come here tonight?" I gasped. I was genuinely interested in the answer, but Ikeda obviously thought I was playing for time. He circled me, and I allowed his katana to pin me to the spot.

"I didn't. I have many enemies. I'm always on my guard and I sleep very lightly," he said simply. "You were remarkably quiet. If you hadn't called out, you might even have been able to finish me before I knew you were there."

As he spoke, he lunged forward and his blade caught my shoulder. The pain was agonizing, but it was a welcome reminder that I had to be careful. The gods would not help me unless I helped myself first!

"Ah! That hurts!" I yelled.

"You see?" Ikeda thrust again and I jumped to one side, poking with my katana. My thrust was careful to just miss and I saw caution in his eyes. "Do put your sword down, dear girl. I have no wish to hurt you. You have my word for that."

"You'll have to take it from me first!" I spat.

Ikeda was quick. Far quicker than I had expected. His body moved fractionally to the right. I thought it was a feint and dodged to the left. I was wrong, his sword followed through to the right and missed my own sword arm so narrowly I felt its passage on my skin.

Enough. I had been a fool, but would be no longer.

I closed my eyes. So quickly it took less time than a single heartbeat, I was one with my katana. It—we—sensed when Ikeda swung his sword and together we parried his blows effortlessly. Ikeda grunted; when I understood I was still depending on my hearing, I closed down my five senses just as my sensei, the old warrior-priest Riku-san had taught me in our dojo on the family estate.

"You have a good brain, Keiko-san. That can be a hindrance to one who wishes to become onna-bugeisha. Your brain can show you fear. It can tell you to do a certain thing when your instinct tells you otherwise. Learn to control your mind rather than have it control you. When you can do that, you can do anything."

I had tried so many times to follow his wisdom. The harder I tried, the less possible it seemed. I knew that Riku-san could do it. I had seen him close his eyes and stand stock still, waiting for me to move. And when I approached him on silent feet, holding my breath so he could not hope to hear me, he had evaded me so effortlessly it seemed he had moved even before I knew where I was about to strike.

Finally, I had cried out loud in my anguish. "I cannot do this! I am a failure. I will never become onna-bugeisha. Please, leave me. I'm not fit to be taught by you."

To my sorrow, Riku had bowed gravely and walked away without a word. I stood in the middle of the dojo with my katana scratching the clay and my head lowered in despair.

I heard no noise. Saw no movement. Rather, I felt the air become displaced behind me and the warmth of a living body in its place. I swung and lifted my sword at the very same moment, stopping the blow as the point of my katana came to rest against Riku's heart. He smiled at me and I felt the world come back around me.

"You see? Don't try. When you are one with the elements, then you are truly onna-bugeisha. You have no need to wonder if it is possible. No need to summon it. When you have need of it, you know that it will come to you. Most men cannot tame the beast within them and make it obedient to their call. You can. Use the gift wisely."

Ikeda had moved. He was behind me. I sensed that he thought I had given in, that the flower was ready to be plucked. His katana swept up; I felt it slice empty air and knew that it was going to fall with the blunt side against my neck, close to the hilt. He intended to disable me rather than kill me. Also, I knew that he was aroused. I could smell the odor of his awakening coming from his body in stinking waves. The violence of our contest and the surge of power he felt when he thought he had me at his mercy had worked an unclean magic on him.

I opened my eyes. Not logical, I knew, to reject the gift of instinct, but still I felt I had to do the honorable thing. I was about to give Ikeda the death he deserved. At the very least I should do it fairly.

His sword was still falling toward me. As I had sensed, he was aiming the hilt and blunt side of the blade at my neck. The blow would have felled me easily. If it had hit the nerve at the side of my neck in the perfect place, I would have fallen to the ground helplessly yet still been able to see and understand. I would have felt all of the horror of Ikeda taking me.

I moved away. To me, it seemed that I moved slowly, but it could not have been so as I had time to see the flash of disbelief in Ikeda's expression before I was out of his reach. And then my katana was lifting high above me. My wrists bent in the perfect stroke. Still I thought that I gave Ikeda plenty of time to duck away from me, but I was wrong. Before his katana could touch my skin, my ancestor's blade was cutting into his neck. I felt barely any resistance, and for a moment, I wondered if I had flinched away at the last minute and my blow had glanced off his shoulder.

Ikeda's mouth was wide open, his lips drawn back from his teeth. He made a sound that might have been an attempt at words, but there was no sense in the noise. He fell to his knees and then toppled back so that the crown of his head touched the tatami. His katana was still clutched in his double-handed grip.

I stayed quite still. He was dead. If I hadn't hesitated at the last possible moment, his head would have left his body. As it was, I had cut through to his spine. Blood was pulsing violently from his neck, but even as I drew breath, it began to slow fractionally. He had died instantly. A quick death that had been too good for him. I waited for some emotion to fill the void within me. I had killed a man. In fair fight, certainly, but I had taken his life just as I had intended. Surely I should feel remorse? Pity? Horror?

I was cold and stiff. Was this what it would feel like when I was an old woman, with joints roughened by the wear of time? I pursued the thought with interest, and then understood that I was using it to shield myself from the horror in front of me.

I had killed this man. Just as my samurai ancestors had tested the blade of their katanas on the necks of innocent peasants to test the sharpness of their weapons, so I had taken Ikeda from this world without a second thought.

I stared hard at the dreadful wound that barely held his neck onto his body and tried to feel...something. I could not. There was no sense of triumph, but neither did I regret his death. I had done what was right.

The gods had chosen me to avenge the horror this man had brought to the women in his life. The same horror that he had gloatingly told me he had inflicted on my younger sister.

How could I feel conscience for a man who had had none himself? I waited, my head to one side, hoping to sense the spirits of Waka-san and the unknown lady who had been Ikeda's first wife. There was nothing, but it no longer mattered. I had killed twice this night. I had given Waka-san the gift of death. I had slaughtered her husband like the foul thing he was.

I regretted neither. I was still holding my katana in a two-handed grip, Ikeda's blood on the blade. I would not defile the steel by wiping it on his clothes. Instead, I tore a long strip off my own robe and wiped the blade carefully and thoroughly before I slid the katana back into its saya.

As I turned to go, I realized with surprise that the wound on my shoulder was suddenly deeply painful.

NINETEEN

How is it I may
Still smell a blossom when its
Life has long faded?

"*I*s it finished? Is Ikeda dead?" Akira demanded urgently.

He had met me halfway between the house and the wall. I listened to his words and waited for my emotions to finally betray me. Tears blurred my eyes, but they were for relief that Niko was finally snatched from Ikeda and the gratitude in Waka-san's voice when I gave her the release of death. Certainly not for any pity for Ikeda.

"Yes. I've killed him." My voice wavered and I cleared my throat, fearing Akira might think it was weakness. "It was the right thing to do. He told me he had taken Niko already."

Akira was looking at me intently. "He was lying to you. But we'll talk about that later. We need to get away now in case the guards wake up."

I closed my eyes in relief at his words, but my pleasure

was short-lived. He grabbed my hand, pulling me toward the wall, and my shoulder shrieked in agony at the movement. I hissed with pain.

"What?" Akira glanced down at me. I had forgotten he was so much taller than I was. Ikeda, also, had been a tall man. But I had still triumphed over him. Nothing could make any difference to Niko, but I wished that he was still alive so I could kill him all over again.

"It's nothing. Don't worry."

Akira was tense, and I sensed his anxiety. If he thought I had taken the slightest injury, he would insist we stop while he patted me down to make sure I was all right. And we had no time for that.

"You're sure?" Akira's grip held me still for a moment. I tugged myself away and managed a smile to reassure him.

"A tiny scratch, that's all. It's nothing, I promise you. I could have taken worse injury from Matsuo nipping me in play. Come on. I need to see Niko."

"Show me." Akira was not fooled and was determined.

I shook my head and scowled at him. "It's on my shoulder. I would have to undo my robe to show you and we haven't got time to waste. I promise you, it's nothing. I was foolish enough to allow Ikeda to catch me with his sword."

I shrugged and Akira wavered, then he smiled with me.

"Quickly, then. But tell me one thing first. Are you glad you killed him?"

"Yes," I said simply. "But that's not important now. Is Niko all right? You're sure Ikeda didn't manage to take her?"

"I believe so." We had reached the wall and once again Akira made a stirrup with his hands for my foot. I found it difficult to believe that it had been such a short time earlier that he had last done that for me. And that so much had happened since. He spoke into my shoulder as I fumbled for a handhold in the stone of the wall.

"She's still very drowsy. While you were gone, I managed to wake her enough to ask if she knew what had happened to her. She was barely conscious, but she still had enough spirit to tell me that he kept her drugged after she cut him with his own dagger not long after he brought her here. She's fairly sure that after that he left her alone. You can look at her yourself, but I think Ikeda was lying to you."

I straddled the wall and waited for him to scrabble up beside me. We glanced at each other and Akira smiled at me. I turned away; I knew my eyes were shining with unshed tears and I wanted to hide my weakness from him.

Akira dropped to the ground first and I slid down clumsily beside him. He crouched and ran for the cover of a copse of trees and I followed quickly. I thought it must be the excitement draining out of my body; my usually excellent sense of balance seemed to have left me. I swayed slightly as my sandals slid on the uneven ground and it took an effort not to stumble. I was angry with myself and determined to keep up with him. The pain in my shoulder increased with every step we took. I gulped the cold night air, concentrating all my efforts on not falling.

"I thought you said the horses were close?" I grumbled softly. Akira paused, waiting for me. He grabbed my hand to tug me over an outcrop of scree that rattled and rolled beneath my feet, nearly unbalancing me.

"You're sure you're all right?" he demanded. I bit my tongue, using the minor pain to distract me from the raging fire in my shoulder.

"Of course I am. It's these sandals. You were right, they're far too big for me. I can barely walk in them."

In a display of bravado, I kicked the shoes off and

walked barefoot. I regretted it at once. The gravel was jagged and bit into my bare feet with cruel delight. Akira shrugged and walked forward again, more slowly. I thought he had slowed out of consideration for me and was about to scold him when I heard the whinny of a horse.

"Here," he said abruptly and parted a thick screen of camphor bushes. In years to come, these bushes would thin themselves until only one tree reared triumphant to the skies. That night, the smell of the foliage rose like medicine beneath his hands.

I scrambled through behind him. The twigs whipped back in my face and clutched at my robe as if they wanted to detain me. I pushed them aside, wincing at the pain in my shoulder. I groaned out loud as I understood that some-where between the wall of Ikeda's estate and here I had lost my precious ability to divorce my mind from bodily pain. That knowledge was almost a great an agony as the pain that clawed at me like a malicious demon. For a moment, I was sure that it was Ikeda's spirit taking his revenge on me and I almost wailed aloud. I couldn't understand it. The wound was nothing at all, and I found the pain it bestowed on me bewildering. I realized that Akira was speaking to me, pointing toward a small body wrapped in a rough blanket mounted on horseback in front of one of his men. Niko. It was only now that I understood how perilous my plan had been, and the joy I felt now at seeing her safe was greater than any pain I felt in my body. She was slumped, supported by the yakuza's arms, and clearly unconscious again.

"She'll be fine." Akira's voice was as faint as if he had been far away from me. "Quickly, get mounted and we will go."

My horse was a short, sturdy pony. I was grateful it took

so little effort to climb onto its back. Akira kicked his own pony into movement and we cantered off, branching onto a dirt track almost at once. I hunched my injured shoulder with the rhythm of his hooves and gasped aloud with the agony the movement caused. I spoke quickly to cover the noise.

"Where are we going? This is the wrong way to Hakone, surely?"

"We're not going directly to Hakone," Akira called over his shoulder. "We'll get on to Tokaido Highway, between Hakone and Odawara. That's the next town toward Kobe on the highway, after Hakone. When we reach the highway, then we'll turn back toward Hakone."

His words made no sense at all to me. I rubbed my hand over my forehead. The night was cold, and I was surprised when I felt sweat on my face.

"Why? Shouldn't we get through Hakone as quickly as possible? Besides, we need to get out of these clothes and wash the soot off as soon as we can. As it is, a blind man would think we were shinobi. Even if a patrol doesn't stop us, the guards on the highway will never let us past."

"That's why we're going toward Odawara," Akira explained patiently. "We're going stop at an abandoned village quite close to the highway. There's a palanquin waiting there for you and Niko, together with two peasants. These particular peasants have no reason at all to love Ikeda. They—together with my men—will be the bearers for your palanquin. There's a change of clothes there for us, and we can wash and make ourselves presentable. We leave these ponies at the village and join the highway on foot. The peasants will come back later and take the beasts as payment for their help." He grinned, a wolf's feral snarl. "Ikeda's body will be found soon after dawn when his

servants go to the house. They'll raise the alarm immediately, but the authorities will be looking for a band of
desperate bandits heading out of Hakone. They will not be
at all worried about a noble lady and her retinue heading
toward Hakone."

In spite of the pain that was beginning to make me feel
light-headed, I was impressed. Left to myself, I would have
taken Niko and gone straight back toward Hakone, skirting
the highway and avoiding the town. I would have made my
way back to Edo by the country tracks, praying all the while
that we would not encounter any patrols. If we had, then my
faith would have been in my katana. I glanced at Niko's limp
body, clasped surprisingly tenderly in the arms of Akira's
yakuza, and I nodded.

I sat very straight on my shambling pony. Each step he
took sent a spasm of pain through my shoulder. By the time
we arrived at Akira's abandoned village, my whole body was
racked with agony. And not just my body; my mind felt
strangely detached from everything around me. As we
stopped, I slid off my pony's back and walked as quickly as I
was able to Niko. Each step took great concentration. Even
greater was the effort needed to walk as if I was not in the
least troubled.

"Niko." I put my arms around her. She lolled against me
bonelessly. I carried on speaking even though it was
obvious she could not hear me. It didn't really matter to me;
the important thing was that I explained everything to her.
"Niko. I have you. Everything is going to be all right, I
promise you." I was repeating the same words over and
over. One of Akira's yakuza took her from me. He carried
her carefully to the palanquin and set her down inside the
curtains. Akira watched approvingly and then tapped me

on the shoulder. It was the uninjured shoulder, but I still bit my tongue to hold back a scream of pain.

"You'll find your kimono in the palanquin. And your wig. Wash in the well and change as quickly as you can. We need to be off. I've planned that we'll arrive at the first checkpoint before mid-morning. I don't believe the guards will bother us, but if they do, remember that you're traveling from Odawara and you're on pilgrimage to the shrine at Hakone."

He paused, waiting for an answer. Although his face was rippling as though I was seeing it through water, I caught his look of surprise when I simply nodded and headed toward the palanquin. I stumbled and it was Akira's hand that steadied me.

It was very difficult changing in the confines of the palanquin. I tugged my kimono on and somehow managed to fasten the obi. The effort of reaching up to adjust the wig was almost too much until I glanced at Niko, apparently sleeping at my side. What was a little pain compared to what my courageous younger sister had suffered? I was deeply ashamed and forced my leaden fingers to adjust the wig carefully. When I was done, I turned Niko on her side, to hide the bruise that covered her cheek, and I pulled the cover over her. She looked as if she was asleep rather than unconscious.

"Ready?" Akira's voice came from in front of me.

I nodded and waited for him to reply and then realized he could not see me. "Ready," I called back. "But take care. Don't disturb Niko."

I found myself racked with silent sobs. I choked them back with a huge effort, but still my body shook. I was bewildered, both by the intense pain I was suffering and my sudden lack of self-control. When I had begun my training in the martial arts, I had suffered much pain. Time and time again, Isamu and Riku-san had struck me with staves and the flat of their swords and their skilled hands. Neither of them had bothered to show any mercy or make any allowance for the fact that I was a girl and just learning martial arts. At first, I had crawled onto my futon at night and wept for the aches and pains in my poor body. Some mornings, when I had performed poorly and left myself open to attack the day before, I had been unable to rise at all, my limbs were in such pain. Once, Isamu broke a rib when he hit me with the flat of his sword. When I whined to him about it, he had laughed cruelly.

"So, little sister, you think I should have shown you mercy? Told you about your error rather than shown you?" I had stared at the tatami, trying to choke back tears of sorrow and self-pity. "You should know that I was very merciful. I hit you with the blade of my katana. If we had been fighting rather than playing, that blade would have gone between your ribs and you would have been unable to moan because you would be dead."

I bowed—somehow—and had one of the maids bandage my ribs tightly. The next day, I forced myself to go back to the dojo and practice with Isamu. Perhaps it was the pain that made me angry, but that day I fought very well. I had expected some praise, but got none.

Remembering that, I was bewildered how the cut I had taken from Ikeda's sword could possibly cause me so much hurt. I tried to analyze the pain, to isolate it, as Riku-san had taught me. If I could do that, I knew that I could lessen it, even conquer it. It had never been an easy task, but today it was impossible. I was confused and that caused me greater fear still until I began to wonder if the wound was so terrible because it had been inflicted by

Ikeda. Was the wound itself infected by his unclean body? I drew a deep breath, curling my lip in disgust at the thought.

Niko whimpered in her sleep and I lay down beside her, drawing her soft little body against me. She snuggled her head into my injured shoulder and it caused me such agony that I almost passed out. I managed to look at her tranquil face and I felt a little better. No matter what I was suffering, I had Niko. Whatever Ikeda had done to her, she was safe now. I had avenged Waka-san and Ikeda's unknown first wife. And of far less importance, I finally had my own revenge as well. I almost felt cheated as I decided that killing a monster like Ikeda had been no worse than putting salt on a slug.

I drifted into an uneasy sleep with Niko's sweet breath on my cheek.

~*~

"We're on our way to the great shrine in the temple at Hakone. Why have you stopped us? What's going on?"

I barely recognized Akira's voice. It sounded rougher than normal, and I grimaced as I heard him hawk phlegm and spit coarsely.

"Never you mind about that. I'm asking the questions. Who've you got in the palanquin?"

"Lady Keiko and her younger sister. The young lady is ill. My lady is not going to thank you if you disturb her."

Akira's voice rose; I guessed in warning to me. In sleep, my body had forgotten its pain for a moment and I almost shrieked aloud as the agony flooded back. I took a shallow breath and called out impatiently.

"What? Why have we stopped? Akira, what's going on? Have we reached Hakone already?"

I heard thumping footsteps approaching the palanquin and I was ready. When the curtains were drawn back, my face was furious and I was every bit the irritated samurai noble, ready and willing to lash out at anybody who offended me.

"What do you think you're doing?" I snarled. I drew back as if I thought that the presence of the guard might contaminate me. "How dare you stop me? Your commanding officer is going to hear about this! When my husband hears about your behavior, you'll be lucky to see the next dawn."

The curtains were dropped hurriedly. I could hear the soldier murmuring his apologies as he walked away, but I carried on screaming angrily anyway. I was quite proud of my performance. I only dropped my voice to a mumble so I could listen to Akira talking to the soldier.

"Problem hereabouts, is there?" he asked cheerfully.

"There are always problems," the guard muttered. "Got your pass, have you? I'd better take a look."

I heard the rustle of paper.

"Nothing wrong with that pass, I promise you." Akira dropped his voice confidentially. "I'd take care to be polite if I were you. You should know that my mistress is the number one wife to a very important man in Edo."

"She would be." The guard sighed. "Just what I need, more trouble. Well, if you could apologize to your mistress for me when she's in a better temper and explain to her that I'm only doing my job, I would appreciate it. The fact is, I've got orders to stop everything that goes past here all day.

Even if the shogun himself chose today to travel unannounced, I've got orders to ask for his pass. What I've done to offend the gods and bring such trouble down on my poor head, I don't know."

"Really?" Akira sounded so amazed, even I believed him. "What's happened to cause such a stir?"

"The local magistrate was found with his head taken off just a couple of hours ago. Done clean as if a vengeful spirit had come in the night and done the deed, or so I've heard. Mind you—" The guard paused and I sensed he was leaning toward Akira so his words were not overheard. "—it seems his wife was found dead as well. Now, I'm not superstitious, but the magistrate was a terribly cruel man in life. It's said he gave his wife nothing at all to live for. It does make you wonder if it wasn't the lady's spirit that did him in to get her revenge on her old man."

Tears glued my eyelashes together. It was all nonsense. But my heart still wondered if Waka-san's spirit hadn't come back to guard me in thanks for the release I had given her. Then my palanquin was lifted again and the jolt sent such agony through my body that I forgot everything but my pain.

TWENTY

I cannot stand on
My shadow. But neither will
I walk behind yours.

*I*t was all wrong. Niko was sponging my face with cool, scented water. My lips were parched, but I managed to open them. I wanted to explain to her that it was I who should be caring for her. That it was she who had been used so cruelly by Ikeda, not me. Before I could force my tongue to form words, the room was spinning around me so dizzily, I thought I was going to vomit, then Niko's face went away.

It happened again and again. Each time, my confusion grew. Each time, I became angrier with myself.

"She's asleep, I think. I mean, properly asleep, not unconscious." Niko's voice came from a long way above me.

"How can you tell?" A man's voice. I listened carefully, trying to identify it. For a moment, I thought it was my brother, Isamu, and I was thrilled. Then I remembered that Isamu was dead. In that case, was I also dead?

"Her breathing's different." Niko again. I was puzzled. Was my poor Niko also in the afterlife with Isamu and me in spite of my best efforts to rescue her? I felt tears run down my cheeks at the injustice of the thought. They were wiped away so softly, I barely felt the touch of the silk on my cheeks.

"Keiko, it's all right. Everything has gone well, I promise you."

Isamu's voice again. But this time I listened carefully and I thought that the voice was not his. Isamu had never spoken to me with such tenderness. But perhaps if we were both truly dead, his spirit had more compassion than he had ever had in life. The hope encouraged me to open my eyes. I managed to pry my eyelids apart a crack, but the light was so intense it caused me to flinch and then clench them closed again.

No matter. It had been enough. A man's face was over me, looking at me intently. A man who was not Isamu. I wanted him to go away. To leave me in peace. If he was not Isamu, he had no place in my life.

"Keiko, wake up," he persisted.

I moved my body, very gently, anticipating great pain. I was sore; my ribs and right shoulder felt very tender. But the pain was not so great. It was...bearable. That pleased me. But still, I wanted nothing more than to lie still for a long time. I thought of my poor brother Isamu again, slaughtered by our own villagers, and I choked on tears of grief. I should have been with him. I *wanted* to be with him now. In death as in life, my place was at his side.

"Go away," I muttered irritably. "Leave me alone."

"No. Drink this." A cup was placed against my lips. I turned my head angrily and a little of the liquid ran down my chin. For some reason, that made me very sad. I sniffed and then growled with anger as the unknown man put his hands on each side of my head and held it still. "Niko, give her the cup again."

Was I a baby that could not even drink by its own effort? I took a mouthful of the cool liquid that was offered to me and spat it in the man's face. I was furious when he wiped his face dry with his hand and smiled indulgently at me.

"Keiko-chan, that was not nice! Akira-san is just trying to help you!" Niko scolded me. I turned my head in the direction of her voice and her face swam in and out of focus. Finally, it stopped bobbing about and I moaned, sharing her pain as I saw the shadow of the bruise that covered half of her face.

"Niko. It is you? Where are we? Ikeda? Is he really dead? Are we safe?"

As the thoughts crowded my mind, I spoke them out loud. Niko took my hand in hers and squeezed it tightly. Her mouth was clenched in a tight line and I guessed she was forcing back tears. For me? Surely it was me who should be weeping for her. I was dizzy with confusion.

Although I had spoken to Niko, it was the man who answered me. "Ikeda is dead. We are safe. Niko is safe." He spoke very firmly. It was, I thought, a voice that was accustomed to being obeyed. Did he also think that I should obey him? If he did, then he would soon discover his mistake.

I felt my mind beginning to wake. It was a strange sensation. I wondered absently if a bear felt like this when the warmth of spring roused it from hibernation. Nothing made any sense. Even my own body felt stiff and oddly unfamiliar to me, as if I was suddenly an old woman. Had I somehow slept the years away and awoken as old as my own grandmother? The thought filled me with such horror that I abruptly patted myself anxiously from neck to stomach, finally daring to dab at my face in search of wrinkles.

I sighed in deep relief as I felt firm breasts and belly and smooth skin on my face.

"Can you eat?" The man's voice again, quite gentle now. The same man Niko had called Akira. Seconds ago, the name had meant nothing to me. Now, I was very still as memories tumbled through my head so rapidly that it was difficult to make sense of them all. But I knew him now, and there was no turning away from the debt that I understood I owed to him.

My gaze flicked from Akira's face to Niko. Both were looking at me with deep worry in their gaze. My lips were so dry it was quite difficult to move them. Still, I managed a polite smile.

"I'm not hungry. But thank you, Akira-san," I said formally. Akira bowed his head; I hoped he knew that I was thanking him for far more than the offer of food. I closed my eyes, as if the effort of speaking had exhausted my strength. It had not. With each heartbeat, I felt my body beginning to renew itself. I was nearly healed, I knew that. In body at least. But I felt that my mind needed far longer.

Akira was smiling at me, his face bright with pleasure. I spoke cautiously.

"It's really over?" I asked. "Niko, you're all right? Did I really kill Ikeda?"

"Yes." Akira spoke instead of Niko. I was irritated; I wanted Niko herself to tell me that she was truly unhurt. But it seemed that my younger sister was content for him to talk for her. "It's over. And Niko really is unharmed." I sighed with relief. "Ikeda hurt her, but his tree wouldn't rise for her. We got to her in time. And Ikeda is truly dead—by your hand. The rumors have reached the Floating World already, and the whole place is buzzing with it. Fortunately, the authorities in Hakone have decided that he was murdered by insurgents out to get revenge against him. It's thought that his wife had a heart seizure with shock at the attack and the poor lady passed away without being touched. The gossip also says that his house was ransacked and that every item of value was stolen."

I stared into space, exulting savagely that it was me who had given the monster Ikeda his death. He had deserved it. I was also glad that I had been able to give his poor wife release from her earthly torment, although my pleasure in her quiet passing was tinged with great sadness that it had been necessary.

But Akira's talk about Ikeda's house being ransacked puzzled me. All Ikeda's possessions had been in place when I left. I could never have brought myself to touch a single one of them. When it was matched against the slaughter that had taken place that dreadful night, it didn't matter greatly, yet I wanted to know everything.

"No," I said firmly. "That's not right. I didn't steal anything. I wouldn't have taken anything he owned. It was all tainted by his wickedness."

"We took nothing at all. Except Niko." Akira smiled. "And she was never Ikeda's property. But the gossip says everything was stolen by the insurgents who murdered him. The only odd thing about it is that they spared Ikeda's guards. When the servants found Ikeda dead, they went running for his guards, naturally. Three of the guards were found with head wounds and still unconscious. The fourth appeared to be unhurt, but he had been tied up securely and gagged. He said a gang of peasants armed with arque-buses had surprised them in the night, just as they were changing patrols. The guard who was unhurt said they had fought like demons, but all the guards had been over-whelmed and he was left tied up so he could tell the authorities what had happened as a warning that the rebels had been pushed too far. Apparently, the authorities weren't too surprised. Even for a magistrate, Ikeda had a reputation for being utterly ruthless, and he was known to be hated."

"I see. And did the guards recognize any of the rebels?" I asked carefully.

"No." Akira shook his head sadly. "The guard who was tied up was certain they weren't locals. The authorities took him in for questioning, of course, but Ikeda had so many enemies, they didn't have any difficulty in believing his story."

"Good." I was genuinely pleased about that.

Akira and I stared at each other silently. Niko shuffled, obviously uncomfortable in the silence. Finally, she stood and spoke carefully.

"I'm sure I heard Matsuo whining. I expect he wants to go out. I'll take him for a walk, shall I?"

"That's a good idea. But take care, Niko," I called as she left. I waited until Niko had closed the shoji behind her before I spoke. "Is it truly over, Akira? We don't have anything to fear from the authorities?"

"It's over. And we're all safe," he reassured me and then paused, obviously waiting for me to speak again. I smiled tremulously and drew a deep breath.

"And Niko? Ikeda really didn't take her?"

"No." Akira bared his teeth in a grin that had no humor at all in it. "Niko said he tried. Almost as soon as he got her back to his house, he took her to the storeroom. She said he stood in front of her, gloating down at her. After a while, he pulled his tree out and tried to get it to rise for her. Niko said it looked like a fat, tea-colored slug. No matter how he tried, it did no good, and in the end, she laughed at him."

I sighed with great affection for my brave younger sister. "What happened? Did he give up?"

"No. Brave man that he was, he hit her. Hard enough to knock her to the futon. Niko said she was stunned, but she remembered him kneeling down beside her and trying to put his tree in her mouth. She said she bit it, hard, and he hit her again. She managed to grab his dagger out of his obi somehow, but he was too strong for her. He grabbed it off her and walked away from her. He left her alone after that, just coming and staring at her now and then and grinning at her. She decided that if he did manage to get his tree to rise for her, she would take it in her mouth and bite so hard that he wouldn't be able to pry her teeth apart. She thought she might be able to hang on long enough so that he bled to death. And if it didn't work, at least she would have taught him a lesson."

"But she would have been signing her own death warrant!" I was appalled. "He would probably have killed her himself. Or if he couldn't reach his sword, his guards would have come running when he shouted and done the job for him."

"I know. Niko knew that, as well." Akira smiled. "She told me she would have died happily knowing that she had honored you by her death."

I closed my eyes. I could do nothing but shake my head. I was filled with such love and admiration for Niko that words would have choked me. Akira waited patiently for me to collect myself.

"She has more bravery than most men," I said eventually. "I'm honored that she's my younger sister." I felt oddly empty as the knowledge that my task was truly complete washed over me. I spoke slowly, feeling very awkward. "It's done, then. Thank you for all your help. I'm sorry to be rude, but could you leave me now? I think I would like to sleep again."

Akira's head jerked back as if I had slapped him. I was sorry about that, but still, I wanted him to go. To leave me alone to think thoughts that I desperately wanted to turn away from, but knew I could not.

"Of course. You've been through a great deal. You need time to recover, I understand that. If you need anything, just call. I'll be close by."

He walked away stiffly, and I wondered what he was talking about. Niko, certainly, had suffered. But there was nothing wrong with me. I supposed I must have been taken with a fever. Perhaps I had been ill for some time. But now, there was nothing physically wrong with me.

It was my mind that hurt.

I stared into space and saw nothing. My vision blurred. I thought I was crying, but when I wiped my face with my hands, my eyes were dry. I had killed two people with my own hands. I recollected that only a few moments ago, I had been proud of it. Now, I was an empty husk, capable of feeling nothing. Surely I should feel remorse? Regret?

My mouth opened and I cried out silently. I desperately wanted to feel *something*. This emptiness was like a small death.

A sudden vision of Ikeda's ruined face came to me and I almost yelped aloud, the picture was so clear. I raised my hands as if I could push the imagined image away from me. He had been a monster. He had murdered his own relatives, infected his wife with certain death. Just as he would have infected Niko—and me—if the gods hadn't smiled on me and not him. Surely he had deserved his death, which had been quick and clean.

Even as I tried to reassure myself, I knew I was lying. A moment ago I had longed to feel something—pain or pleasure, it didn't matter. Now, guilt overwhelmed me and I moaned out loud. Who was I to dictate who lived and died? Even if Ikeda had deserved to die, what about poor Wakasan? I had thought she had welcomed the gentle death I gifted to her, but what if I was wrong? A great horror filled me. I didn't know. I was no longer certain that I had done what was right. But I had followed my precious code of bushido; I had done only what it instructed me to do and no more. I was a warrior woman of the samurai. It was my duty to put right what I saw as wrong.

Why, then, did I find myself in this hell of uncertainty? Why did I suddenly want to do no more than turn my face to the wall and wait for death to claim me as well? My thoughts went around in circles and I put my hands over my eyes, as if by doing so I could divorce my actions from my own soul.

And then I understood with dreadful clarity that the pain I was suffering now was little more than self-pity. I had nothing. My life was finished. Everything I had hoped and worked for was over. How could I ever be truly a samurai warrior if I was going to hate myself for every wrong I tried to put right? If my compassion for those I was about to hurt —even kill—was so great that I felt their pain and could not bear to wound them, and if I was no longer onna-bugeisha, what was I? I answered my own question with great bitterness.

I was nothing.

I opened my mouth and howled out loud.

TWENTY-ONE

We think we are the
True children of the gods. But
The gods know better

J was vaguely aware that Akira had come back, but his presence meant nothing to me. I sobbed, curling my body as far into a knot as I could. He stood at the side of my futon, looking down at me. I could feel his concern, but even more his total confusion. He could take my defiance and my anger, but he had no defense at all against my bitter tears. He watched me, neither speaking nor touching me.

I didn't mind that he was there. It no longer mattered to me that he would see my weakness. I was diminished; now I was nothing more than a woman. My dreams of being onna-bugeisha were dead and gone from me. I wept with sorrow for myself, but also I understood that my tears were not just for my loss. For almost the first time since their deaths, I wept for my father and my brother. And also for the little death of my sister Emiko, imprisoned in marriage to a man she hated. A man who made her shudder every time he touched her. I felt an overwhelming pity for them all. And myself.

I wiped my face, but still the tears came. I was exhausted and empty inside. And the more I cried, the deeper was I ashamed of myself. I had been onna-bugeisha. A warrior woman of the samurai. And now I had lost my heritage. And yet, perhaps simply because I was a woman, even in the depths of my self-hatred I began to feel a small flicker of confusion.

Surely all men felt a certain kindness toward their fellow human beings? Even a samurai must find it neces-sary to learn to overcome his compassion for those weaker than himself. To be able to kill a fellow human being was a very great and terrible thing, no matter how justified the cause. That, surely, should come naturally to no man. Instinctively, I understood that that must be so.

But the knowledge did nothing but deepen my loathing for my frailty.

The code of bushido was meant to ensure compassion for everybody. A samurai must learn to put his own weak-nesses aside in favor of the greater good. Conscience must be set aside in favor of obedience. And if a man—samurai or not—was able to live with themselves after taking anoth-er's life, then they must be able to justify their actions to themselves. That was what I would never be able to achieve.

I had killed two people. One in self-defense, the thought of which made me feel slightly better. But Waka-san? She had been as helpless as a newborn babe in my arms and I had murdered her. But she wanted to die! I had been nothing more than the instrument that gave her the peace she longed for. I closed my eyes as I understood that I would never know if that was true or not. Who was I to decide that another's life had become such a burden that death would welcome?

I wrapped my arms around myself and rocked back and forward. Even the touch of my hands on my own body was repulsive to me. Had I truly thought of the samurai code when I killed Ikeda? Where had been the need to take Waka-san's life? I bit my lip so hard it drew blood as I admitted to myself that at the time I had thought of nothing but my own need for revenge. For me. For Niko. For the women Ikeda had killed because they were in his way. I had been sure I was carrying out Waka-san's deepest wish. Now, I wondered if I had decided in my conceit that I was as wise as the gods and had the right to free her soul.

Even in the depths of my regret, I felt a bitter anger. Such an outflow of self-pity as I was experiencing surely had no place in the code of bushido. There was no place for tears in the life of a samurai. If I had to grieve, it should be from compassion for those whose lives I had taken. And I knew I was crying not just for them, but also for myself, and that surely should have no place in the life of a samurai warrior.

I thought that I had plumbed the depths of shame. I was wrong. Along with the shame and pain came a darker knowledge.

I would never be able to kill again. The very idea of causing somebody pain made me feel sick to my very soul. I was a disgrace to my family's tradition. I was finished. It was with that self-knowledge that I knew I was truly no longer onna-bugeisha. Perhaps I had never been so. And once I acknowledged that, I knew that there was only one way this could end. Only one way in which I could regain my lost honor.

I thought that Akira must have become bored watching me sob. He slid his hand cautiously on my shoulder. I slapped it away and turned my back on him. His hand came back, warm and comforting. I wanted to turn back, to bury into his body and let him cuddle me as if I were a child, crying for some minor hurt that was easily relieved. The very thought appalled me.

"Please. Where is my father's katana?" I asked stiffly. I wondered if he would notice that I had said my *father's* katana, not *my* katana. It was no longer mine. I had surely forfeited the right to use it.

"It's safe," he said evenly. "You have no need of it for the moment."

"I would like to see it. To make sure it didn't take any harm," I lied fluidly. I managed a bleary smile as I watched Akira's face. If he would only bring the katana to me, all would be well again. Once before I had held the noble blade to my own throat. This time, there would be no hesitation. I knew how sharp it was. There would be no pain for me. All I had to do was lean against the steel. The katana would do what was necessary. It would not betray me as I had betrayed it and all that it represented.

"It's safe," Akira repeated. "I'll take care of it for you until you feel better."

My bitterness was a sour taste in my throat. I lashed out at him uncaringly. "Leave me alone," I snarled. "If you won't bring me my katana, you're of no use at all to me."

"No," Akira said simply.

I raised my face and stared at him through my tear-dulled eyes. His face seemed to waver, so I could not see his expression, but I thought he was looking at me with pity. That infuriated me.

"I will not bring you your katana. And I won't leave you. I'm staying here. You need me," he said.

Instead of snapping at him, telling him he was talking nonsense, I spoke from my heart. "I *need* nobody. And nobody can help me except myself. Please, bring me my katana and let me end my miserable existence."

I watched his expression turn stony. I wanted to beat my hands against his body until my flesh bruised and we both hurt.

"You don't understand. I've betrayed everything that ever mattered to me. I'm not worthy of being called onna-bugeisha anymore. I'm not brave enough to fight again. I could barely bring myself to swat a fly. I've disgraced myself. I'm a coward. My katana will know that. It will help me end my miserable existence."

I had spoken so quickly and vehemently that I was panting for breath. Akira grabbed my wrists and held them very tightly. I couldn't even be bothered to struggle to free myself.

"Listen to me. You don't know what you're saying. You've hovered at death's door for weeks. It was only your own strength that pulled you through. Ikeda's sword barely cut you, but he nearly killed you anyway."

His face was very close to mine. I could not make out any features except his eyes. They were lit with a cold, angry light that held my gaze.

"What are you saying?" I was suddenly dull and empty of all feeling. I couldn't even be bothered to try and persuade Akira to bring me my katana. It didn't matter. I had made my mind up. When he finally left me, I would ask Niko to bring it to me. If she refused, I would wait until I was alone and find it myself. It didn't matter greatly where Akira had hidden it. It would cry out to me.

I had contemplated taking my own life once before, when I had stumbled upon the slaughtered bodies of my father and brother. It would have been better if I had acted then. Still, I was grateful to the gods for giving me a second chance to redeem my honor.

"Ikeda poisoned you." Akira put his hands on each side of my head and forced me to look at him. I guessed he knew I wasn't really listening to him. "You were unconscious and shaking with fever by the time we arrived back in the Floating World. I couldn't wake you up. I thought you were going to die."

I pushed his hands away and stared at him. Ikeda had poisoned me? How? What nonsense was this? Then I actually saw Akira's face and I was deeply sorry for him. Akira, the most feared yakuza in Edo, the man who was said to be so terrible that strong men trembled at his name, was so full of hurt that he had not disguised his weakness to me. I was filled with amazement. For a moment, I put my own shame aside as I felt the need to thank him by at least pretending interest in his words.

"Is that possible? How did he poison me? I didn't eat or drink anything when we raided his house. Was it his poor wife? Did I take something from her as she died? Did he avenge himself on me through her?"

That made complete sense to me. I had held Waka-san against my body to release her spirit. She would never have hurt me. But Ikeda? Infecting me through his wife would have delighted him. I could barely catch my breath at the thought; if this was so, then I was surely right. Committing seppuku with my own katana would be a clean, honorable, and, above all, quick death compared to enduring a slow, living death from the plum poison disease.

I watched Akira's face intently as I spoke. He spread his fingers in a soothing way and shook his head. I tried to breathe slowly and calmly as I waited for him to tell me that Ikeda had truly taken a terrible revenge on me.

"No. You didn't catch anything from Waka-san." I was both puzzled and relieved. I remembered the thinness of her poor body and suddenly I was sure that I had been right when I heard her breathe her thanks for the tranquil death I had given her. I gave thanks for it. Akira hesitated and then spoke strongly. "That wretch Ikeda must have infected her with the plum poison years ago. She might have lingered for much longer, but I think he was starving her as well to bring her to death quicker. He was a coward as well as a ruthless killer. He wouldn't have dared take the risk of doing anything to her that was obvious. She came from a good family, and they would have made sure she got justice if there was the least suspicion about her death. I would guess Ikeda simply told everybody she refused to eat. Nothing to do with him. If she wouldn't eat, he couldn't force her."

In spite of my own agony of spirit, I bared my teeth in anger. "If it wasn't through his wife, how did he poison me? You're lying to me. He had no idea I was going to be there that night. He couldn't have gotten anything ready. My illness, if that's what you want to call it, was nothing to do with Ikeda. It was just my own conscience. I brought the illness on myself." The words were flowing from my mouth in an unstoppable stream. "I could never truly be onna-bugeisha. It was all just a dream. I'm not worthy to bear the name. My first test as a samurai warrior and all I can do is cry because I did what I thought was my duty. I'm just a weak woman, no better than any yujo who's earning her living walking the streets. I'll never be able to lift my katana against a fellow human ever again. Niko has a dozen times the courage that I do. I'm finished."

There. It was said. The burden that tainted my soul was out. If I hadn't felt so full of disgust for myself, I would have been bitterly amused by the irony of the situation. Akira would never understand what I was talking about; he probably thought I was babbling with my fever.

I fell silent, my thoughts running through my head so quickly they came in a flood that threatened to overwhelm me all over again. What use was an onna-bugeisha who could only fight in the dojo? Whoever heard of a warrior who crumpled into tears after the battle was over? I had played at being a samurai warrior woman all along. When it mattered, I was a silly, useless girl. And my dear Niko would have died happy in the knowledge that her death would have made me proud of her! My shame grew until it was a physical pain in my belly.

"You don't understand," Akira persisted. I listened courteously. I would not cry again, no matter what. I owed that to myself. And to Niko. "Listen to me, Keiko-chan. Why would I lie to you? The truth is that Ikeda almost killed you. It's a gift from the gods that you have survived. More than that, it's your own strength that pulled you through. I called in the best surgeon in Edo as soon as we got back. Dragged him off his futon and away from his favorite concubine. He examined you and said you were going to die. There was nothing at all he could do. I threatened him with a long and lingering death of his own if he didn't save you. He was terrified but insisted there was nothing either he or any other surgeon could do for you.

"It was the cut on your shoulder, he said. I could see that

it looked very bad by then. Ikeda's sword hadn't gone deep, but the cut was a long one and it was festering already. But I had seen worse on my own men and I told the surgeon so. He shook his head and pointed to a red line that was running from the cut down across your breasts and onto your stomach.

"'It's not the wound that's the problem,' he explained. 'I could treat that easily enough. The real problem is that there must have been poison on the blade that made this cut. I can see it's a fresh wound, but it's infected badly already. The poison has already spread into her blood. Look —you can almost see that red line moving as you watch. And she has a high fever. I don't know what the poison is. If I did, there might be a faint chance I could give her an anti-dote. But as it is...'

"He looked at me with fear in his eyes. I told him if he didn't save you, I would kill him and every one of his family without any mercy. He flinched but still shook his head.

"'I will not give you false hope,' he said. 'There's no point. I can give her medicine, but it will do no good. There is no cure for this. I'm sorry. If you killed my family in front of me, the answer would be the same. I cannot help her. Nobody can. The only thing I can do is give her opium to try and soothe her pain and help her to sleep.'

"I believed him." Akira sighed. "He knows me, that surgeon. He knew I would keep my word. And he is the very best in all of Edo. If he could not help you, then nobody could."

He wiped his hands over his face and incredulously I saw that he was wiping away tears. I turned my face away so the burden of me seeing him weep wouldn't be added to his shame.

"But I'm alive," I said cautiously. "What happened? Did he find something to cure me after all?"

"No." Akira sniffed and pretended his nose was running. "I knew as soon as he told me about the poison on the blade that he was right. I've lost several men that way, to rival yakuza gangs. Once, it was no more than a scratch from a dagger, but it went bad and my man died eventually." His face darkened with anger and his voice was bitter when he continued. "I know that to a samurai, a yakuza is nothing but a riverbed beggar. We have no place in your life. But we —or at least some of us—still have a code of honor. If I cannot beat an opponent in a fair fight, I would never consider such a dishonorable trick as poison."

"I understand that," I said. And I did. Akira looked at me as if he doubted my words, then shrugged.

"Thank you. Anyway, when the surgeon told me what Ikeda had done, I guessed the poisoned sword was not meant specifically for you. He no doubt simply kept something deadly smeared in the blade on the grounds that if he needed to use it in his own home, then he was going to be sure he won."

"That can't be right," I interrupted. "By the time we fought, he knew he had lost Niko. He told me he was going to take me in her place. In that case, why would he want to kill me?"

"If it were Ikeda's poison, he would also know the antidote," Akira pointed out. "He could cure you any time he wanted, but why bother? You would have taken days, perhaps weeks to die from the poison. He probably had hopes that you were still whole, but even if you weren't, he had nothing to lose. Even if you couldn't cure him, he would still have taken huge pleasure in watching you die. He could have visited a witch for his potion at his leisure. If he needed it, that is. Seeing you helpless and at his mercy might easily have given him such pleasure that he didn't need a potion. His tree might well have risen for you out of sheer delight at the thought that he had won.

"If Niko said anything, it wouldn't matter. He knew that nobody would believe her word against his. And you had done him the favor of killing his troublesome wife. He could obtain his cure at his leisure and then think about finding another wife with plenty of money."

I grimaced, my mouth sour at the picture Akira had drawn. He was right. Yet still, my mind twisted and came back to one thing. I was alive. My body had healed itself of Ikeda's poison somehow. If the surgeon had been unable to help me, how had it happened?

"If your surgeon couldn't help me, how did I survive?" I asked bluntly. I stared at his face as I spoke, determined to know the truth.

"You healed yourself," he said quietly.

I laughed out loud. "And how did I manage that? I was unconscious. My blood was poisoned. I don't believe even the gaijin have anything that could cure that. What? Did I simply dream myself better?"

I knew I had spoken bitterly, but I thought Akira was playing games with me. Teasing me with my own shame. I was astonished when he smiled and nodded.

"When the surgeon offered to give you opium to dim your pain, I was tempted. Then I looked down at you and saw that even though you were unconscious, you were gritting your teeth. Your whole face was intent and I changed my mind. I told the surgeon to go and think himself fortunate he was still alive. I sent Niko for the kannushi from Jokan-Ji Temple. I knew about his past life and I wondered if he might know something the surgeon did not. Even if he couldn't help, I wanted him to tell me if I was doing the right thing."

"He's a good man," I said quietly. "Was it he who helped me, then?"

"No. He was deeply sorry, but like me, he had seen wounds that had gone bad and infected the blood. He knew there was no cure for it. I explained that I had refused opium for you and why. He thought about if very briefly and then nodded his agreement.

"'If it was any other woman except Keiko-chan—or man, for that matter,' he said, 'I would have said to give her as much opium as it takes to dull her pain. But not Keiko. The pain will make her angry. She will fight it. If she has no pain, then she will have nothing to fight against and she will die. As it is, if the gods will it, she will live. And it will be through her own strength as much as anything.'"

"You both thought better of me than I do," I said stonily. I had a sudden memory of Adam's miraculous morphine pills. Perhaps they also had their limitations. If they had taken away all my pain, might it have been that I never awoke but simply slipped into death? "So I cured myself, did I? Even though I was unconscious and had no idea where I was or even what was happening around me?"

"Yes," Akira said seriously. "That's exactly what you did. You're alive, and you have nothing but your own stubbornness to thank for that."

I smiled thinly. How strange that two such strong, determined men should believe that I alone had had the ability to save myself from death. If they really knew me, they would not have been deceived so easily. My life—like all the rest of us—had been in the hands of the gods. The simple fact was that my time had not come.

"Not me. The gods decided it wasn't time for me to die, and I suppose I should be grateful for that."

"You're too hard on yourself." Akira frowned. "I don't believe there's another woman in the whole of Edo who could achieve what you have. But still you think you're not strong enough."

"I have failed," I barked. Why couldn't he understand? "Would a true onna-bugeisha weep with weakness? Did the great samurai warrior woman Tomoe Gozen cry when she knew her man was sending her away so she wouldn't see him die? I'm not fit to bear the name of samurai. When I was a child, my amah was fond of telling me to be careful what I wished for in case I got it. I used to think she was silly. Now I understand that she had great wisdom. I wanted something that was far beyond me. I had no right to try and attain it."

"You think less of yourself because you regret doing what you thought was right?" Akira asked curiously. "Tell me, Keiko, if the shogun was to summon you to his presence tomorrow and tell you that he had discovered that the men who killed your father and brother had escaped punishment but he had them now and was offering you the chance to execute them yourself, what would you do?" He was talking nonsense, of course. I shrugged my shoulders, but he persisted. "You told me you felt no need for vengeance against those men. That you knew that they had been driven to kill only by their great desperation. But I understand that the essence of the code of bushido is to obey the shogun, no matter what. So, would you obey your samurai code and kill them even though you knew them to be innocent of deliberate hurt?"

My senses spun. Akira was right. Obedience to the shogun was everything. But could I kill in cold blood at his command, knowing that I thought his decision was wrong? Could I have done that even when I truly believed myself to be onna-bugeisha, before my courage had left me?

"No," I said in a small voice. "It wouldn't be right. I would kill myself before I did that." Which was, of course, exactly what the shogun would expect for my disobedience. The thought gave me no comfort at all.

"Of course you couldn't do something that you knew to be wrong," Akira spoke urgently. "Listen to me, Keiko. In killing Ikeda, you did what was right. Even more importantly, you did what you *thought* was right. You gave the release of death to his wife, and if she could, she would have thanked you for it. You still don't believe that, do you?"

I opened my mouth and then closed it again. His words seemed to make sense, yet at the same time, I couldn't believe him. His logic was flawed; it had to be.

"I'd like to believe it, but I can't. Who am I to say who should live and who should die? No matter what the code of bushido says about honor and obedience, I can't follow it any longer. I'm a failure," I said simply. "I'm sure my conscience wouldn't allow me to inflict hurt on anybody ever again. I know now that I'm not a samurai. I'm a woman, nothing more."

"And I suppose you think if you say it often enough, it's going to be true?" Akira said cruelly. "I tell you, you are greater than any samurai who has ever followed the code of bushido. You *think* about your actions instead of following the code of bushido with blind obedience. I told you, your brother tried to persuade your father to give your peasants rice. He knew your father was wrong in denying them food. Yet when the time came, he still died alongside your father knowing he was wrong. But he followed the code of the samurai blindly."

I was so furious I almost gagged on my anger. "And who are you to criticize my father and my brother? They were honorable men. You're a yakuza who murders and steals for nothing but your own profit. How dare you talk about something that is beyond anything you could ever understand?"

I was panting with anger. If I had had my katana in my hand at that moment, I would not have hesitated to take Akira's head from his body.

"I speak as I see."

A pulse of anger was beating beneath Akira's right eye. For some reason, it fascinated me. I kept my gaze fixed on it as he finished speaking.

"I don't pretend to be noble. I'm not. To you and all your class, I'm simply trash. But I know what's right and what isn't. And so do you. You would never do anything that you knew to be wrong. You would face your own death first. You talk about Tomoe Gozen. Do you really think she didn't know why her man was sending her away? Of course she did. She pretended to follow the samurai code, but only so that he would die knowing that she was safe. She was greater than her man, just as you are greater than any man who bears the name of samurai. You have a woman's love and pity, as well as the courage of the greatest of warriors. You would never hurt anybody, still less kill, without being certain that it was the right thing to do. That it was justified by their actions. And unlike any samurai man, your heart would always weep with pity for what you had done."

He had spoken almost without drawing breath. I knew that he meant every word, and I was almost undone all over again by his admiration.

"Thank you," I said finally. "Would you leave me alone for a while, please?"

Akira stood without saying another word. He bowed and walked away without looking back. I stared into space, trying not to think. Suddenly, I realized where I was. This was Akira's house. He had brought me here and taken care of me. I sniffed the skin on my arm and found I smelled sweet and clean. I flushed deeply as I understood that I had been bathed, probably every day that I had been lost to the world. Niko could not have washed me so thoroughly without help.

I had ordered the man who had helped me back to life out of my presence as if he was no more than a servant. I closed my eyes and cringed at my own arrogance. Another trifle to add to the burden of my unworthiness.

I sat very still for a long time. The fingers of sunlight crept across the tatami and began to touch my futon. I was very thirsty, but I did not want to call for tea. I knew if I did that Niko would come running, and I couldn't face her yet. I bit my lip at my cowardice, and before I knew I was going to speak, I heard my own voice calling for my younger sister. I was right; she was there so quickly she must have been hovering outside the shoji.

"Keiko-san, you are well? You've come back to us fully at last? Please, let me pull your kakebuton over you. You must be cold. Would you like some tea? Something to eat?"

If I spoke, I knew I would cry. Instead, I held my arms out to Niko and she threw herself against me so hard we both crashed back on the futon together. She began to giggle, and I smiled with her. I wiped away tears again, but this time without any shame. These were tears of joy and pride in my younger sister.

"Niko-chan, I promise you, I'm well again." She was patting my arms with her hands, moving up to my face as anxiously as a mother with her baby. My heart nearly broke with love for her. "And I think I have you to thank for my recovery. Did you care for me while I was ill?"

"I did," she said proudly, then she puffed out her cheeks and shrugged. "Actually, we all did. Me and Akira and Aisha. We all took turns to sit with you. You were never alone." My pride—that I had thought could sink no lower—shriveled completely. What had I ever done to deserve such loyalty? I, who had thought of nothing but myself, had somehow inspired these three people to give up their normal lives to care for *me?* "Actually, Matsuo sat with you longer than anybody. I had to drag him away from you to make him go for a walk now and then."

I felt the faintest of smiles twist my lips. Worship from my dog, now that I could take. And yet...was it so different from the love that these three good people had given so freely to me?

"So," I said with mock severity. "You not only cared for me, you took care of Matsuo as well?"

"Sort of." Niko frowned. "To be honest—" She lowered her voice to a conspiratorial whisper. "—Matsuo was so determined to stay with you, I had to bring a litter box in here for him in the end. I hope you didn't mind."

Niko's down-to-earth words brought me crashing down. She was right; I was wrong. The things that mattered in this life were the basics. The love of friends that was given freely and without demands being first amongst them. Even the instinctive devotion of my dog—that was surely as impor-tant as any high-minded code of honor.

And I was alive. No matter how it came to be, I was alive and going to be well in mind and body both. And I no longer wanted to die. I might not be the onna-bugeisha I had wanted to be, but still, I could and would do my best to live a good life. I could surely ask for no greater blessing.

Joy flowed through my body, lifting me like the kiss of sunshine on a cloudy day. I hugged Niko tightly, and she spoke into my breasts, her voice muffled by my body.

"I knew you would get better. I told Akira and Aisha that. I told them you would never let death take you. Not you. But now that you're well again, what are we going to do, Keiko-san? There's no need for you to play at games any longer. So, what's next for us?"

TWENTY-TWO

Each new day is bright.
Each dawn, I should rise anew
And greet my fresh life

*N*iko raised her head. She was looking at me with such hope in her expression, it was all I saw, and it took a moment for her words to mean anything to me. After a while, I realized I had no answer for her. Still less for myself. I had achieved everything I had set out to do. I had made all my dreams reality. I had truly been a samurai warrior woman. If Akira was to be trusted, I had succeeded far better than I was allowing myself to believe.

Truly, all my plans had been realized. I had taken my revenge on the daimyo, Lord Akafumu, who had refused me my birthright. I was comfortable in my own mind that by giving him his just punishment, I had also avenged the deaths of my menfolk and taken vengeance for the dishonor he had brought on my ancestors. The three men who had tried to buy me from Hana had suffered for it. And out of those three, only one had died. And even then, I had killed Ikeda in a fair fight.

I frowned as I recalled Akira's words to me earlier. It shocked me as I began to wonder if he knew me better than I knew myself. I could have murdered my daimyo, Lord Akafumu, and escaped without notice. But I did not. I had used his own weakness against him and enslaved him to opium. If he had possessed strength of mind, he could have saved himself. I had given him the choice. I had turned Sato-san's father against him, so he was cut off from his only source of income and could no longer live the life of luxury he depended on. But I had not hurt him physically; it was his own greed and flawed character that had undone him. And Hara-san? I had done nothing at all to him. I had handed him over to Akira, secure in the knowledge that he would punish him for his betrayal of Akira's father.

I covered my mouth with my hand in surprise as I realized that Akira had been correct. I had used each of my enemy's weaknesses against them, just as I had been taught to deal with my opponent in martial arts. And—apart from Ikeda—I had shown mercy to each of them. I could have killed. I had chosen not to do so.

Niko was watching me hopefully, still waiting for her answer. I dragged myself back to the moment and put my hand up, asking for her patience. I needed to think.

Even though I smiled confidently at Niko, my mind was in turmoil. Although I felt Akira's words had been flattery, designed to drag my thoughts away from taking my own life, slowly I began to feel that perhaps I did have a future in this world. But at this moment, I had no idea at all what it was to be.

I took a deep breath. No matter my own doubts, I would

not lie to Niko. We had been through too much together for that. Of all people, she deserved to hear the truth from me.

"I don't know," I said finally. "I haven't looked beyond getting vengeance for my family and for myself." Niko looked so disappointed, I forced a smile. "But in a way that's good, you know. It leaves us free to do whatever we like."

She wriggled with pleasure at the inference that we would be together, and I cursed myself silently. Not only had I no idea what *I* was going to, I had now committed to taking Niko on life's journey with me.

"Of course it does." She smiled at me adoringly, her face crumpling with concern when I yawned. "Are you tired? I'm so sorry. Of course you must be. I'll leave you to sleep."

She jumped to her feet with all the agility of youth. At the door she paused, looking at me hopefully, obviously waiting to make sure there was not the slightest thing I needed. I waved her away with a smile.

A smile that faded as the shoji shut behind her.

In spite of my brave words to Niko, I felt that I was no more than an empty shell. I had nothing left for me. I reminded myself roughly that I did have something, something far more precious than was gifted to most people. I had friends who cared for me. But I could hardly spend the rest of my life relying on Akira's charity. And Aisha was the kannushi of an important temple and an old man. If I went humbly to him and asked for his compassion, he would accept me as his burden gladly. But that good man had enough responsibility already. The idea of inflicting myself on him made me flinch. Niko would follow me willingly and happily wherever I went and whatever I chose to do; I smiled at the thought. The smile faded quickly as I realized that she was part of the problem. Niko was my responsibility. Her welfare mattered far more than my own.

I tried to consider my options rationally. The man my father had selected for me to marry thought I was dead. I could hardly rise up and present myself to him as his bride. My family was dead. A ghost of hope rose as I remembered that was not strictly true. As far as I knew, my sister Emiko was still alive and presumably well. I doubted she was happy. She had done everything in her power to avoid marriage to Soji-san, the man she had been betrothed to as a child. But Father's will was not to be denied, and she had married Soji not long before my menfolk had died at the hands of our starving villagers.

Could I then go to Emiko and humble myself before her? Throw myself on her—and Soji's—charity? Soji had been fond of me when I was younger. His gentle courtesy had been virtually all the affection I had ever received. I squirmed as I remembered how I had thought myself deeply in love with him. But still, I shied away instinctively from the idea of thrusting myself on them. Unless Soji had changed significantly since his marriage, I had no doubt that he would be courteous enough to at least pretend to welcome me as family. But my sister? She had always treated me at best like a tame dog, there to amuse her. At worse, I had been nothing more than her servant, told to fetch this, do that. It was Emiko who had convinced me that I was ugly and worthless. Having learned to lead my own life and found that I did have value, could I really go back to existing as a nobody who depended on somebody else's kindness for every bite of rice, every robe in my closet? I had no need to think about it. It was unthinkable. I would beg in the streets first.

I beat my fists against my knees in sheer frustration.

I was angry with myself, and slowly I began to understand that it was my own anger that was clouding my judgment. Nothing was impossible. There had to be an answer to the way forward, and it was up to me to find it. I chided myself firmly; had I forgotten all I had ever learned?

Slowly, I began to seek the calmness of spirit that I knew would drive away all the doubts and fears. I relaxed as my mind began to empty. After an unknown time, I thought I had fallen asleep and was dreaming. I was walking in the temple that Father sponsored. Once again, I was standing in front of the old monk who was enduring self-mummification so his spirit could remain on this earth and help his fellow monks. Only now, I felt no fear at all.

I sat on the ground before him and waited silently. I sensed he was still alive and aware of my presence. He did not speak; perhaps he was already beyond forming words. It didn't matter. Gradually, the tranquility of the temple crept into me. I stared at the monk and felt his placid joy in the certainty that what he was doing was right wash over me.

And slowly but surely the answer was with me.

"Thank you," I said softly. I rose and turned to leave him. I had no physical sensation of coming back into my living body, but suddenly I was aware of the warmth of the kakebuton around me and the softness of my futon.

I had my solution. It would mean betraying Niko's trust, and I was deeply sorry about that, but she was young and resilient. Eventually, she would come to understand that I had acted for the best.

I was confident that if I made Akira listen to me while I explained to him what I had decided and why it was necessary, he would take care of Niko—for me. In time, Niko's memories of her older sister would dim. She might even come to think of me fondly. I hoped so.

My mind was focused. I had the answer I had searched

for. Tomorrow, I would go to Jokan-Ji Temple and seek a formal audience with Aisha. I would beg him to be my sponsor. He would, I thought, be joyful for me. Above all, he would understand my decision. Had he not lived the greater part of his life as a shinobi before he had been called to life as a priest?

I would enter a monastery. Shave my hair and put my past life behind me. Commit myself to a life of contemplation. I was sure that Isamu had told me that the great Tomoe Gozen had become a contemplative after the death of her beloved husband had crushed her heart. If the greatest onna-bugeisha who had ever lived could put herself away from the world, then surely I could follow her example

I called to Niko. There was no reply, and I guessed she must have taken Matsuo out. I had been so deep in my own thoughts I had not heard them go. I was relieved. Telling Niko of my decision could be postponed. But there was also someone else who had to be told, and the words would be every bit as difficult for me to say to Akira as they were going to be when I finally spoke to Niko.

I found it very strange that I—who even now would face death with a sword in my hand without a second's hesitation—should find it so very difficult to hurt others.

I ordered my thoughts very carefully. I watched Akira's face intently as I told him of my decision.

His reaction astonished me. He laughed. I was deeply disappointed at the effect my words had had on him. Had the man no understanding of how important my decision was? After all we had been through together, could he not see that this was a fitting end for me? I stared at him, schooling my face not to show my feelings. When he finally wiped away his tears of laughter, I spoke with icy calm.

"I'm delighted to have given you such pleasure Akira-san. Perhaps it can go a very small way toward repaying you for all the kindness you have shown to me in the past."

"Kindness?" Akira raised his eyebrows in apparent thought. "Now that is a word I never expected to hear you say, Keiko-chan. It is such a...*mild* sort of word. Not like you at all."

"Then it's a good word for me to choose," I said firmly. "As a nun I will need to be moderate. And kind. You will take care of Niko, won't you?"

"You mean it, don't you?" Akira's amusement faded. He stared at me as if I was a stranger to him.

"What alternative do I have?" I spoke honestly. Suddenly, my patience was at an end. I had no desire to play games; we had been through too much together, this man and me, to bother with pretense. "You have to understand, it's an honorable tradition for me to follow. I suppose it was the obvious answer all along, it just took me a while to understand that. What else is there for me? My menfolk are dead, I have no home to go to. The man I was supposed to marry thinks I'm dead. So does the rest of the world, come to that. I was raised as a noblewoman, so I couldn't hire myself out as a servant—I can't even wash or cook. I suppose if there was a war going on, I might persuade somebody to hire me as a mercenary, but I doubt I would even be able to do that. Even if I could convince some general I could be useful, they would say a woman soldier would just be a distraction for his troops. The gods have smiled on me, Akira. They have allowed me to achieve all I wanted to do in my life. This way, I have a chance to repay them for their generosity."

"And what about Yo?" Akira asked brutally. "Have you given any thought to him? Do you think he's not going to come back to Edo? If he does come back and finds you in a monastery, what will you do then? Change your mind and go back to him?"

"I don't think that's going to be a problem," I said. I wondered if Akira was jealous of Yo, but not for long. His expression was simply interested. "He obviously didn't want to take me with him when he went off on his adventures as a shinobi. And if he does come back, I have no wish at all to stay at home as a traditional wife, worrying and waiting for her man to return to her side. Besides, I think he must have forgotten about me. Or perhaps he's changed his mind about me. He's been gone for months with no word."

"If he has forgotten about you, or changed his mind, then he must be the greatest fool the earth has ever seen," Akira snapped. "In any event, put all thoughts of Yo aside, along with your plans to become a nun. You're not going to go back to Yo no more than you're going to go join a monastery. I'm not going to let you throw your life away on either."

I was both astonished and furious at the confident arrogance of his words. I stared at him in disbelief and spoke slowly and clearly, as if I was addressing a naughty child.

"Who gave you the authority to decide what I am going to do with my life? I thought you were more than just my lover, Akira. I thought you were my friend. But neither gives you the right to make decisions for me. Yo doesn't own me, and neither do you."

"I know that," he said quickly. It was clear he had seen his mistake in trying to bully me. "I'm sorry, Keiko. I spoke without thinking, but believe me, it was from my heart. Will you listen to me? Please? There is another future for you. And a far better and more meaningful one than dying slowly of boredom and regret in a monastery."

"So tell me," I said wearily. What did it matter? Whatever Akira said, he wasn't going to change my mind.

"You've really thought about this?" Did he think I was a fool, to commit the rest of my life on a whim? I stared at him in astonishment, and he spoke quickly. "I'm sorry. Of course you have. But you do have another option, Keiko-san. You can stay here, in Edo. With me."

Was he asking me to marry him? I was shocked and skeptical and amazed all at the same time, and then immediately ashamed of my reaction. I had taken Akira as my lover. Even more, I had considered him my trusted friend. He had been more than acceptable to me in both ways. I liked him more than I wanted to admit, even to myself, and I owed him a debt of gratitude I could never repay. But none of that mattered at this moment. True, I had become a ronin by my own actions; I was a samurai with no master. But for all that, I was still a samurai and always would be. I didn't think myself *better* than Akira. We were just so different, we were worlds apart. Surely, he must understand that. He must know that the gulf between us made it impossible for me to marry him. The thoughts tumbled in my head and kept me mute. I was shaping my face into an expression of polite regret when he spoke again, urgently, as if he needed to get the words out before he lost them.

"Keiko-chan, please, listen to me for just a moment. I know how much you value your traditions. I understand that, and I would never insult you by asking you to marry me. I know it would be impossible. How could an honorable samurai woman ever contemplate marriage with a humble yakuza? It would be like asking the moon to mate with a toad."

I cringed inwardly with humiliation, deeply thankful

that I had not spoken. "You do yourself no justice at all, Akira," I managed to say.

Confusion shouldered aside embarrassment rapidly. If Akira wasn't proposing to me, then what was he talking about? Did he think he could become my danna? A patron such as a geisha took? A man who would set me up in a luxurious house somewhere in the Floating World, where I could live relatively freely, so long as I was available to him when he chose to visit? So he could gloat to his friends about having a samurai woman for his concubine? A moment ago, I had felt almost sorry for him. Now, I knew how foolishly I had mistaken his intentions. I was grateful I had no weapon to hand to strike him with.

"I understand that you think going into a monastery is the only way forward for you. The only honorable option you have." Akira was leaning toward me, as if to emphasize his words. I sat very still, listening with apparent courtesy. "Just try and forget about your code of the samurai for a moment. Think of yourself. Is this truly what you want? To be shut away from the world for the rest of your life? To do nothing, see nobody except your fellow nuns. To spend your days in prayer and contemplation and nothing else? Even the gods would weep that you had left the world behind you for such a life. It's wrong for you, Keiko. You would suffer every moment of every day. And you don't have to waste your life in that way. I promise you, there is another way."

"You haven't listened to a word I said." I was quite surprised by how calm I sounded. "It's not a matter of wanting to enter a monastery. I haven't suddenly discovered I have a vocation. No matter what you think, I have no other choice. I have nobody and nothing in this world except my poor Niko, who would no doubt willingly enter the monastery with me. But I hope that isn't necessary, that I can rely on your charity to care for her."

I put a light emphasis on the word "nobody," hoping he would understand it was aimed at him.

"Of course I'll take care of Niko." Akira sounded so surprised that I needed to ask that I felt ashamed yet again. "If you insist on following this nonsense, then it will give me pleasure to take care of her. At least she would remind me of you. Just think, we could spend the long, winter evenings together exchanging our memories of you. Of how selfish you were in insisting that you had to sacrifice yourself. How you were so blinded by the code of bushido, you had no thought for anything else. And above all, how you were so proud of your samurai tradition, you could never lower yourself to the level of us common folk."

It was not the answer I had expected. My fingers bent and ground into my palms. I was so enraged, I could barely breathe. Was Akira deliberately refusing to understand what I was telling him? I had taken this thug for my lover, even believed that we were equals in most things. I winced as I understood how very wrong I had been about that. And no doubt about much else.

"Thank you for your kindness toward Niko, Akira-san." I spoke icily, as though his words had left me untouched. "Since Niko's welfare is settled, I shall go with a light heart. I hope the kannushi at Jokan-Ji Temple will be my sponsor. Thank you for all you have done for me. I will be sure to remember you in my prayers."

I stood up. I had sat for too long and my muscles were cramped. I stumbled slightly as I walked and my awkwardness annoyed me even more. All the way to the shoji, I expected to hear Akira's voice calling me back, apologizing, explaining that he had spoken in anger and he regretted it. I heard nothing at all except a sharp clap of his hands as I slid the screen back.

TWENTY-THREE

My back is straight as
Reeds that stand above a pond.
Like them, will I break?

I was immediately as tense as a warrior's bow pulled taught and ready to fire. Had Akira's signal been to summon his yakuza to stop me from leaving? Was I about to be faced with as many armed men who could crowd into the doorway? I took a deep breath, relishing the conflict to come. I was unarmed, but it didn't matter. I would die rather than be taken in battle. The thought was sweet. I would meet my end as a true samurai warrior after all. How much better than to spend the rest of my life in contemplation. If I survived long enough to speak, I would thank Akira for his kindness. I was delighted that I had misjudged him, that he had understood me all along.

My absurd sense of anticlimax was so deep I groaned out loud. There was not a single man in the corridor. Not even a servant. I bent to pat the dog that stood before me, barely reaching my knee with the top of her head. Marika,

Akira's beautiful, white shiba inu. Marika and I were old friends and I was surprised when she bared her teeth at me and growled, deep in her throat.

"Marika," I scolded. "Have you forgotten me?" Shiba inu are famous for their vocalizations. If they are excited or very pleased to see someone, their usual response is to throw back their heads and scream like a woman—the famous shiba inu scream—and also Marika's normal greeting for me. I put my hand out for her to sniff but snatched it back as she snapped at me.

"Marika will not hurt you. Not unless I tell her to." Akira sounded smug. I turned to stare at him, and he clicked his fingers crisply. Marika moved forward immediately, herding me in front of her implacably.

I knew it was ridiculous, but the dog's aggression upset me. I had thought her my friend—just as I had thought her master my friend.

"Why have you turned her against me?" I demanded. "Marika, let me pass. I want to leave."

Marika wagged her tail and growled deep in her throat at the same time. I clicked my fingers at her, but she stood her ground.

"I'm afraid she will not let you pass. Not until *I* tell her to let you go. And the gods will walk the earth again before I do that." Akira's voice sounded perfectly reasonable in spite of what he was saying.

"You're mad," I told him.

"No, not at all." Akira clapped his hands again and then dipped his hand toward the tatami at his side. Marika moved forward relentlessly. When I didn't move, she darted forward and nipped my ankle. Her teeth barely grazed my skin, but the shock was far greater than any pain she had inflicted. I backed away and sat down where Akira had indicated, stunned into obedience. "I knew you would never hurt Marika. If I had shouted for my men, you would have been delighted. You would have died a happy woman if it had been necessary."

How well the damned man knew me! And how very dishonorable of him to use my own weakness against me. He knew I loved animals and that I would never dream of kicking out at poor Marika, who was only doing her duty and obeying her master. As soon as I sat down, she stopped growling and threw herself at me, fawning and whimpering in apology. I accepted her regrets and scratched behind her ear.

"Such a lucky dog," Akira said wryly. I refused to answer him, staring straight through him as if he wasn't there, and spoke only when I was certain I had my anger sufficiently under control that my voice did not shake.

"You've made your point. I understand I can't leave until you allow it. But that doesn't mean I have to listen to you."

"I suppose not." Akira spoke calmly, but I was certain I detected something hidden in his voice. Anger? No, not anger. Pain. I was certain of it, and it confused me.

His expression was open to me, and I knew at once that I was right. I could read pain in his eyes, those beautiful grey eyes that normally glinted coldly but were now soft and deeply unhappy. His mouth, too, was oddly vulnerable. It was a strange thing. I had been prepared to inflict hurt on those men who I knew deserved punishment and until recently had thought nothing of it. I had seen myself as no more than the mechanism to inflict that punishment. Yet the sight of Akira's naked, troubled expression inflicted deep regret in my soul. I spoke hesitatingly.

"You can't keep me here forever. I understand that you don't agree with my decision, but it's the only way forward for me." Perhaps if I repeated that often enough, he would understand.

"You haven't listened to a word I've said," Akira said very softly. I began to protest, and he raised his hand to stop me. "No. Let me speak. This time, listen to what I'm saying. When I've finished, if you still want to leave, I promise I won't stop you."

"Very well. Tell me. Again!" I shrugged and tried for lightness, and then wished I had not. It was evident that Akira was deadly serious.

"If there really were no other option for you, then I would agree. Painful as the thought is, a monastery would be the only place you could live out your life with any sort of purpose. And it is, of course, the traditional route for a woman from good family who wishes to renounce her life. But it's not for you, Keiko-chan. There is another way for you. Stay here, in the Floating World, as my partner."

I was shaking my head before he finished speaking. We had already been through this! Akira had said bluntly that he understood we could never marry. I had surely made it plain that I agreed with him. So why was he persisting with this nonsense?

"I heard you say that the first time," I said bluntly.

"You didn't listen then, and you're not listening now," he said wearily. "I am making a proposal to you, Keiko. But it's purely business. Not pleasure, I assure you. I'm asking you to be my business partner. Everything I inherited, everything I've built up myself, I want you to be part of it. I want us to work together. Between us, I know we can achieve true greatness."

I stared at him intently. I was sure that if I stayed silent long enough, his serious face would crack and he would laugh. Hold his hands up and admit he was doing no more than trying to detain me, to put off the moment when I finally walked away. Or perhaps he was genuinely hurt by my decision and this was his way of trying to get back at me, by mocking my ambitions.

I gritted my teeth with anger as I thought that if he was ridiculing me, then he had succeeded all too well. His proposal was even more ludicrous than the notion that he wanted to marry me. It was appalling nonsense. Me, the daughter of a samurai, enter willingly into the nasty, dirty business of the most feared yakuza in Edo?

"Thank you." Akira was watching me intently. Very well. He would get his answer. "It's an interesting proposal. But what would you see me doing exactly? Am I to visit merchants who haven't paid their tea money to you and threaten them into paying up? Or perhaps you see my role more as a protector of your tea houses? Or am I perhaps to take over Hana's role and peddle her flawed jewels to those who have the inclination for something different? And the money to pay for it, of course."

I was smiling widely, as if I really was amused by his offer. I hoped Akira would be deeply hurt by my words. Just as deeply hurt as I was by his insult. What a fool I had been. I had trusted this man. I had taken him as my lover, and I had really thought that he understood me. Perhaps even loved me. Well, let this be a lesson to me for the future. Trust no man. And I had even thought I saw pain in his expression earlier. What a consummate actor he was.

"Have I been very foolish, I wonder? I'm normally an excellent judge of character." Akira was staring at me as if he was trying to read beyond my expression. "I thought from the first moment I met you that you were the woman I had dreamed of. That you would understand my hopes and ambitions like nobody else, and that I in my turn would respect your ideals. That we would be perfect together, just as the gods intended us to be. But now it seems as if we're so far apart that we don't understand a single word the other is saying, as if we're speaking to each other in languages neither of us understands."

Marika put her head on my knee and sighed heavily. I patted her absently. I was bewildered. He sounded so weary, I wondered reluctantly if it was I who had misunderstood him. I hesitated, and then spoke softly.

"I don't understand, Akira-chan." I saw the faintest of smiles lift his lips at the endearment. I gathered my thoughts and spoke very carefully. "A while ago, you said our worlds were so far apart that you could never dream of asking me to marry you. And now you say you want us to be business partners. It seems to me that either way, we would be dependent on each other. That our paths in life would follow the same route." I paused and shrugged. "And I have to tell you, I know even less about any sort of business than I do about being a wife. I imagine I would be equally bad at either."

The tension broke with an almost audible snap. Akira smiled and I smiled hesitantly back. I wondered why, if he was as good a judge of character as he thought he was, he didn't see that my smile was as brittle as thin ice?

"I'm sure you're right," Akira said. I pretended to be hurt that he was agreeing with me. When I realized I *was* hurt, I carried on smiling. "It would mean a great deal of learning for both of us. Just like you, I've always walked alone. I've never trusted anybody but myself." I bowed my head silently in acknowledgment; were we so very far apart, after all? "But I know I could trust you—with my life if necessary. And I hope that you feel the same way about me."

He paused and I broke in and spoke my own thoughts

out loud. "Forgive me, Akira. I have to be honest. You are yakuza. You don't buy anything. You don't sell anything. Your money is earned through fear. Merchants and tea houses give you tea money to protect them. They pay you rather than other yakuza because they fear you more. I don't know, but I suspect you trade in opium, probably in slaves as well, keeping the brothels supplied with new women. And no doubt there are other unsavory dealings that I don't even want to think about."

I had spoken impulsively. Did I regret my bluntness? I decided I did not. Akira spoke of trust. Now was surely the time to be honest.

"Yes, you're right," he said simply. He held his hands up, palms out toward me. "All of that. And as you say, much more. I am feared, and there is good reason for that. If you want me to tell you everything I find it necessary to do each and every day, everything I have done in the past, then I will tell you everything. I can't change anything that's gone already. But if you agree to commit to me, then in the future, my hands will be perfectly clean."

Akira had raised such a conflict of emotions in my mind, I was dizzy. I put my hands to my head, tugging at my hair as I tried to drag what mattered to the forefront of my mind. All at once, I knew that he was right about one thing, at least. The prospect of spending the rest of my life in a monastery was literally unthinkable. I had been wrong to consider it. But was Akira's most bizarre of offers any more worthy of consideration? Could I help him bully and cheat and lie? Inflict pain on those who did not deserve it simply for profit? Probably even kill and torture just to maintain his reputation? Could I do that and live with myself? Of course I could not. Nor could I ever help him come to terms with what he did.

He was still holding his hands up. I stared at his palms, clean and white but calloused from the grip of his sword, and I wondered all over again if he could truly believe what he was saying to me.

"You're a yakuza. Just as I'm a samurai," I said hesitatingly. "Neither of us knows anything else. I can't change. Can you?"

"Yes." The answer came so quickly it startled me. "I can change. I can't erase what I've already done. It was my tradition just as much as the code of bushido is yours and I must live with my past. But I've changed already. *You* changed me. Do you remember telling me about the Shop of Dreams? How the merchant, Ota-san, said that only I would be able to save him and the tradition of his shop when the gaijin came and changed everything in our country?"

"I remember," I agreed. I also remembered Akira's delight when I had passed Ota's strange message to him. "But what does that have to do with...with us?"

"Everything. I have power now. And money. I'm feared. Mothers use my name to frighten their children into doing as they're told. But it's not enough, Keiko. I'm a young man and already I have achieved all my ambitions. Just as you have. And just like you, I've wondered what's left for the rest of my life. But unlike you, I'm not hiding from it," he added shrewdly. I frowned at him, but he carried on anyway. "I want more. Far more. I don't want to die as just a yakuza, not even a powerful one. When the day comes that Ota-san needs me to defend him and the whole of Edo—who knows, perhaps even the rest of our beloved country—I want to be able to do it. Cleanly and openly and with honor, not underhanded through fear and pain. I want to be remembered as a great warrior who saved our country in its hour of greatest need. Do you understand that? Do you understand *me*, Keiko?"

"Yes."

I wanted to say more, but the words wouldn't come. I felt an overwhelming pity for Akira. His dreams were ashes already. There would never be a time when a yakuza—no matter what he achieved—would be seen as anything but riverbed beggars by those who thought themselves above them. The world would be turned inside out before that could be. And I understood now why he wanted me by his side. Not for love, but for what I was. I was samurai by birth. I held the keys to doors he could never open. I spoke a language that was foreign to his tongue. I knew—had known—the *right* people. With me to help him, he hoped he would surmount the mountain he could not conquer alone. I knew I had to destroy his dreams, now, before the hurt could be even greater. For the sake of both of us.

"Will you come to me, then?" Akira turned a shining face toward me. "At least at first as a business partner?" I wondered at his words, but I barely had time to consider what he meant before he was rushing on. "You must know I would never ask you to dirty your hands, to do anything that was at all dishonorable. But I need you to help me. To teach me manners. To stop me insulting my *betters*—" His voice was ironic as he spoke that word. "—without realizing I'm doing it. To help persuade those who I need to recognize me, not to look through me as if I'm nothing more than a burakumin. I want you to guide me. To be at my side. I'm not going to ask anything else of you now. I know any other sort of bond between us would be impossible, at least at the moment."

You might as well ask the moon to mate with a toad, he had said. Would that be so very impossible when Akira the yakuza became Akira the respectable and respected member of society? When the world turned on its axis and everything changed? The thought frightened me. Even more terrible was the knowledge that I had allowed myself to fall at least a little in love with this man. And even as I acknowledged it to myself, I thought about what he had just said. Was I fooling myself when I thought that Akira also cared for me? Was his offer of a business partnership actually just a tentative beginning of something else entirely between us? And if it was, did I want it?

I was thrown completely off balance. Life had been so much easier when I had relied on the code of bushido to guide me. When emotions had been unnecessary and everything was clear and sharp. Suddenly, I understood that there was far greater pain than anything that could be inflicted by my sword.

"Akira, it's not going to happen." I would deal with the practicalities first. Head before heart. At least that way I had a little more time to think. "You know how society is structured. The shogun rules the daimyo and the daimyo rule the samurai and the rest of the world is simply beneath all of them. That's how it's always been, how it will always be. And you're forgetting that I now have no status at all. Lady Keiko is dead. I'm just as much a nothing as you are. I have nothing left that could help you."

If I could have snatched the words back, I would have done so instantly. Akira was offering to share everything he had with me and I had thrown it back in his face contemptuously. I was both relieved and surprised to see he was smiling.

"You think so? You haven't heard about the new production at the kabuki, then?" I stared at him in confusion, wondering if he had run mad completely. "No, of course you haven't. You were ill for weeks. The new play is already a tremendous success. It tells the tragic story of the samurai lady who had the courage of a samurai warrior. The lady who was cheated out of her inheritance by her daimyo and committed suicide rather than allow herself to be married off to an old man. That wouldn't be enough on its own, of course, so the kabuki has added an amazing twist to the tale. In the play, the samurai lady's spirit comes back to earth to take vengeance on the daimyo who cheated her. I understand the theater's packed for each performance. The authorities are not at all happy about it. I've heard that they feel it will incite the insurgents even more. But of course, there's nothing any of them can do about it. The kabuki and the bunraku puppet theatres have always been above the law in the same way that they have always been the voice of the people. And I promise you, the people are very much on the lady's side. You see? You think you're nothing when in reality, I should be on my knees before you, begging the new legend of the Floating World if she could possibly help me in any way she saw fit."

I stared at him, literally lost for words. How many times had I reproached Niko for confusing reality with a kabuki play? And now—if Akira was telling the truth—I had become the heroine of a play myself. It was absurd, yet I felt a smile tugging at my lips.

"If you're basing your whole future on a silly play, then I beg you to think again," I said firmly. "You know the Floating World much better than I could ever hope to. This play might have caught the imagination of the people today, but next week there'll be a new sensation to take its place and I'll be forgotten."

Akira shook his head. "No. It's you who doesn't understand. The play was produced because the kabuki heard of the interest in you. They could hardly not have heard. The whole of the Floating World is buzzing with the gossip. It's fate again, you must see that. Ota-san asked you to help him."

I put my hand up to silence him. "No. All Ota-san asked me was to deliver the message to you. It's you who's going to save the Floating World, not me."

Akira was shaking his head. Although his body was still, I sensed eagerness in the way he was leaning forward.

"And have you never thought why he chose you to deliver the message, Keiko-chan? You must see, our fates are entwined. Together, we can do great things."

I bit my lip in indecision. The kabuki was irrelevant. In spite of that, I was proud that it appeared my deeds had met with approval. Could Akira and I together really influence the future of a whole country? My natural modesty made me want to shake my head at the idea. And yet, when Akira spoke of fate it seemed to be...sensible.

I spoke before I knew what my words were going to be. "If you're right, if the gods will it, then perhaps. But you must understand, above all I'm still a warrior woman of the samurai. That is the path in life I've chosen for myself. I've gone too far to leave it behind now. And I don't want to. I know now that I haven't failed the code of bushido. And I have no intention of doing so in the future. It will always come first with me, and I will never do anything that would go against it. Does that make you change your mind about wanting me as your business partner? Knowing you would be second to an ideal?"

"Not at all," Akira said promptly. "Your ideals are what make you unique. That's why you've become a legend, a heroine of the people. You can't abandon them, Keiko. You've given them hope that things can be questioned.

Perhaps even changed. All of that is why I want you by my side. All I ask is that you stay here and help me if your conscience allows it. I truly believe that together, we can do great things."

I wanted to believe him. Wanted to think that somehow I could right wrongs in a way that had never been possible in the past. He was staring at me intently and I thought, "Why not?" If he was wrong, then I could walk away. And if he was right? Ah, who knew what could happen.

TWENTY-FOUR

The rose is lovely.
Beware! Her thorns can rip and
Catch you unaware.

I reassured myself constantly. I had not committed to Akira in any way. We had parted with understanding. I had promised him that I would not run off to a monastery. That I would return to him with an answer. Although I knew what my answer was going to be.

I could not forget Ota-san's simple conviction that only Akira could defend the Floating World when the time came. And if Akira was right when he insisted that Ota-san had chosen me to bear his message for a reason, then it was only right that I took Akira up on his offer. And apart from that, surely it was my duty under the code of bushido to help turn this terrifying yakuza into a truly decent man. Others might think it a strange way of expressing the code of the samurai, but to my mind, it was perfectly logical. At least, it was if I didn't think about it too deeply.

And of course, there was the business of the kabuki play

written about me. I would ask Niko if that was true. She would know, and if it were true, she would be delighted. I wondered absently why she had not mentioned it to me and decided almost at once that I knew the reason why. She would have thought I would be angry about it after all the times I had scolded her about not confusing art with reality.

The sun was shining serenely. Even the Floating World looked as if it had been cleansed by the light. It seemed to me that the people I passed in the streets were happier than usual; that their normal, brisk pace had slowed to a stroll. Even the constant whine of the beggars was less irritating. I threw a coin to one woman and instead of howling her thanks loudly, she simply smiled and clapped her hands.

I was so delighted by this other face of the Floating World that I was surprised to find that Niko wasn't at one with the perfection of everything.

"Keiko-san, where have you been all this time?" she scolded as soon as I slid back our shoji. I had intended to tell her about my conversation with Akira at once. I wanted to reassure her that whatever happened, all would be well for her. That in time, she would come to regard him more than I did. Not with liking, at least not at first. That was asking too much of my stubborn younger sister. But surely it wasn't too much to hope that she would show him respect for the good qualities I was sure lurked beneath his cold exterior?

I was very thankful that I hadn't told her of my decision to enter a monastery. Now, the idea seemed so desperately wrong it made me blush with embarrassment to even think of it.

"Why such a hurry, Niko?" I asked casually. "I had some business I needed to discuss with Akira-san. You had gone out. I couldn't tell you where I was going. Were you worried about me?"

"Yes, I was. But it's not that." Niko was fidgeting in impatience. I felt my anticipation for our future life begin to ebb away as I saw her anxious expression. I wanted to shake my head, tell her that whatever news she had for me, I didn't want to hear it. But Niko carried on anyway. "It's Aisha. He sent a priest with a message for you. He wants you to go to Jokan-Ji Temple straight away. When I told the priest you weren't here, he said it was very important and could you please go to the temple as soon as you got back."

"Did he say what he wanted me for?" Anxiety was laying cold fingers on my heart. I looked at Niko, willing her to tell me it was good news.

"No. I asked him, but the priest said Aisha hadn't told him anything else. Just that you were to go to the temple at once."

"Well, in that case, we'd better get on our way."

Niko brightened immediately at the idea that she was to come with me. I felt tenderness for her and wondered absently how I had come to love my younger sister so greatly when not long ago we had been strangers to each other. Was this how a mother felt for her child? Yesterday, the thought would have been ridiculous; today, I understood it perfectly.

Niko fell into step behind me automatically. One day, I was sure, she would be her own woman. She would step in nobody's shadow. Perhaps all women would be like that in the far distant future. I remembered the gaijin, Adam, telling me that in his country, men were courteous to women, putting their needs before their own. At the time, I had thought it beyond belief. Now, I wondered. The thought was both pleasant and deeply disturbing. Surely, if women ever came to be worshipped almost as goddesses, there would be no need for onna-bugeisha to fight for their place alongside their men. And if that was so, what need would there be for the likes of me?

I shrugged the thought away. No matter what the future held, it would never be perfect. Mankind would always covet what it did not have. I was certain there would always be the need for a code of honor to put right the wrongs of the world.

Lost in my thoughts, I walked quickly. Poor Niko was almost panting when we reached the temple. The door was flung wide and the temple was already crowded. None of the male pilgrims stepped aside for us; so much for my thoughts of a world where men were unfailingly courteous to their women! I was about to use my elbows to push our way through, but I had no need. A muscular young monk strode toward us, parting the crowd effortlessly before him.

"Keiko-san." He bowed politely to me. "The kannushi asked me to keep watch for you and bring you to him as soon as you arrived."

I felt the eyes of the crowd watching us with interest as we followed our escort to Aisha's apartment.

"Keiko-san." Some of my apprehension flowed away as I looked at the kannushi's face. As always, he seemed perfectly serene. "I apologize for summoning you in such an abrupt manner. I assure you, I would never have done so if the matter hadn't been important."

He glanced at Niko and smiled. "Niko-chan, would you like to go to the kitchen? I believe the cook is making wagashi as a treat for us. I'm sure he would be happy to spare you a few of them."

I was about to tell Aisha that Niko was entitled to hear whatever he had to tell me, then I saw her greedy expression and I smiled. It was far too easy to forget that Niko was still a child who was easily tempted by the offer of sticky cakes and sweetmeats.

"Go on," I told her. "But don't eat so many that you're sick!"

Niko hesitated for a moment, then her greed won out. She was gone in a heartbeat.

"Aisha-san." I smiled politely. The kannushi must have read the anxiety in my body. He sighed heavily and stared at me with his old man's rheumy eyes. I knew instinctively he had bad news for me. Was I fated to always bring this good man pain? "What is it, Aisha-san? What's happened that you needed to speak to me so urgently?"

"I'm sorry to have summoned you so hastily, Keiko-san." He pursed his mouth and his top lip almost disappeared in a nest of wrinkles. "It's important, or I would not have disturbed you. I have had a message from Yo. It came this morning. I sent the messenger for you as soon as I read it."

I wanted to give Aisha my apologies and then stand up and walk away without hearing any more. I had thought Yo was gone from my life. I had come to terms with that. Surely the gods could not be so cruel as to snatch me back from the very threshold of my new life?

I would not let it happen. I had made my decision. Yo had walked out of my life. I no longer had any obligation to him. Whatever Aisha was about to tell me, I did not want to hear it. I noticed absently that my lips felt parched. They rasped when I licked them. I took a deep, calming breath. Surely it was possible that Aisha was going to tell me that Yo had written to tell him he was not coming back. That he was sorry, but he had found that he no longer cared about me. Perhaps Aisha's obvious distress was because he thought he was about to inflict pain on me. If that were the case, I would be only too pleased to reassure him that he was wrong.

I knew I was lying to myself almost before the thought was finished. Yo would never do that to me. If he were too ashamed to come back and tell me to my face that there was no longer anything in his heart for me, at the very least he would have written to me. In his own way, he was an honorable man. Just as Akira had honor. I winced at the thought, wishing I had not made the comparison.

"Is he on his way back to Edo at last?" I asked drily. My head was pounding. Why did it have to be today that I heard from Yo? Not fair! Not fair at all!

I knew Aisha felt my distress, and I understood he was disturbed for himself as well. Yo was not just his friend, but they had been brothers in arms. He did not speak but reached into his sleeve and handed me a slip of parchment. The message was brief, and I saw before I read it that it was not in Yo's hand. I frowned. Why would he seek out a calligrapher for such a short message?

Aisha.

I am afraid that my business here is taking rather longer than I anticipated. Please, do not worry. I will be back as soon as I can.

Yo

"Oh." I frowned with surprise and disappointment. I had hoped for closure. This message was nothing but another postponement. "I'm sorry, Aisha. I don't understand. This message doesn't seem at all urgent. Why did you want to see me straight away?"

I watched him, understanding instantly that there was more to the brief message than I knew. The kannushi's face was set and his eyes were heavy with worry. He tapped his finger on the parchment.

"It's not supposed to seem urgent. You must understand, we have a code, Yo and I. It was always so amongst the shinobi brotherhood. When one of us went on a mission, it was arranged beforehand that if there was danger and it was possible to get a message back, it would contain a certain word. I will not waste your time now explaining the system of words. All that matters is that he has written the word 'afraid.'"

"Yes," I said reluctantly. "But surely that's just politeness? Yo apologizing that he will be away for longer than he expected?"

"That is the point of a code word, Keiko-san," Aisha said quietly. "It has to appear to be nothing important. And do you really think he wouldn't have mentioned your name if he was not writing this under duress?" I tensed and he reached out and patted my hand. "This is difficult for you, I know. He did not mention you on purpose, to ensure that there was no danger for you. I am sorry. The word 'afraid' means that there is great danger for Yo. He has been taken. He dictated this message and it was sent by his enemies to make us think that all was well with him."

I sat very still. My eyes were focused on the tatami, but I did not see it. Aisha was silent and did not move. He knew what was going through my thoughts. Old he may be, but none of his senses had been dimmed by the passage of time. He knew—or guessed—that the message from Yo was not welcome to me. He probably regretted having to give me the message, but he understood that when it mattered, the samurai code of honor would always come first for me.

Yo had been taken. And he was calling for me to help him. I could not refuse him, no matter what the decision meant to my future. Ice gripped me as my vision narrowed to that one simple fact. I had no choice. I had embraced the way of life that was onna-bugeisha. I had known all along that there was no turning back from it, even when I had tried to fool myself into thinking I could somehow dilute its demands.

Without the code of bushido, I had no honor. Without honor, my life had no meaning. Still, I tried to reason with myself. I had thought Yo was in my past. Just because he had suddenly stepped back into my life as if by magic, did that really mean I had to put my own my life aside for him?

Aisha was staring at me silently. I glanced at him, hoping I would find something in his expression that would help me. His face was open and very calm. I understood dully that he could not help me. The choice was mine and mine alone. But I had no choice. I had forfeited the right to choice on the day I became onna-bugeisha. Of course, I could still walk away. I could shrug and tell Aisha that I was very sorry, but my relationship with Yo ended the day he left me behind. I was about to begin a new life with Akira. I intended to do a great deal of good in that life. Surely that was a reasonable enough excuse for stepping away from Yo's cry for help.

I could do that. And if I did? If I betrayed the man who had been both my lover and my friend when he called out to me for help? The man who had risked his own life to free me? I sighed. What was the point in even considering it? If I left Yo to his fate, then I would end my own life. Oh, surely, my body would continue to function. I would wake each morning. I would do my best to help Akira achieve his ambitions. I would make sure that Niko had a good life. But the essential me that lived inside my flesh would have changed. Whatever I did, I would live with the knowledge that I had walked away from a man who loved me because it no longer suited my plans to help him.

My life would be grey from the moment my decision was taken. And I would deserve it.

I was so sorry for myself, I wanted to cry. The knowledge that I had only myself to blame was the final weight that tipped the scales. Why hadn't I been content with my life? If I had obeyed my father, been a dutiful daughter and married the man he had selected for me, I would not be in this predicament. If I hadn't been determined to become onna-bugeisha, I could have lived my life in contentment. If I hadn't been weak enough to be tempted by Akira, I wouldn't have been torn like this.

I raised my head and saw Aisha smiling at me.

"One cannot change one's fate, daughter," he said calmly. I smiled back wearily. Of course not. Just as nobody could turn back time. I had decided on my path in life. Whether I regretted it at this moment mattered not at all. I almost laughed as I remembered thinking that I was no longer fit to be onna-bugeisha. That I would never be a true samurai warrior woman.

I had almost convinced myself. Almost, but not quite. And now I knew that I would never be free of the burden I had chosen for myself, no matter how painful the decisions I had to make were.

Yo, I am coming for you. My mind spoke to his mind, and I hoped he would hear. Also did I hope that all he heard was my message of faith, and none of the uncertainty that lay behind it.

"Is there anything I can do to help you?" Aisha's asked quietly. Just like Yo's note, his words seemed innocuous. I took his wrinkled old hand and held on to it, wishing I could explain how my feelings were tearing me apart. I met his gaze and I knew there was no point. He knew. Just as he had known all along what my decision would be.

"No, I don't think so. Not at the moment. But thank you," I said politely,

"I'm sorry, child. Life can be difficult. But one must always follow one's heart."

I stared at the scroll behind his head, wondering bitterly if he could hear my heart breaking.

TWENTY-FIVE

Even if I choose
To ignore it, the path I
Tread is still jagged

*H*ave you ever stood on a sandy beach and watched as a gigantic wave pounded the shore? If you have, you must surely have wondered how it was possible for the sand to be no more than just a little wet when the wave went back to its home in the sea.

Nothing but a pleasant, philosophical musing, that. Nothing at all compared to how I felt as I watched Akira's face. I saw him nod thoughtfully and I wondered if it was possible for him to be as truly unsurprised as he appeared to be at my news. As unmoved and unchanged as the unfeeling sand once the sea has left it.

He was smiling in obvious anticipation when I walked into his home. He rose to greet me, his hands held out in welcome. He must have intuited something was wrong. Before I could speak a word, his smile faded and he stared at me seriously.

"Keiko, welcome." He paused, obviously waiting for me to speak.

I had been in a daze on the walk across the Floating World from the temple to his house. Now, I wished I had thought a little about what I was going to say. How I was going to break my news to him. As it was, I blurted the words quickly, simply anxious to get it over and done with.

"Aisha has received a message from Yo. He's in serious trouble, and he needs me to go to him straight away to help him."

I knew at once I had used the wrong word. I had said *needs* not *wants*. Akira picked up on the difference immediately, I could see in his expression. Had I said *wants*, there could have been some leeway in the matter. But I had not. I had said he *needed* me. And bound as I was by the code of bushido, how could I refuse a cry for help that came from the heart of a...friend?

"You're going to him," Akira said flatly.

"I feel I have to. Yo saved me from Hana when she had me imprisoned. If nothing else, I have to repay him for that."

"I would have saved you." Akira's voice struck like a lash. "If I had been in the Floating World at the time, you know I would never have allowed Hana to keep you for a moment."

"But you weren't in the Floating World." I tried to speak reasonably. "It wasn't in your power to save me. The gods decreed that it should be Yo. And now it is my turn to save him."

"One man, Keiko?" For a moment, I was puzzled. I stared at Akira, trying to make sense of his words. "For one man, you would abandon all our plans to save the whole of Edo when the time comes? Does Yo weigh so heavily on your heart that you would be prepared to do that?"

Fool that I was, I was pleased by Akira's words. I had an answer for him, one that would make everything right again.

"I feel I must go to him. But I will come back, Akira. And when I do, then we can begin our partnership. It's just put on hold for a short time, not finished."

I was so satisfied with my solution it took me a moment to see the hurt in Akira's face. Before I could do more than wonder at it, his emotions were under control and he spoke quietly.

"I see. Of course, you must do what you think is best."

He steepled his fingers beneath his chin and looked at me calmly. All at once, he was a stranger to me.

"It's not a matter of what I think is best. Yo needs me. I have to go to him. But I will come back, I promise you."

"I suppose you will come back. But I'm afraid that when you do, the time will have passed for us. You can come back, but it will not be to me."

I was bewildered. We had agreed that no matter what, I would never abandon the code of bushido. Couldn't he understand that my response to Yo was governed by that? I had said I would come back—to Akira—as soon as I possibly could. What was it that he was unable to understand?

I was hurt and bewildered. I spoke abruptly, wanting to goad him into telling me what was behind his curt words.

"I don't suppose it will make any difference to your plans whether I'm here or not. I seem to remember that Ota-san was convinced it was you that mattered. All he wanted me for was to pass his message on to you."

"Really? I had forgotten that. No doubt you're right. In that as in so much else." Akira bowed his head politely. "Thank you for coming to give me the news yourself. I appreciate the courtesy. Now, I expect you'll want to go as soon as possible. May I help with your plans in any way? Are you taking Niko with you, or would you like her to stay here with me? Do you need any help with documentation?"

I shrugged. It was a casual gesture that said nothing of my mental struggle. I cleared my throat and spoke as colorlessly as Akira had a moment before. I would take my lead from him. We would part as friends, with neither anger nor regret between us. That was surely the best thing for both of us. I was lying to myself, I knew that perfectly well. But I had no other option.

If I forgot myself so far as to humble myself before him and beg him to wait for me and to understand what I needed to do, could I do that? And if I did, and he was still ice, what then? No, better not to take the chance.

"That's very kind. But I'm taking Niko with me. She'll be quite safe, I'll make sure of that. If you could help get the right passes for both of us, I would be very grateful." How very polite I sounded! As if Akira and I were discussing things that mattered not at all. "As you know, I'm not that good at practical matters. I intend to travel as a merchant's widow out to visit my sister in Kyoto who has fallen ill. Niko will travel with me as my maid."

Akira inclined his head. "Of course. That's the least I can do." Marika was sitting on the tatami between us. She seemed to sense the strangeness between her master and me. Her head swiveled between us and her eyes were puzzled. I patted her gently, lowering my head so I couldn't see Akira's face. "You'll be taking Matsuo, of course?"

"Naturally." As soon as I said it, I wondered if I should have asked Akira to take care of him for me. Absurdly, I felt as if I was deliberately removing every trace of me from his life.

"I'll have the passes for you tomorrow morning. I'll send them to the temple for you." Akira rose and bowed.

"Thank you." There was nothing else I could say. His final words hung between us, a barrier that I could never surmount. He did not want to see me again, just as I had no reason ever to see him again. The thought made me want to cry. Surely this could not be right? After all that had passed between us, how could I walk away as carelessly as if I was going to return tomorrow?

He came to the shoji with me and watched as I slipped on my zori. My feet were on the garden path before he spoke again.

"It is I who should thank you, Keiko-san. I understand now that I have been very foolish for some time. I thought I could leave my old life behind me and start a fresh life. Forget the traditions of my ancestors and become something I am not." He paused. I was about to speak—although I had no idea what words would come out—but Akira raised his hand abruptly and silenced me. "We are what the gods will for us. I understand that now. I believe it is past time that I showed some solidarity for my own men. That I reminded them that I am truly one with them and will never leave them." I almost reared back with shock as he pulled his robe apart to bare his chest. "You are the last woman who will ever see my naked flesh. Tomorrow, I will arrange for the irezumi tattooist to come to me. As soon as he can do it, my body will be hidden by the glorious tradition of yakuza."

I put my hand out and laid it flat on his warm flesh. "I'm sorry." I choked. I felt him flinch and snatched my hand away. It was unexpected, but a flash of understanding came with the touch. Akira—the yakuza who was so feared that strong men quailed at the sound of his name—was jealous.

He thought that I had put Yo before him and he could not live with that. Almost did I say then that I would stay. I could not forget Yo, but oddly I guessed that if I appealed to Akira to help him, then he would not hesitate to agree.

Akira was staring at me. I knew that he was waiting, hoping that I would change my mind at the last moment. And I wanted to do that almost as much as I knew I was and always would be a warrior woman of the samurai. That the code of the samurai would always come above my own desires.

I was once again onna-bugeisha. And I had no choice.

"I hope you are successful in your quest." Akira lowered his head, and I thought for a moment he was going to kiss my cheek. Instead, he shook his head as if brushing away an annoying fly. "Goodbye, Keiko-chan."

I had hoped at the very least that he might say he was sorry, perhaps even try and persuade me to change my mind, but he did not. I turned away and heard the shoji slide shut firmly. There was a curious pain beneath my ribs, and the sun was no longer shining. I remembered feeling the same pain when I had found the bodies of my father and brother. But then, of course, I had had Yo to rescue me from my despair. Just as I was now going to rescue Yo.

It was odd, but the knowledge left me untouched.

Marika's desperate howl followed me as I walked away. I shared her pain.

THANK YOU FOR READING

We hope you enjoyed *Chameleon*. Keiko's journey is not at
an end yet! *Spider* is now available!
https://www.amazon.com/dp/B0863BFMV4

Make sure you never miss a new release by following India
Millar on Amazon
https://www.amazon.com/India-Millar/e/B01392F7DK

and Goodreads
https://www.goodreads.com/author/show/
13686311.India_Millar

and by subscribing to our mailing list.
http://redempresspublishing.com/subscribe/

SPIDER

WARRIOR WOMAN OF THE SAMURAI BOOK 4

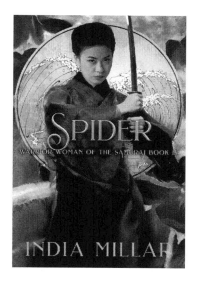

Amazon

When Keiko chooses duty over love, she wonders if the code of the samurai is worth the heartache.

Leaving Edo to save the life of a man she once loved, Keiko

must give up everything she has worked for. She vows one day to return, but she has learned the hard lesson that the gods have a dark sense of humor.

The city of Kobe seems a world away from Edo, a place where she could disappear, become whoever she wants to be, and leave the way of the samurai behind her.

But the code of bushido is not so easily discarded.

Even as Keiko makes new friends, new allies, and explores new dreams, her duty calls to her. Torn between a life of joy and a life of honor, Keiko knows that she can never truly have both.

ABOUT THE AUTHOR

 India Millar started her career in heavy industry at British Gas and ended it in the rarefied atmosphere of the British Library. She now lives on Spain's glorious Costa Blanca North in an entirely male dominated household comprised of her husband, a dog, and a cat. In addition to historical romances, India also writes popular guides to living in Spain under a different name.

Website: www.indiamillar.co.uk

ABOUT THE PUBLISHER

VISIT OUR WEBSITE
TO SEE ALL OF OUR HIGH QUALITY BOOKS:

http://www.redempresspublishing.com

Quality trade paperbacks, downloads, audio books, and books in foreign languages in genres such as historical, romance, mystery, and fantasy.

Printed in Great Britain
by Amazon